ANKARAN
IMMERSION

Will Weisser

ANKARAN IMMERSION

Will Weisser

For Juliet

1

"DID YOU HEAR that?" Evie pushed aside a branch and looked over the clearing. The sound was already retreating, a deep, thunderous boom—on a clear spring day. Sunlight filtered through dense leaves above, casting a greenish-yellow glow over a field of brush, and the grey metal fibers running through it. The strand lay all around here, burrowed in the earth, wrapping the trees, giving off its electric hum. Nothing unusual. Whatever had made the booming sound was too distant to trouble her. For now.

Evie vaulted through the branches and landed on a spot of bare earth, then hopped eastward across a broken path of strand-free soil. It was still early morning, and if she kept a good pace, she could get to the pond where the moonseed grew, harvest the berries, and return to the safety of their home field before noon.

If she kept a good pace.

"Hunter!" she yelled. "Hurry up!"

A rustling came from behind her, followed by a muffled "ouch" as her half-brother passed through a thorn bush she had avoided. At the edge of the clearing he leaned forward, hands on his knees, red scratches on his cheek. He closed his eyes tight and opened them again, then puffed out, "I want to rest."

"Father gave me an order. If I don't get the berries as fast as possible, I'll be breaking the law." The second law of the Pure, to be exact: youngsters must follow the will of their elders. Even Hunter couldn't argue with that.

"He also said you had to…" He paused to blink hard again and swallow. "Take me with you."

Evie made no effort to hide her annoyance. She didn't expect an eleven-year-old to be able to keep up with her at sixteen, but everyone else his age knew when it was appropriate to speak. "He said you could come, not that I had to sit around waiting for you."

She headed off, only looking back once she had left the clearing. Shoulders hunched, Hunter stepped gingerly through the high grass, avoiding the strand as she had, but taking longer to do it. Evie wiped a sweat-soaked lock of hair from her face and kept moving. The air was heavy with moisture, her leather shirt stuck to her skin. Unseasonable heat for early spring, and not a good sign. The tribe would have to migrate northward within weeks. Hence this trip for the berries—they didn't grow in the mountains up north, and the shaman needed them to make medicine. Already their home field was swelled with neighboring families preparing for the migration. Tents, food, tools, everything had to be packed and carried. No possession could survive the coming of the silver strand.

The trees thinned, and the patches of dried leaves gave way to a carpet of flexible, fibrous metal. The blight surrounded her now, patches of thistles and clovers pushing through the strand, coming up brown as if the effort had robbed them of vitality. Evie didn't like this place. The square plots where the Ancient's buildings had once stood lay marked in the ground, the stones long ago colonized by blue strand, turning them to flat metal plates inscribed with square-patterned designs. Gray strand grew thick between, bunched together like muscle and wet with strand-oil, forcing her to wend her way through the grid to avoid it. There was so much of it here that Evie could see slivers moving as it grew, and the whole place seemed to pulse in its mechanical rhythm.

Hunter appeared at the edge of the blight behind her and let out a tired sigh. He made up time by making his way through in more or less a straight line, even if it meant his foot brushed the strand occasionally. Evie shot him a reproachful look the first time it happened, though since it was Hunter he would never notice. Touching gray or blue strand was unlikely to pose a danger, but if they did happen to come across the silver, such recklessness could spell disaster. Silver strand could slither along the ground at incredible speed, or even form itself into walking, bloodthirsty monsters. And if it caught you, it could hook its tendrils inside you, steal your spirit and make you a puppet to its will—a fate worse than death.

On the far side of the blight lay the Ancient Road, a wide swath of crumbled black rock, dotted with patches of blue strand and natural detritus. The ancients had built other roads out of the same material, she knew—one often saw chunks of it half-buried in the forest—but for some reason in the Southern Pines only the Ancient Road had survived. Remembering the booming sound from earlier, Evie stared down its flat, straight length, but saw only the horizon.

"Wow," Hunter said, though his voice remained its usual monotone.

He was facing the wrong direction, away from the pond. The morning haze had burned off, and far out over the road the spires of the Tainted City rose over the Riversea. Evie could only remember getting this clear a view of it a handful of times in her life. If she squinted, she could see coils of strand hanging off the leaning towers.

"Look how close it is," Hunter said.

Evie put a scold in her voice. "You're looking at people who choose to live among the strand. Even take it into their bodies. " She suppressed a shiver.

"I know." But he stayed in place anyway, his eyes fixed to the city.

She quoted the third law to him, mimicking her father. "Do not be concerned with the will of the strand."

"I'm not concerned." After a long pause, Hunter turned to follow. "I was just…wondering."

The first time he had focused on anything that day, and it had to be *that*. Evie shook her head. "Just be glad they're over there, and we're here. Come on."

She set off at a jog down the road. Her half-wit half-brother. Everyone knew there was something wrong with him, but the adults tended to ignore it, or acted like it was something he'd grow out of. Evie knew better. He meant well, and one soon got used to his strange movements and speech, or the way he avoided eye contact in conversation. But his preoccupation with the strand—though he tried, poorly, to hide it—was going to bring them both trouble. It was only because they were the closest in age among her step-siblings that she was expected to watch over him all the time. Well, she had to do it, it was her duty as the elder, but she didn't have to like it.

The pond lay not far from the road, beyond a meadow alive with tiny white moths and winged ants. Ducks scattered at their approach, leaving expanding circles on the water's surface. Evie got to work, kneeling in the shallows and using the knife from her belt to cut moonseed berries from their stalks. Hunter arrived and made some half-hearted efforts to help, then got distracted staring at frogs. Evie said nothing, glad to be left alone.

She found a tangle of vines and pulled them apart, rough bark chafing her palm. Hunter followed a frog out to a series of rocks. He leaned forward too far, slipped and fell in. Evie yelped and wiped the splash from her face.

Hunter stayed submerged for a few seconds, then rose with a confused expression, a lily pad resting on his head.

Evie clucked her tongue and moved on. Another couple weeks, then a month on the trail, and she would be spending her summer in the mountains. Resting in the cool air, swimming in spring water, spending time with her older brothers, who she seldom saw now that they had moved to other fields to start families. And best of all, Hunter wouldn't bother her there. He always seemed to wander off once they—

Ka-thoom.

A rumble in the distance shocked her to awareness. The same as she had heard before? It had to be.

Ka-thoom.

The sound grew louder. A lump formed in her throat. Hunter's eyes were wide. Something was very wrong. She shouldn't have come here, should have turned back to the field when she heard it before. How many times had she been told that no matter the season, life among the strand meant eternal vigilance?

The air was quiet save for their breathing. If they left now, maybe she could get away with it this time. Lesson learned, she wouldn't—

Ka-THOOM.

"Hunter," she whispered. "Get over here."

A line of trees exploded, and a giant strand monster tumbled into the meadow. The thing was as tall as a full-grown pine, and the ground shook as it rolled onto its knees to face a second giant following at its heels.

Evie grabbed Hunter by the wrist and splashed out of the water, then hid behind a smooth stone. The first beast was vaguely human-shaped, but bulkier, its limbs composed of lumps of rock and debris held together by silver strand. The second was more insect-like, taller, with sharp appendages extending from its shoulders and thorax. They must have come from the south—creatures like this shouldn't have walked the pines until late summer.

Hunter shook in her grasp, and she hugged tighter to still him. She had to keep her thoughts calm, resist her instincts. *Just stay out of their way. Giants don't bother much with humans. Stay hidden and wait.*

Another bone-jarring crash, followed by thudding vibrations. The insectoid giant had swung at the other, which had ducked out of the way. Evie peeked out enough to catch glimpses of the beasts struggling, screeching and growling. How agile they were despite their size, the strand in their limbs flexing and pulsing. The one that had retreated through the trees feinted low, then leapt forward. Its pursuer changed shape, reforming its upper body into a loop of strand, and caught its foe in mid-air, redirecting it toward the pond. Before Evie could respond, the giant smashed into the water, and the sound blasted her eardrums. A lily-filled wave rushed past her knees, nearly dragging her away from the rock.

Evie opened her eyes. Her arms were empty. Panic gripped her, but then she saw Hunter a few feet away, covered in mud.

"Come on!" They might not get a better opportunity to run. She grabbed Hunter and pulled him along, not daring to look behind. She had to get around the pond, head west back to their home. Thundering footsteps came from her right, followed by another crash. The human-like giant monster had been knocked over again, taking trees down with it. A blinding cloud of dust enveloped her. She jumped a brook, turned, and stopped short, too frightened to breathe.

The giant was lying a few paces ahead, its face to the side, staring at her. Its eyes were massive glass orbs, and she watched in horror as smaller black circles within them shrank, focusing. She froze, trapped in its glare, but the thing did not move. Hunter gasped, and his arm shuddered in her hands. She ran, her fingers putting divots in the flesh of Hunter's wrist. The thing's eyes rotated to watch her flee.

Ahead, an ancient stone dam lay at the pond's outflow, its crumbling surface replaced with long stretches of gray strand. If she could just get across, then nothing would lie between her and home but a stretch of familiar forest. She stopped at the dam's edge, habit preventing her feet from touching the metal. To her left, water trickled down a flat, strand-infested embankment to a drainage tunnel far below. Climbing down would take too long, but the law said she couldn't cross the dam, couldn't use the strand as a bridge.

The insect giant screeched as the two resumed their battle. There was no other way; she had to cross, just this once. She gave Hunter a yank to keep him close, then set off along the narrow causeway. The fighting behind her sounded more ferocious than before. A dozen steps, and she was halfway across. Hunter puffed and wheezed, struggling to keep up with her strides.

Below her feet the strand changed shape, writhing, separating. She stumbled, then lost her footing. Hunter yelled. The dam had formed into a ramp, dumping them both down the embankment. Evie tucked her limbs, but they flew apart when she slammed into the hard stone.

Pain erupted through her. She tumbled and tried to call, "Hunt—"

Another jarring thud, and the world went black.

2

ONO PULLED UP his walker on a ridge overlooking the Gwyer Plain. Below, strand covered the flat ground. At the center of the plain, a tavern rested on stilts. Though its structure was made of wood, it was bound and covered by the same cords of metal that surrounded it, not so much rising above the plain as forming a raised nub within. Ono knew the place well, one of several gathering spots on the road between Jolon and the coast, catering to merchants and fishers on their way inland— and the less savory types looking to prey on them.

With a mental command through his implant, he urged the walker forward, jerking him back as they began their descent. Before he reached the bottom of the hill, a slight tingle arose in the bottom of his skull. Ono knew that feeling well. It meant Aunio was aware again, listening, waiting, growing stronger.

Not good timing. But then again, unwanted guests were rarely appreciated, especially inside one's own head.

Ono spurred the walker again, and it accelerated across the plain, rocking him gently, its six legs darting back and forth with mechanical precision. A few drops of rain struck the strand of his right wrist, beading on the oiled surface. Sunlight still shone in patches of sky, but not for long; he had been traveling ahead of a storm all day.

When they neared the tavern he bid the walker to halt, and it flattened to the ground, spreading the strand of its body to take in as much sunlight as it could. Ono dismounted and headed up the stairs, then pushed aside the strand hanging over the doorway.

The tavern's long wooden struts ran through into its interior, and more like them were laid at right angles, running overhead as rafters, with a flatter piece along the side of the room functioning as a bar. Its builder had used strand to tie the joints together, which had since grown and burrowed into the adjacent wood, so that the place looked as if it were being eaten from within by long, metallic caterpillars. A dozen locals sat at half as many tables, mostly silent, their eyelids twitching—playing games on the strand, or else letting it shock their brain into a near-catatonic state of inebriation.

Ono kept his hood up and his coat closed as he entered, though he couldn't hide his uneven gait, *tap, clank, tap, clank.* Everyone present had at least a little strand in their bodies, but the sight of a man with nearly his entire right side replaced with metal would still be intimidating, and Ono wanted to keep a low profile. He took a seat at the bar, by far the classiest thing in the tavern, old and polished to a sheen, with hardly any strand in it. The bartender wandered over, a tall man named Tokkan with a shock of gray through his long hair.

"Hello…" Tokkan looked up and his eyes went wide. "You! That is…good to see you." He made a quick check of the tavern's other occupants. "You here on business?"

"Just sniffing around," Ono mumbled. "I'm not looking to drag one of your customers back to Jolon this time." He avoided mentioning who exactly he *was* looking for. A few patrons had no doubt taken note of Tokkan's reaction to him, and if he uttered Fesso's name aloud, he'd lose what was left of his low profile.

Down the bar, a gray-haired man slammed down his empty glass and glared. Ono couldn't recall having met him before, though that didn't mean he hadn't come across Aunio. But whatever his grievance, silence might resolve it better than words. Save for a tiny wire of strand that ran across his eyeball to his iris, the old man appeared clean. Ono, itching down his centerline where the implants joined his skin, shifted his weight until his stool creaked under the heavy lengths of metal. That was enough; after a grumble, the man took his glass and moved to a table in the far corner.

"Need anything?" Tokkan asked.

"Some gluce would be fine." Sugar water, produced from specially tailored strand. Ono's body could synthesize it using the wireless power it pulled from the grid, but he had turned that system off to help keep Aunio at bay. Unfortunately, it hadn't worked—in the time since he had entered the bar, the buzz in his head had only grown louder. "And the local news, if any."

"Strand's moving early this year."

Ono scowled at his clinking ice. "I ask for news, you give me the weather."

Tokkan shrugged. "Folks are worried, is all. The roads will be dangerous, and The Mystic of Tumsiever died last week. We asked the church for a replacement, but in the meantime we have no one to pass our prayers to the Ints."

"Mmm." Typical frontier griping. "Anything else?"

Tokkan shrugged, and turned to the endless supply of bottles, glasses, taps and other paraphernalia that bartenders could clean when they wanted to look busy.

So be it; time to risk a direct approach.

Ono said under his breath, "Have any of Fesso's Children been through lately?"

Tokkan's hand tightened on the glass he had been wiping. He set it down slowly on the bar, eyes narrowed. "Now that's bad business. Did Serr really send you to take one of Fesso's lieutenants? Didn't think he wanted to stir up those hornets again."

"Something like that." Serr was the City of Jolon's autocratic ruler, and Ono could hardly think of a better way to attract attention than mentioning him and Fesso the same sentence. He checked the bar to see if anyone had heard. A few of the larger patrons looked back his way. "You didn't answer my question."

"You're right." Tokkan walked away.

Ono sat back and swirled his drink, imagining Tokkan's reaction if he knew the whole truth. Tracking down Fesso's lackeys was one thing—most of the wrongdoing in the plains could be traced back to her one way or another. But actually finding the old gangster herself, bringing her back to Jolon alive—that was a suicide run. He would never have accepted a job like it before he had grown so desperate. Before Aunio.

As if responding to his name, Aunio's buzzing rattled behind Ono's teeth, pressing on his thoughts.

"Tokkan."

"Hmm?"

"I was at the Church the other day. You know, the big one in Jolon."

"Uh huh."

"I spoke to the High Mystic while I was there. Perhaps when I return I could put in a word for Tumsiever—"

A breeze passed to the left, and a chunk of strand hit the bar beside Ono with an ear-popping *slam*. The mass of metal was shaped like an arm, but twice as thick as any arm should be. Ono turned slowly to meet the limb's owner, a man whose massive chest came up even with Ono's head.

"You have a lot of balls coming back here."

"Sylas!" Tokkan yelled. "The bar!"

"Good to see you again." Ono gave a gracious nod. In fact, he had never seen the man apparently named Sylas before, which could only mean one thing: this was another of Aunio's acquaintances.

"Good?" Sylas's sneer parted over brown teeth. Strand ran above his lips, coming from his nose and across up his cheek, then looping around his left ear on the way down to his oversized arm implant. "Just wait till we get done with you."

With his flesh hand Sylas motioned to his two companions, muscled and mean but possessing relatively little strand. Not Fesso's Children, then—her gang tended to come better-equipped.

"Tell me," Sylas continued. "Why'd you do it, eh?"

Ono searched in vain for some memory of how Aunio had wronged this man, but his alter ego had left him with no recollection of the period when he had taken over their body. He shrugged. "I don't suppose you'd believe me if I told you it was someone else?"

Sylas cocked his head. "You think I wouldn't recognize a skinny creep with half a body's worth of strand?" The words built in anger as Sylas readied himself for the fight.

"Now, Sylas." Tokkan's voice from behind. "Let's just take it easy."

"I'll take something." Sylas slammed his hand down on Ono's forearm at a speed beyond reaction, pinning it to the bar top, strand on strand. His friends drew closer. Ono had a split-second decision to make: risk Aunio's return by using his implants, or risk a serious beating by not fighting back. Neither option seemed clearly superior to the other.

The strand in Sylas's arm flexed, then oozed down, covering Ono's own. A string of lights flashed across Ono's ocular implant, warning him of network probes searching for vulnerabilities. Sylas may have looked a brute, but that arm had a few tricks— by throwing enough raw data Ono's way, he might render his implants useless before the fight began.

With a tinge of regret, Ono enabled his counter-measures, engaging parts of his internal network he had previously left dormant. As more of his implant's functions came online, Aunio responded, pressing against his bonds at the edge of consciousness. The buzzing intensified. Sylas raised his meaty fist to strike.

Ono dodged to the side, leaving his strand arm behind on the bar. Sylas's hand thumped the bare wood where Ono had been, then he swiveled and lunged in pursuit.

Ono kept moving, using the crowded bar-room for cover. Thin cables trailed from his shoulder back to his detached arm, drawn out like a snaking river over the floor. One of Sylas's friends charged, and Ono hopped onto the wall with a powered boost from his strand leg, then kicked off and landed up on a rafter. The man crashed into a table full of glasses below, raising howls of protest from other patrons. Tokkan screamed at them all to take it outside. Ono jumped across to the next rafter, then the next. He hopped down to the floor, breaking his fall with another table, leaving it smashed to pieces beneath him.

The three toughs regained their bearings and advanced again, Sylas in the lead. Behind them, Ono's arm crawled along on its fingers, still trailing the cable that looped up and over the ceiling.

The buzz in Ono's head pulsed, became a growling voice only he could hear.

Kill them, you coward.

"Shut up."

Do it. They're scum; I should have finished them when I had the chance.

Sylas, noticing his apprehension, grinned and cracked his knuckles.

Ono whispered, "Be helpful for once and tell me what you did to him, so I can talk us out of this."

"What?" Sylas raised an eyebrow.

Aunio chuckled in his mind. *His cousin had a warrant. Sylas wouldn't give him up, but his wife would. She has a fetish for men with extensive implants. I gave her what she wanted, and she returned the favor.*

"Great." Not likely he could talk his way out of that.

Sylas growled, "You think mumbling to yourself like some sort of nut is going to save you?"

"No."

Ono's detached arm leaped. The fingers elongated and splayed, encircling the thick flesh of Sylas's neck. Ono took hold of the cables running to his shoulder, jumped and tugged down with his considerable weight. Sylas rose a foot off the ground, hands at his throat, emitting a choking noise that would have been a scream.

Very nice. I like the style.

"Sorry about this," Ono said.

Sylas's friends took a step forward. Ono shook his head. The strand squeezed Sylas's neck, evoking another gurgle, causing the men to hesitate.

"This is probably the last time I'll be allowed in here," Ono said. "So I'll make the best of it. Who's seen Fesso's Children lately?"

At once the room fell deathly silent, save for Sylas's rasps.

"Come on. She always has crews skulking around these parts. One of you must know something."

The only answer came from Aunio.

They're scared.

"I know that," Ono mumbled. "Don't tell me you're sympathetic?"

They're scared of Fesso, but they should be scared of you. Show them you're more dangerous than her. Strangling this buffoon to death should prove the point.

Ono sighed and released the cable, dropping Sylas to a coughing heap on the floor. He watched the two men run to his side, studied the look on Sylas's purple face, the stares of the onlookers.

Aunio was right. Fear dominated this place. The farmers and fishers feared the outlaws, the outlaws feared Fesso, and everyone, high and low, feared the strand and the Ints who controlled it from within. And if he was going to succeed, he had to use that fear to his advantage. But not the way Aunio wanted; he wasn't in control of their body yet, and he didn't get to call the shots.

"Listen, all of you. I know you don't trust me. Maybe you don't trust anyone from Jolon. But this time is different: I'm not working for Serr anymore. I'm going after Fesso herself.

The Children are nothing without her. Once she's taken down, none of them will threaten you anymore."

The crowd mumbled, processing his words. Perhaps some wanted to believe him, but was that enough? Life out on the Plains meant facing hard reality, and they likely understood how little chance he had of success. What good were his promises of protection from Fesso if he was dead?

Sylas coughed. Several of the onlookers shuffled their feet, eyes on the floor, but said nothing.

"Two of them were here yesterday."

All eyes went to the far corner, to the old man Ono had seen at the bar.

"Here? In this tavern?" Ono flashed Tokkan a look.

"Quiet, Ger!" came a call from another table.

"Shut it. Those two knew what happened to my boat. They tried to act like they didn't, but I'm no fool."

"Your boat?" Ono said.

"Went missing at dock a week ago. Just replaced half the strand in the hull." The words sloshed drunkenly from Ger's mouth. "They laughed at me, you know, when I asked for it back. Said they had bigger things to worry about. Well, I don't care if they find out I talked. You hear that, everyone? If I can't feed my family, what good am I alive or dead?"

"Where did they go?"

"South."

"There's nothing south but wilderness."

Ger sneered. "You think I don't know that? That's the direction they went. Was I supposed to run after and ask why?"

"No." Ono reeled in his arm. "You've done enough."

He headed for the door, passing wide around the three toughs.

You got lucky. But the lead is weak, and you're weakening. You really think you'll be able to bring Fesso in without my help?

"We'll have to see." Ono nodded to Tokkan. "Sorry for the damage." He closed one eye, found the tavern's key on the local net and sent a small amount of coin to its account, all he could afford. "Thanks for the tip, Ger. I hope you find that boat."

At the bottom of the stair, the walker rose slowly from a pool of rainwater. Before them, the oily Gwyer plain had turned iridescent from the moisture. A mile distant, the edge of the forest loomed green.

That's a lot of land out there. Plenty of space to get lost. Go back inside and give me control. Let me find out what else these people know.

Ono set about re-attaching his arm, muttering curses when the water interfered with the connection. "We need to disappear. I told them too much; now Fesso will find out I'm after her."

Then you should have told them who we're working for. These yokels are so superstitious, one mention of the Ints would have shut them up good.

Ono mounted the walker and dug his fingers into the loose strand atop its neck. The walker tested a few hesitant steps, then splashed forward. "If we get the Ints what they want, they'll keep their end of the deal. You'd better keep yours."

You're going to spend weeks combing those woods, and in the end find nothing.

Ono hunched against the rain and snorted. "At least I'll have the pleasure of your company."

3

EVIE DREAMED OF rushing water. She was a young child again, her mother bathing her in a chilly stream. She knew it was her mother by the smoothness of her touch, the melody she hummed, but no matter how she squinted or focused she couldn't bring her face into view. She wanted to see, to remember what her mother looked like, and as the frustration grew she cried out, an infant's wail.

The scene shifted. She was older again, her true age, and kneeling before her father. The dark lines of his face and his deep voice were stark and familiar.

"What have you done, Eveningstar?"

"Strand creatures…they were fighting…they were huge."

"You used the strand to escape." He folded his arms, his voice cold as the stream. Why could she never please him? "You crossed it on purpose."

"I had to. I'm sorry." A dull pain throbbed in her limbs. She was waking up, re-entering her body.

"You broke the law and you'll pay the price."

"Yes. Yes Father, I understand."

"Watch your brother. Without me, you must protect him as the elder."

"Wait! Don't go." But too late. The dream faded, and Evie opened her eyes.

She was sitting waist-deep in stagnant, cold water, her whole body aching. Light streamed in from above, quenched to a dim glow by a long tunnel. They must have fallen into the drainage pipe, an underground passage the ancients built to take water away, now infested by the strand. Hunter lay beside her, whimpering softly. Evie shook her head, forcing herself out of her stupor, and rose on unsteady legs.

She tested her weight and rubbed her arms—nothing broken, thank the spirits.

"Hunter." He didn't respond, so she knelt close to him. "Are you hurt?"

He looked up and fixed her with his far-away stare, only this time with a face smudged with mud, blood dripping from his nose. He looked placid; did he even know what had happened?

"Did you break anything?"

Hunter wiped his nose and wiggled it, wincing at the pain, but ultimately shook his head no. He tried to rise as she had, then yelped and fell back down with a splash, clutching his foot.

He held it up. In the dim light, she could just make out blood dribbling from his instep. She took the foot in her hands and wiped it off. Hunter yelped again. The cut wasn't that deep, but she would have to stop the bleeding. She pulled a length of cloth from her belt and wrapped the foot, then tied it tight on top.

"Try not to put much weight on it."

A length of strand behind him slithered across the wall. Evie jumped back, her heart skipping a beat. The strand was a strange type she had never seen before: glittering, almost translucent. The entire chamber was covered with it, the walls shimmering when she turned her head. Evie wasn't sure what it meant, but it didn't seem good.

"We have to climb out of here. Let's go."

Hunter pulled his knees to his chest. "Just wait."

"What?"

"Those monsters are up there." Hunter blinked hard and cleared his throat. "We should wait here. Father knew where we were going. He'll come and find us."

"Father..." She remembered the dream. *Without me, you must protect him.* "Hunter, the tribe can't come look for us. Don't you see? They have to leave right away. If those giants are here, it means the silver strand is coming. If we hurry we can warn them."

"But the shaman said..."

"We had half a month, I know. She was wrong. The silver strand has come early before. Come on."

Hunter stayed sitting, studying the water, and began to rub his foot with one hand. Anger rose in Evie's chest, and she was about to shout when his head snapped up. But instead of looking toward her, he stared into the darkness down the tunnel.

"What is it?" she asked.

"I..." He cleared his throat and blinked again. "I heard something."

"I don't hear..." She stood for a few moments, listening to the burble of running water, until the skittering sound rose above it.

Something was crawling up the tunnel. Clicking. Metallic. Large. She pulled Hunter up by the elbow, and he gave no resistance.

The narrow drainage pipe entrance was covered in strand, but there was truly no other way this time. She cursed as she dug her fingers between the fibers, holding against the slickness of water-covered metal, and climbed up in long pulls. Hunter puffed behind. Between each of his breaths, the skittering grew louder.

"Come on!" she yelled as much to herself as him. In her haste, her hand slipped, and she skidded down the tunnel, bracing herself against the sides just before she crashed into Hunter. A high-pitched rattle came from the dark behind them, like the call of a giant cicada. Evie hooked Hunter around the waist, grabbed a hand-hold with her other arm, and boosted him up with an effort that nearly tore her shoulder.

Pull, step, pull. Just above, daylight streamed over the lip of the tunnel. Evie hauled herself over, then helped Hunter up and crouched, panting and listening. The forest around them was quiet, no thunderous booms or cries of battle from the giant monsters. Tentatively, she edged near the hole and put her ear down. Distant echoes, nothing more. Whatever had been advancing up after them seemed to have stopped, afraid of the light. Evie sighed relief and collapsed face-up on the weed-covered embankment.

Seeing the sky, she knew something was wrong. The sun was at the wrong angle. It was already well past noon—how had they lost so much time? She rolled over and scrambled higher up the embankment, until she rose to the level of the forest floor.

"No."

Across the wide field of yellow grass, patches of silver fibers reflected the daylight.

"Hey," Hunter gasped, hopping up behind her on one foot. "You have to wait…" He caught sight of the field and the words audibly stuck in his throat.

Evie struggled to catch her breath. Think, she had to think. Small tendrils of silver strand were everywhere, slithering over the ground, around the trees, coming from the south. Could the tribe have managed to leave in time? There was still so much to pack for the migration, they wouldn't be ready. If it reached them unprepared…

"We have to get back," she said. "We'll head northwest. We can outpace this wave, then circle back south to the field."

Hunter nodded, and Evie took off into the woods.

There were no complaints about the pace this time, though she tried to keep it reasonable, knowing each step on Hunter's wounded foot must have been agony. She dodged through the trees, focusing on her breaths and the uncomfortable sliding of wet clothes over her limbs, turning left or right when she caught a glimpse of silver strand on the ground, making sure to give it a wide berth.

Even at a run, having to detour north through the lake

country meant that the sun was already dipping below the tree line by the time they neared home. Evie stopped at an ancient wall, a place where the older children in the tribe would sometimes climb, racing one another to the top. She found a spot of crumbled stone free of strand and put her back against it, facing the direction she'd come so she could watch for Hunter's catching up.

While she'd been in motion she'd outpaced her worries, but now that she was still, they caught up in force. What if something terrible had happened to the tribe? For the past month they had been gathering at their home field for the coming migration, the elderly and infants among them. Surely the silver strand wouldn't have moved that quickly; they would have had time to at least get out of its way. But what if those giants weren't just an isolated skirmish...

No. They were fine, they had to be. Her father, her brothers, all of them. Falling into the underground tunnel had been a harsh judgment from the spirits, punishment for her indiscretion, but she had learned her lesson. She was lucky she and Hunter were young, their bodies so resilient; another member of the tribe couldn't have taken such a fall and been running home within the day. Hopefully they'd return before searches went out, warn the others that the silver strand was just south of them, and come away with no more than a harrowing tale to boast about for the summer and beyond.

Hunter slipped out of the tree cover to the north and began making his way through the field of half-buried strand surrounding the wall. Evie waved to show her position. Seeing they were close to home, Hunter broke into a hobbled run, favoring his cut foot.

A whisper of instinct led Evie's gaze to the path in front of him, where a star-shaped formation of gray strand splayed in a circle.

"Stop!"

Hunter froze a few paces from the outer reaches of the fibers. His eyes widened as he recognized what they were. The dark gray color was only camouflage—the strand-trap would spring to life as fast as a cat's claws if anyone stepped on its tendrils.

Evie jumped up and strode toward him. "Be more careful! You should know better!"

He said nothing, turning away and looking at the ground with a hard blink. Something about his guilty face, sweaty and flushed, compelled her to speak again.

"I'm sorry..." Too late she realized the absurdity of apologizing for his mistake. "...but you're never mindful enough. If I'm going to be responsible for you, you need to help me."

He nodded, then looked off past the wall. "We might be too late. Do you think they could all be dead?"

"Shut up! Never say things like that." She remembered who she was talking to and shook her head at the futility. More than anything, she wished she had an answer. Behind her, the sky had settled into a purple-gray haze as the sun began to disappear. Evie swallowed and headed off through the final copse of trees.

Their home field lay beyond a dense, protective tangle of brush, with a ring of strand inside, forming a threshold. The magic her ancestors had laid here kept the gray strand at bay, and so it piled up in a thick coil on the outskirts.

Already, in the pit of her stomach, Evie knew. The field ahead was too quiet, no patter of feet, grunt of labor, whispers of gossip or whoops of laughter. She pushed through the final tuft of grass and leaped over the ring.

Silver strand lay over every surface, worming its way through broken tents, slithering into carefully tilled soil. Random belongings were scattered among the ruins, a wooden bowl half-buried in the metal, leather straps frayed to pieces.

Evie's legs grew weak and she sank to her knees. Hunter stepped out beside her and took a deep breath. She waited to hear him cry out, but nothing came. He stood impassively for a few moments, surveying the destruction, then said, "What now?"

She didn't know. The field was deathly silent. Was anyone in their family buried under that metal? It was too much to take in. Beside her, Hunter continued to stare impassively. What was he so calm about? He turned and noticed her glare, and his face became confused.

"Aren't you worried about them?" she asked.

"No." He pointed. "Everything's gone, see? Anything we need on the trail, they took with them. The tools, the steel. And they had time to harvest the potatoes, and the other food that will keep."

He was right. The tribe had obviously left in great haste, but they had left. Someone had noticed the strand coming north just in time, and her father and the other members of the council had organized them well enough. She didn't want to think of how much trouble and worry she and Hunter must have caused by being missing on such a day, but it was over now, and the tribe was on its way north.

Just without them.

"We're going to follow the trail," Evie said. "We'll be all right. Just stay by me. Whatever I say, you do, got it?"

He nodded.

Evie stood and quickly wiped her eyes. "We're leaving."

She made sure her knife was secure and checked her belt for supplies—she had just the small amount of food she had packed that morning, but she could forage for more on the way. She was a Pure, after all. She shouldn't have doubted the spirits' ability to guide her.

She turned and leaped back over the threshold, toward the route the others had chosen this year. To catch up with them would take a couple days at most.

Rain trickled off the tip of Evie's nose. She sneezed, sending drops in all directions, only for more to replace them from above. The water soaked her through, as pervasive as her misery.

What was the tribe doing in the storm? Had the council noticed it coming and directed them to a natural shelter? Or were they huddled in temporary lean-tos of stakes and skins? Those kinds of nights were always Evie's least favorite on the trail, given that she preferred to sleep alone, unlike most of the others. If she were with them now, she would probably elect to stay with her aunt, keeping warm beside the pillow-like lumps of her breasts, trying to ignore her uncle's body odor and gaseous emissions.

But as uncomfortable as that arrangement was, she would have preferred it a thousand times over to what she felt now: utterly lost.

A large shape appeared in the distance of the dark forest, and Evie pulled up short, raising her knife.

She rubbed the water from her eyes. No danger, just a clump of dead trees. That might be the last time she'd be able to tell the difference; the last of the evening light was fading, and the night would be crow-black.

"Evie? Are you up here?"

She bit down on a sigh. "Just hurry, please." Hunter was young, and hurt. She had to be patient, or so she had reminded herself again and again. Evie's stomach growled, and the tail end turned to a painful cramp. She wiped rain from her eyes again, but only succeeded in turning a dark blur into plain darkness. Somehow they were going to have to make camp—if only the rain would stop for a little while. How could it go on so hard, for so long? Or did it only seem longer than usual?

In any case, they couldn't stop here; they were on the border of a patch of blight, and there was too much strand around to be safe. As Hunter picked his way through the brush behind, she stepped forward into a puddle. A shape slithered out of it. Evie yelled and jumped away.

Only a snake—probably. A reminder from the spirits. The rain was miserable, but it wouldn't kill them; failing to stay ahead of the advancing strand would. Despite their numbers, the tribe could move quickly on the trail when they needed to. And now she and Hunter had to outpace them, on empty bellies over unfamiliar terrain. Any thoughts of rest had to wait.

A flash came, and the thunder followed before her next heartbeat. Hunter stumbled and fell beside her. She waited for his silhouette to rise, but he remained crouched.

"What's wrong?"

He didn't answer, but she knew already. She knelt to examine his foot.

The flesh surrounding the cut was still swollen. Its color was imperceptible in the dark, but Evie could not imagine the redness had abated, either. No wonder he didn't want to speak of it—Hunter knew as well as she did just how bad such a wound could get. But what could she do? She was no shaman, and she had no medicine to give him.

"Climb on my back."

He lifted his arm, and she hefted him up. She had already resolved to walk all night; what was one more burden? She grunted as she started forward, but there was a hint of satisfaction in it, a feeling of atonement for her earlier breaking of the law. She was the elder, he the younger. If the spirits wished to punish her, she would protect him at her own expense.

A nice idea. But it took only twenty paces before the ache in her lower back told her how foolish it was. The pain grew worse as she slogged forward, her feet sinking deep into the mud. The ground sloped down and she slid, nearly losing her balance. Hunter's wet hands grasped tight on her neck, making her head pound. He mumbled with his lips near her ear.

"What is it?" she said.

"Stop."

"Why?"

"…make a plan…can't just stumble around."

She set him down on the soaked earth. A flash of anger hit her. Stumble around? What was that supposed to mean? He had no right to question her. Who did he think he—

A sound in the distance made her jerk her head. It sounded almost like a muffled…bark?

"What's wrong?" Hunter dug in his ear with a mud-covered finger.

"Ssh." It was nothing. Please, let it have been nothing.

A long howl came, drifting from high to low. Evie's blood ran cold.

Even though she was sixteen, standing tall in the rain, in her mind she may well have been six again, kneeling in the dry dust with her brothers. With a hoarse shout her uncle had come running and pulled them toward the center of the field. Evie remembered his face well—she had never seen her uncle scared before.

All she had of that day were scattered images, events blurring across the addled mind of a child. People were running, grabbing weapons, yelling. Intruders. Evie spun in a circle, trying to catch a glimpse, and between running legs she saw one in the distance. Gray and sleek, large. Wolves.

The animals growled and bayed on the border of the field. Why were the behaving this way? Wolves never attacked the Pure like this. More shouting, and the tribe's warriors coalesced at the northern border. Time seemed to slow. The tribe fell back as the thing jumped into the fray. It must have been big even before it was tainted, jaws slavering oil with hundreds of metal teeth.

The warriors charged with their spears. The tainted wolf

lunged, its leg changing shape, and sunk a two-foot-long claw into Great-Horn's chest. Evie's scream still rang in her memory. She ran into her older cousin's arms, tears soaking her face, crying and crying.

"No!" She belted the word into the night, shaking in her mud puddle.

Hunter looked up at her, confused. "Evie?"

"*Quiet!*" Something moved on the hill above. Evie held her breath, eyes fixed on the black and gray shapes in the distance.

Lighting flashed. Against the clouds, stark and clear, stood a silhouette on all fours, tail and triangular ears raised.

Evie screamed. It wasn't until Hunter yelled behind her that she realized she had taken off running without him. Shameful. Horrible. No, she had to get away. She ran and jumped, couldn't see, a gleam of strand in front, couldn't turn, slipping—

The strand reached for her. A trap, like the one Hunter had almost walked into before. Evie screamed and twisted as the tendrils grasped her wrists and thighs. Oil-coated wires touched every part of her. She heard Hunter yelling, running after her, and she screamed back, telling him to get away, but the strand wrapped around her throat, probing into her mouth.

Another flash, and she caught a glimpse of Hunter's arm wrapped in strand. She struggled hard, not caring whether she ripped her own body apart, but the strand was implacable, squeezing tighter the more she pulled. Metal climbed into her nostrils and hovered before her eye, preparing to stab.

A voice called out. Deeper than Hunter's. A man. Not a cry of panic, either, almost a questioning tone, in a foreign language.

From a corner of her eye Evie saw a figure approach. The metal locked her jaw shut, cutting off her warning. The strand reached for the man, and he reached for it at the same time. Something happened, quick movements in the dark, jerking and shivering, like a contest of wills. Then the strand fell limp and slithered away, and the entire trap followed suit, withdrawing from her body, leaving her prone on the ground.

Evie rolled over and gagged. Her throat hurt. The world spun, purple spots whirling in her vision. A horrible thought came: she could be a Tainted now. Her hands ran up and down her body. Nothing. No holes, no metal. Blessing of the spirits. The relief came strong and let her inhale again. She sat on her knees and coughed.

Beside her, Hunter slowly rose as well, coughing and blinking furiously. Finally, he took a deep breath and stared up at the strange man.

The man surveyed them both, then spoke again in his foreign tongue. Evie rubbed her eyes, focusing on him for the first time. The man wore a cloak with a hood. He extended his left hand to her and she took it and let him pull her to her feet.

"*Ko oko wen?*" the man said.

"What?" she swallowed. "I mean, thank you…"

Lighting flashed, and she saw his other arm. The man's right hand was strand. *His right hand was strand.* Another flash, and beneath the hood the right half of his face shone bright, mechanical eye glowing red.

Evie tried to speak, but her mouth opened and shut, useless. The man stayed still, watching and waiting. A wave of horror built inside her, and she screamed, grabbed Hunter, and took off into the woods.

4

"COME ON, YOU stupid pile of scrap." Ono yanked and spurred the walker, but it maintained its languid pace through the woods, choosing each step carefully as if the ferns contained viruses or other malware.

It's too damp.

Ono wiped the drizzle from his chin and sniffed. It had been years since he had been out in the wilderness, and the dense, earthy smell nearly made his head spin. "It's damp, all right, but try to be positive. We're experiencing nature."

I mean for the strand. It needs to be specially formed to operate in water. It's a problem for our implants, too; I can feel the moisture seeping in.

Ono felt slight satisfaction at Aunio's discomfort. He had turned off most of his internal monitors to help keep Aunio in check, but his alter ego was always in tune with his mechanical side. "At least it's cool. When the weather turns hot again, I might have to take you and this useless walker for a dip in the Jolon River."

You know what else has grown cool? The trail. The network here is as spotty as it is barren. This place is an information wasteland.

Ono grunted. As much as he resented Aunio speaking in his mind, he resented him more when he was right. But he wasn't ready to give up yet.

"Come on..." He attempted and failed to convince the walker to step over an apparently insurmountable obstacle, which resembled to Ono a medium-sized puddle. "I expected better from Jolon's armory."

You could ask for a refund, if you hadn't stolen the thing.

"Borrowed. Not like I had much choice, with my city accounts frozen."

Aunio stayed silent at that. There were possible retorts, ways to shift the blame away from him, but all of them led down a road neither of them wanted to tread: what Aunio had done during the period when he had taken over their mind, how exactly he cost Ono his livelihood, his friends, and most of all his wife and daughter. He was sure Aunio would never voluntarily reveal what he had done to make Ana and Clerie refuse to speak with him; his obstinacy and pride wouldn't let him. And Ono didn't want to ask, because the subject was simply too painful.

The rain kicked up again, and soon Ono was guiding the walker as best he could through a twilight stained black by the storm. The water pelted him, hammering on top of his hood, and after nearly an hour of the walker's feet sinking in mud he had nearly decided to give up the search for the night.

A wolf howled in the distance, then screaming came from the woods: fearful, panicked, strangely high-pitched.

Look at the strand.

He didn't need any network monitoring to see it; the metal was pulsing, responding to some nearby event. The pattern led downward, past a slope lined with thick brush. Ono dismounted and half-scrambled, half-slid down the steep bank of wet leaves.

"Who's out there?"

It was even darker down in the gully. Ono risked empowering Aunio by tuning his right eye to infrared. At the bottom of the hill, tendrils of strand, glowing yellow with their internal heat, writhed around small human shapes. Two children, caught in a snare. Ono stepped forward and the snare's arms grabbed for him. He held out his hand to interface with it, opening his personal firewall, letting the data flow.

As he had expected, the snare was a mild sort of virus, adapted to eating passing animals. It stood no chance against the weaponized cleaning routines in his personal network. In moments, he wiped the bug from the immediate surroundings, and without its commands, the snare fell limp.

The two children coughed and sputtered on the ground.

"It's all right. You're safe, now." He helped the closer one up. "What's your name?"

She mumbled something and looked up at him. Then it was Ono's turn to be shocked.

She was an Ankara—obvious from the strange words she mumbled, the way she dressed, and her wild, rugged nature. Ono had grown up among the street children of Jolon, who considered themselves quite the rowdy bunch, but they had been mild-mannered compared to these offspring of the forest.

The Ankara girl's gaze flitted to his implants. Her whole body quivered. Before he could speak again, she took the boy's hand and dashed off with him out of sight.

Ono stood there a while, dumbstruck, before the awareness settled that he was standing alone, at night and in the rain. He made a rote check of his network integrity as he stumbled up the hill and back to the walker, tumbling the encounter over in his mind.

It wasn't anything important, really. Just two Ankara children, likely siblings. He had never imagined he would meet an Ankara in person, but that wasn't what stuck with him. It was the girl. Aunio had seen it too, and was staying quiet on purpose.

By the Will of the Ints, she reminded him so much of his daughter.

The next morning, Ono headed north again. The forest lay wet, drops coming off the pine needles to spatter on the walker's legs, but now all was quiet, save the gentle buzz of the strand as it absorbed the tree-filtered sunlight.

Ono still wasn't able to get the girl out of his head. She didn't look much like Clerie, but she must have been nearly the same age, and she had the same bearing about her, those determined eyes, skeptical but not yet jaded.

Clerie. Ono had thought her perfect, once. From the day of her birth, practically small enough to fit in his palm, she could do no wrong in his eyes. In latter years he had grown more distant at times with both her and her mother, but if he had neglected either of them in favor of his work, it was only because he had never expected to lose them both so suddenly. She was still so young, had so much more growing to do. If he couldn't capture Fesso, couldn't get the Ints to resolve his problem with Aunio…

To the left, a gap in the bush led to a path where strand did not cover the ground. A ways along, a footprint lay in the mud.

"Them again."

Aunio grumbled. *Because you're intentionally following them.*

"They're taking the most direct route north, same as us."

They're on foot. You're riding slow, otherwise we would have passed them easily.

Aunio was right, of course. Still, he had kept quiet about Ono's tarrying thus far, because he had wished to avoid the subject of Clerie. It must have been heavy annoyance indeed that caused him to speak up.

"I suppose I'm curious," Ono said, keeping up his side of the pretense. "What could they be doing out here alone? They're supposed to travel as a group."

A few steps further on, a voice came from a nearby copse of trees. The girl. Their language was unfamiliar, but Ono knew the sound of cursing when he heard it. The forest was beginning to thin, and the closer they drew to the great solar fields, the more numerous the strand became and the harder it was for them to avoid.

"They must be lost. They're ahead of the energetic strand to the south, but they've come the wrong way."

If they're lost, what does that make us?

Ono spurred the walker ahead, into a clearing, and waited in silence for them to appear.

In a few seconds they obliged, mud-spattered and looking miserable, the boy grimacing in pain. They saw him and froze, much as they had the night before. This time Ono purposefully left some distance between them. He hoped he might appear less threatening in the morning light than in the gloom of the storm, but when the girl looked him and the walker up and down, an expression of disgust crossed her face. The boy blinked heavily as he stared, exhausted, too caught up in his own misery to despise the stranger before him.

"I'm a friend." Ono tried to make a hand gesture indicating as such, but without thinking he brought up the right limb made of strand. The girl shrank away. Ono put it back down. "Do you need help? You understand? Help?"

The pair of them stood silently for a moment, the girl half-crouched as if waiting for an attack. When she realized one wasn't coming, she snarled, hissed, and ran back into the trees with her brother in tow.

Ono sighed.

Are you convinced yet this is a waste of time?

He was getting there. But perhaps wasting time was half the point. Aunio wanted them to return to Gwyer, but Ono disagreed that they would find more information at the tavern. That left two choices: move on to some other town without a lead, or stop avoiding the one place he knew he should be going.

The Gridlands. Rumors had spread months ago that Fesso had moved her headquarters to that blighted place. Miles upon miles of strand-coated ruins, crackling with energy, stalked by creatures of strand. And worse things, like Fesso's Family.

For decades the old gangster had made a habit of collecting stray children. Some of them were the offspring of her former enemies, others abandoned or runaways, but all were brought up in the brutal confines of her underground enterprise, educated solely in the ways of power and weakness, and what one could do to the other. If there were a way to raise a personal army more dedicated and ruthless, Ono didn't know it. That was why the idea of catching two of her henchmen here, isolated, where he could easily tail or interrogate them, had been so tempting.

It's a lost cause, Ono. Get me back to where I can make some difference.

"You're too impatient. The Ints didn't give us a timetable."

That doesn't mean they'll wait forever. For all we know they wanted Fesso delivered to them yesterday.

"Hmph." Ono urged the walker forward again, but this time he felt a tug inside his head. Aunio wouldn't wait forever, either. The summer sun was pumping more energy into the strand, charging his implants and making his alter ego stronger. If he didn't stop at some point and find a tech to drain his power reserves, he might not be making the decisions for them much longer.

With a wide jump the walker cleared a line of rock and landed in an open field of strand. The next tree line lay a few hundred yards distant; beyond, less than an hour's ride separated them from the triangular plain of Gwyer.

Look. Aunio had picked up something on their strand-enhanced right eye.

"You know as well as I do that every time I use that, I hand over more control."

Something tells me you'll want to see this.

Ono acquiesced. Zoomed and motion-detected, two shapes flitted between the thin trees on the clearing's eastern border. The children again. "They're going to run right into Gwyer, if they're not careful."

Careful has nothing to do with it. They have no idea where they're going.

"I should warn them. Tell them to go around somehow. They'll want nothing to do with that place."

They want nothing to do with you, either.

"If the choice is me or some of those Gwyer folk, they'll be glad they met me first."

Ono put the walker in stealth mode, and it scuttled softly over the metal-laced turf. Once again, he found a place beyond where the Ankara would emerge from the wood and waited for them to approach.

Their voices preceded them, having some sort of argument. Then the two of them stepped around the remains of an ancient building and found Ono waiting. He smiled and put up his left hand this time.

The girl growled and turned away, not even keeping an eye on him, as if she was starting to view him more as an annoyance than a threat.

"That's progress, isn't it?"

Aunio chuckled derisively in his mind.

The boy trailed after her. He was coated in sweat, despite the rain having broken the heat wave. He walked with a pronounced limp, the lower half of his leg bright red.

After stumbling ahead ten paces, the boy turned back and took a long look at Ono.

Interesting.

Ono nudged the walker forward, barely enough to keep pace with them, watching the boy. He knew that look for what it was. Not fear, or desperation, but something potentially more powerful: curiosity.

The question was, how long would the boy last?

Ono watched his clock tick one minute, then two. The boy turned and stared again, even harder, drinking him in with his eyes.

Ono tapped his chest. "Ono."

The boy opened his mouth, then slapped it shut and looked at his sister. She hissed a reproach at him, then continued on.

But it was too late. Once again the boy kept glanced back. Ono repeated his gesture.

"Ono."

The boy tapped his own chest. "Hyanta."

The sister whirled, furious. She launched into a long diatribe, and the boy hung his head in shame. Or at least, he appeared to be trying to look ashamed, but his feet still refused to take him as far away from Ono as the girl seemed to demand. Finally, she threw her arms up and stomped away. The boy called after her, and she held her hands to her ears and sang some sort of chant at the top of her lungs.

Ono held back a chuckle at that. He made no further attempts to communicate, but kept his ten-pace distance. Gradually, the boy began sneaking looks his way again. When he seemed to realize the girl was no longer going to interfere, he half-whispered a question.

Ono shook his head. A few of the words sounded familiar, but the boy spoke far too quickly for him to pick up anything meaningful. He started again from the beginning.

"Ono. Friend. Ono Friend Hyanta? Yes? No?"

"Frin?" Severe puzzlement. "Hyanta." The boy pantomimed thrusting with a spear, making a small animal with his fingers and slaying it. "Hyanta. Mais."

"Hunter? You're a hunter?" Ono mimed back and pointed. "I am hunter, too. Ono is Hunter, see?" He considered forming his implant into the shape of a spear to illustrate, but thought better of it and settled for mimicking the boy's hand motions.

The boy seemed unsure, opening and closing his mouth. He tapped his forehead, then repeated the hunting gesture again, then tapped his heart and shook his head. Ono stared in confusion.

He says that's his name, not what he does. His name is Hunter.

"Decided to be helpful, have we?"

No reply from inside his mind.

Hunter cocked his head, thinking he was meant to understand Ono's mumbles. Ono cleared his throat and said with a raised voice, "Hunter is name. Name, Hunter. Name, Ono. Right?"

Hunter nodded. "Du. Right."

They continued on for a while as they traveled, exchanging words and phrases back and forth. The girl, never far away, interrupted with hissed warnings at first, but seemed to soften when she noticed how the boy had forgotten his discomfort. All at once Hunter had gone from withdrawn to single-minded, attacking the problem of understanding Ono like strand crushing rock, forceful and unremitting.

Ankara words flew at Ono in rapid succession, terms for the sky, trees, woodland animals and especially different forms of the strand, for which the Ankara seemed to have an extensive categorization system, which did not at all mirror Ono's experience with the living metal. At the same time, Hunter interrogated him for the equivalent words in Plainspeak, and had no trouble recalling almost everything he was told. From the boy's growing vocabulary, Ono teased out information, none of it particularly useful; the girl was in fact his sister, and her name was Evie, short for a word of unclear meaning; they were heading north, on some trip concerning their family, who had apparently left ahead of them.

The walker pulled up short as it sensed a network boundary and scanned the new connections for threats. Ahead, the Gwyer tavern was just visible through the haze coming off the overheated strand. Time to say goodbye to his new friends.

"Hunter. Ahead are many Karin," Ono said, using the word that as far as he could tell meant "anyone who isn't an Ankara."

"Understand?" Ono added a generous application of hand motions to his words. "Do not go north. East is more trees. Go east, then north."

Hunter fixed him with sharp brown eyes, and after some calculation seemed to follow his meaning. He turned and relayed the message to Evie, who was kneeling at the edge of the ridge. She responded with a question. Hunter turned back to Ono. His eyes went wide and he pointed and yelled.

Ono felt the swing coming through the air. He braced and shrugged, and the blow caught him on the shoulder instead of the head, knocking him off the walker. He landed in the dirt and skidded, leaving a large divot behind.

A man and woman stepped into view. Fesso's Children, he could tell from their tattooed faces and colored jewelry. The man had replaced the lower half of both his legs with strand. Curiously, he also held a bundle of loose strand over his back, which sparkled in the noon sun. Ono couldn't see any implants on the woman, but given that she was the one who hit him, she must have been packing intramusculars under her taut skin.

"We takin' this?" The man rubbed his hand over the walker admiringly.

"Must be keyed to him." The woman nodded at Ono.

The man sneered and took a slow look around, seeking another target. He found it in Hunter, standing stock-still with Evie quietly sneaking up behind to drag him away. With two long strides, the man reached him first.

"We'll grab these two." He took hold of Hunter and Evie darted back, teeth clenched. Her body began to shake, her rage so palpable that Ono doubted a word existed for it in their language or his own.

"Fesso won't want her, she's too old," the woman replied, disregarding Evie's reaction completely. "And what about the Big Int? We're supposed to be here delivering the stuff, nothing else."

"Lay off, Kaia, the Ints don't care 'bout stray kids disappearing."

Ono rolled up to a sitting position. In the time the pair had been yammering, the throbbing in his neck and shoulder had grown almost bearable.

"Who are you?" Kaia said.

"Just a concerned citizen, looking out for the welfare of children."

"Rat droppings," the man spat. "Look at the size of that implant. He's that hunter from Jolon, the one who tried to take in Demerian."

Kaia snarled and cracked her knuckles. "Wait here. I'll kill him and we'll take the body back to Mother."

She came forward and Ono rose, aware that Aunio was watching, waiting for his chance to take over. Punches came at superhuman speed, slicing through the air beside his ear as he slipped and dodged. She was strong, yes, but she telegraphed every blow. Ono stepped back, baiting her, waiting until she was off-balance, then stepped to the side and fired his right knee into her sternum. With a muted grunt, she crumpled.

The man flew through the air toward him before she hit the ground, propelled by his strand-augmented legs. He came too hard and too fast; Ono had no choice. He whipped his right arm forward, extending it to a long metallic rope and wrapping the end around the man's head. Dropping to one knee, he pulled the rope, slammed the man to the ground and watched him skid past.

That had been too much. Ono stood again, his head buzzing, perception drifting as if he were in a dream. Aunio was loose inside his mind, taking control of his nervous system. Kaia pulled out a knife the length of her forearm and stepped in to slash, and Ono's strand arm came up as a shield. The steel blade sliced through the softer metal, nearly severing it. Ono stumbled back, though he felt no pain; his head was swimming from Aunio overwhelming him, his vision doubled. Two copies of Kaia raised their knives to stab him in the heart.

She grunted and fell forward, rolling away from the walker, which had rammed her from behind.

That was Aunio's work; he was in enough control now to send a message to the walker. But the strand-creature wasn't built for fighting; Kaia popped back up with knife held high, and all it could do in response was to back away sheepishly. Kaia screamed and plunged the knife into its head, metal scraping on metal, shredding a deep hole down its centerline. Before she could pull it out, Ono watched as his arm folded into the shape of a battering ram and knocked her down again.

No. He had to keep control. The world was growing dark, the air thick. Ono felt numb, floating, yet still aware of his body and the other persona inhabiting it. He tried to move and Aunio shook him off, stretched their muscles, and walked them over to the prone Kaia.

"Hey!"

The man stood a few feet away, holding a shocked Hunter in one hand and a furious Evie in the other. A stream of blood ran from his nose as he spoke. "Get away from her, or I snap their necks."

Ono's hands reached down and pulled Kaia up by the back of her shirt.

"You think I care about the brats?" Aunio formed one finger into a sharp point and pressed it against Kaia's neck. "I'm the one who will make the threats, fool."

"Let her go!" The man's hands shook as the Ankara struggled in his grasp. What would he do if Aunio drove him to the point of desperation? If Aunio did kill his "sister," as Ono knew he would, would he crush the children out of spite?

Ono steeled himself. The world was hazy, indistinct, but he had to make one final push. All his focus went to the hand on the back of Kaia's neck. The effort of moving one finger felt like lifting a thousand tons.

"Stop," Aunio mumbled. "We have them."

You stop...he has...the children...

They let go of Kaia's neck. She rolled, then scrambled away, the fight gone from her.

"Come on, Mager!"

The man took one last look at Aunio, growled, then dropped the children. He picked up the bundle of strand he had been carrying and ran after Kaia. Hooking his arm around her waist, he bent low, then sprung upward, clearing a row of trees and landing thirty yards distant down the ridge.

Aunio stared after them. His anger, always close to the surface, bubbled forth. He examined the walker, which had only begun repairing the damage to its head, and gave it a swift kick.

"You imbecile!" he yelled. "At least you could have let me put a trace on her."

I saved their lives.

"You let yourself get distracted in the first place. That's why they got the jump on us." Aunio gritted his teeth and spoke in a low voice. "It won't happen again."

"Ono?"

Aunio whirled toward Hunter. The Ankara were gathering themselves up, still shocked. The boy stared, confused at Aunio's sudden rage. His eyes were large, his face small. Very...cute.

No.

Aunio grinned. To Fesso, her Children were more than soldiers in training. Collecting them was a hobby, a passion. The Ankara boy was unusual. A unique opportunity. Once Kaia and Mager brought word to Fesso about their encounter, she would know that such a tempting prize was hers to come and collect.

Stop. I won't let you. You're not going to use that boy as bait.

Aunio tapped into the strand. A small burst of electricity flared in his own skull. Ono fell silent, blacked out, cut off from the world and from memory.

"About time you shut up."

Hunter shook his head, still confused. Evie shouted at him harshly and pulled him away. He glanced once more at Aunio, then joined her.

They had gone thirty paces when Hunter stumbled and came to a stop. Evie turned and yelled something about the

"Karin," but this time Hunter wasn't looking back. His hands went to his head and he swayed, staggering as if drunk. Evie yelled at him again, shriller this time, as he collapsed face down into the dirt-covered strand.

5

HUNTER BLACKED OUT. Then he came to again. He was staring at the sky. He couldn't have been out too long, because the sky was still blue and bright, and clear like it had been all day. He blinked hard. When he opened his eyes again, Evie was above him, frowning.

He had seen this particular frown a lot, lately. Hunter knew that frowning meant someone was upset. That was easy. But there were other things behind a frown that were too subtle for him to tell. Usually, if Evie was upset, it was safe to assume she was angry at him. That worked well most of the time—once he made the assumption, he could leave her alone for a while, or act sorry for what he did, even if he didn't really know what it was. But this frown was different. None of the things he usually did made it go away.

"Hunter? What's wrong?"

Now he understood. A *worried* frown. Worried about him. But if he answered her question, told her what was wrong, that would only make her worry more. There was an ache running through his bones, his lungs and especially his head. He was slightly nauseous. The sickness rushed through him in waves and throbbed behind his temples. He knew instinctively that it was deathly serious.

Evie's fingers touched his forehead. His hair was wet.

"You're burning. We need to get you to a shaman."

That didn't make sense; obviously there wasn't any shaman

around. Hunter tried to shake his head and correct her, but his temples hurt.

"I'm going to help you." Evie's voice had a strange shake to it. Was she scared? Probably she was, since she must have known what was happening. She remembered the story of Cats-ears as well as he did.

Hunter closed his eyes and recalled.

It had been Cats-ears's own fault, all the elders agreed. The spirits of the forest took as well as gave, and a cut from an antler meant the deer's soul was not satisfied upon death. The smart thing to do would have been to return to their home field as soon as possible. But Cats-ears had continued on the hunt. Out of pride, they said. By the time the others carried him back, the infection had spread from his shoulder into his chest.

That had been the first time Hunter had heard that word, *in-fec-tion*. Tiny animals spreading in Cats-ears's blood—that was what the old tales said. The elders clucked their tongues at his stubbornness. But they stopped when the shaman couldn't control the fever anymore. Then they only walked with their heads down, muttering prayers to comfort themselves, and to help drown out the screams.

Hunter opened his eyes again. Evie was still staring at him. Maybe she didn't know what else to do. The wave of nausea had passed, but Hunter's body had started shaking.

The sky grew dark. But not from a cloud. Ono was standing over them. Evie leaned over Hunter, putting herself between them. Ono ignored her. He knelt down and inspected the swollen leg. He was frowning. He asked a question that Hunter didn't understand. His tone ended with a harsh snap Hunter hadn't heard from the Tainted man before.

"Sick," Hunter said.

"Sick," Ono mimicked the Pure word. Then he switched back to the Tainted tongue. "If help, Hunter not *dyen*."

Dyen? Dying. "What does that mean, 'help'?"

"Ono can help Hunter."

Ono held up his tainted arm, reached over and peeled a length of strand from it. He brought the metal close to Hunter's foot. Evie yelled and slapped at it. Ono pulled away, scowling.

"What's he doing?" Evie said.

"I don't understand," Hunter said to Ono. "Why?"

"Hunter knows. Strand helps Hunter. No dying."

"What?" Evie yelled.

Her voice hurt Hunter's ears. He blinked hard and coughed, then answered, "He says the strand will help me."

Evie stared at them wide-eyed for a moment. Then she crouched, her body shook, and she launched herself at Ono. Her speed surprised him and he stumbled back. Her nails found his human cheek, clawing him, opening three wide scrapes. He let out a clipped cry of pain and stood, scowling.

The flesh side of his mouth turned to a sneer. His strand-arm dropped to his side and the fingers elongated, separated, became writhing tentacles. Evie pulled her knife from her belt and crouched, teeth bared.

"Stop!"

Both of them looked down at Hunter.

"Don't fight. He's trying to help me." Hunter put his head back on the ground. The yell had exhausted him. "He...he doesn't know our ways."

"He knows what he's doing," Evie said in a low growl. "He's trying to infect you with the strand. You'll be one of them. You won't be a Pure anymore!"

Ono stayed still, tense, eyes flicking back and forth between them. The strand hung slick and glistening in his left hand. Hunter had seen and smelled the stuff every day he'd been alive, but he had never thought about having it inside him. It was strange, but it didn't seem terrible.

"What if he's right?" Hunter said.

He had spoken without thinking, but as soon as he said it,

the idea bloomed in his mind. He mouthed the next words slowly. "Maybe he really could cure me."

"What..." She grimaced. "What difference would that make? You can't become a thing like him. You have a spirit, Hunter. You can't just give it up, become nothing forever."

Hunter tried to respond, but a chill ran through his body. He turned and doubled over. Evie returned to his side and held him until the convulsions stopped.

"Evie," Hunter mumbled. "I'm going to die."

"Don't say that!"

"But it's true. If you let him work, I might live, otherwise I'll die. It's your choice."

"Don't do this to me. I'm the elder, it's up to me to stay true to the law. *Use no strand, take no strand into your body.*" She quoted the fourth and fifth to him. "It's not fair for you to make me do this!"

Fair? What difference did that make? He was too tired, and her words too confusing. "I spoke the truth. If we do nothing, I die. And you killed me."

Evie's eyes grew wide. She bit down hard and her jaw ground back and forth. She stood, showing him her back, then out a great scream and walked away, pulling her hair. Ono remained where he was; he had not moved at all since Evie had scratched him.

Evie stopped yelling and looked out over the plain of strand. She stood there, breathing raggedly for what seemed like a long time.

She spoke through clenched teeth. "Ask him if he'll take it out again."

"What?"

"Ask him!"

Hunter wet his lips. "Ono?"

Ono approached, standing over him much as he had before.

"Can you...*remove?*" Hunter spoke the Pure word and mimed the motion. "Strand *remove* from Hunter?"

Ono narrowed his eyes for a moment. He touched his finger

to his ripped cheek, then held out the tip in front of him, stained in red. "What is?"

"Blood?"

"Yes. *Blood.* Strand goes in blood. Remove sick from blood. After, remove strand from Hunter."

Hunter said to Evie, "He says he can. I think."

Evie growled. She approached Hunter, and for a few moments looked back and forth between Ono, the strand, and her brother. Then she knelt, took a deep breath and whispered into his ear, "You don't tell anyone, you understand? When we get back to the tribe, *no one* finds out I let him do this."

Hunter nodded. It had taken him a long time to understand how the others in the tribe felt about such things, and that talking about them could get him in trouble. Even now, though he knew the law, and could predict Evie's reactions, deep down he still didn't understand why she was so upset.

He remembered once when he was younger, wandering in the woods with his cousins. He had come across the body of a possum. Two days dead, perhaps. Maggots had coated it inside and out. Then as now, he knew the others wouldn't like it, but he didn't know why. Hunter knelt and observed the carcass for a while, watching the worms coming from its ears and eyes. He was so focused, he didn't hear his cousins sneaking up from behind, pushing him...

His eyes snapped open and he shivered. He was slipping in and out of consciousness. Ono stood over him. Hunter guessed he was waiting for an answer. He blinked hard, cleared his throat and spoke.

"Do it."

Even if he didn't know the words, Ono seemed to understand. He studied Hunter's foot, then changed his mind and wiped an area clean on his neck. Evie made a sound of protest, but didn't move. The chills were getting stronger. Ono placed his tainted hand on Hunter's chest to keep him still while he manipulated the strand with the other. The pressure of the oiled metal on top of him was an interesting sensation, but he was soon distracted by what was happening to his neck. Hunter felt a sharp prick, and then the length of strand writhed, worming its way inside, flipping and shaking.

Evie turned, hand on her mouth, nearly vomiting.

Hunter closed his eyes. His neck throbbed, but otherwise he couldn't feel the strand anymore. Brown splotches danced on the inside of his eyelids, and he faded into unconsciousness.

———

He came to with a deep breath, his whole body quaking. Hands held him down, but he couldn't tell whose; his eyes were too heavy to open. For a long time he writhed in agony—not pain, but a deep discomfort that touched every muscle and organ.

He may have blacked out again after that, perhaps several times. All he knew was that when he opened his eyes, his head still hurt, but the rushing feeling had subsided. Sunshine warmed his skin. The chills were gone. He tried to sit up but his muscles ached.

Evie was there. "How do you feel?" She touched his head. "Your fever's down."

"Not...as bad." How long had he been out? The sun was still high. Could the strand really have worked so quickly?

Ono said something at his side. Hunter felt a slick pull in his neck as the Tainted removed the strand from inside him. He felt cloth on his neck, a makeshift bandage. Ono demonstrated how Hunter was to hold it on himself by roughly shoving his hand against it. Blood bloomed wet on Hunter's fingertips through the cloth.

"We have to get out of here," Evie said. "Those Tainted could come back. We need to get away from this one, too. Go far away, forget all this happened. Can you move?"

Hunter didn't answer. He was distracted by Ono stepping back, holding the strand up in the light and examining it. Ono frowned, then said something that sounded like a curse.

"What?" Hunter said. "What is it?"

"Hunter sick," Ono said flatly. "Dying."

Hunter pressed his fingers to his eyes and rubbed out the remnants of his headache. "No. Feeling better. No fever." He touched his palm to his forehead and shook his head.

"Yes," Ono said. "Hunter sick. Blood is sick. More fever comes. Ono cannot help. Seeker can help. Seeker to the northwest."

He tossed the piece of bloody strand into the bush, then headed to his tame strand creature.

"Hunter rides. Comes north. Seeker helps, no dying."

The strand on the creature's back stretched and reformed into a pair of basket-like seats. Ono mounted it in front, then jacked his thumb toward the empty spaces.

"What?" Evie said. "What did he say?"

———

By the time they reached the outskirts of the Midlands, Evie's lips were shut so tight, Hunter wondered if she'd ever speak again.

"How can you trust him?" she had said, after his eleventh or twelfth attempt at explaining.

Hunter had glanced at Ono. He hadn't looked very trustworthy at that moment, scowling at them from his creature. But he was telling the truth. Hunter could feel it deep in his bones: something was still wrong with him, suppressed for now, but ready to flare up worse than before.

"He helped me already," Hunter replied. "And he's going to take us north, where we need to go, anyway." He had left out the "west" portion of Ono's intended direction.

"Listen to me, Hunter," Evie said. "Every time we break the law, something bad will happen. That's *why* the laws exist in the first place! Remember the bridge over the dam? I ran across it when I shouldn't have, and that's how we ended up in this mess. This is all my fault, because I didn't heed what my elders told me."

"How do you know?"

"What?"

"How do you know the bridge was trying to hurt us? What if it was saving us? The giants were coming behind, we had to get out of the way—"

She grabbed him by the chin and turned his face, fingernails digging in his jaw. "Do *not* be concerned with the will of the strand."

"We don't know." He ripped his head free. "If I can't be concerned, then I don't know, and neither do you."

They had argued more after that, while Ono looked on, giving occasional annoyed grunts. But Hunter had known he would get his way eventually. He knew now that no matter what she said, Evie wouldn't risk letting him die.

She had refused to ride next to him at first, insisting on running alongside the creature. But she could not keep up with its long, six-legged strides, and after much barking by Ono that she was slowing them down, she had finally agreed to sit. Hunter had tried to speak to her once after that. The sound she made in response reminded him of the tales his tribesmen told of the noise of bears preparing to strike.

"Ono?" Hunter said, turning his attention from his sister. No answer came back. "Where are we going, again?"

"Bordertown," Ono mumbled.

"*Bordertown.*" Repetition would help him remember the word. He had been trying to learn more of Ono's language, but ever since their encounter with the other Tainted, Ono had been less eager to speak. Almost as if Hunter or Evie had offended him in some way. But he still seemed willing to help them, even if his mood had soured.

Hunter looked over the field of strand to his left. They must be in the Midlands now, because the ground was mostly blue strand, carved into square-shaped dips and monolithic rectangles jutting upward, an endless maze of right angles. He had passed through them every spring, but he didn't usually get such a good view—the Pure took secret routes on their way north, through abandoned ruins and riverbanks where the strand did not grow. He couldn't look for too long though, because gazing to the side of the moving creature made him sick to his stomach.

He waited until the nausea began to set in and then closed his eyes. "This man we're going to," he said in his best approximation of the Tainted speech. "Seeker. He will use the strand to help me?"

The answer came after a long pause. "Seeker has many kinds of strand. One kind can help Hunter. Seeker will give, if Ono can *convis.*"

"*Convis?*" Con, con…convince. Of course. The word was almost the same in Tainted as in Pure. "Why do you need to convince him?"

Silence again. Hunter took a deep breath. He was starting to feel sick again, through his whole body.

Convis. Bordertown. Memorizing words was a game he knew well.

He remembered the previous summer, the tribe's arrival in the mountains. The smell of the northern trees, the cool air after a month of walking in the heat. And especially the crowds. That was why the Pure went south in the first place; there wasn't enough room in the highlands, and the spring harvest would run out in a few months. But no one was worried about that yet; the arrival was a time for celebration. Their mountain cousins brought out fermented honey and played music, and everyone danced while haggling over where to set up their camps.

Hunter didn't like those gatherings. Too many strange people and loud voices. Boys stared at him, some around his age and some older, their faces having grown wider and meaner in the past year. Two of them, Beetle and Growler, whispered to each other while they glanced at him. Hunter had coughed and blinked hard, then sidled up to his father.

"Father?"

His father's eyes flicked toward Hunter, then back to the short, bald man he was sharing a drink with.

"I'm going to explore the north woods."

No response. Hunter went off, up one gently sloping mountain and down another. He listened to the birdsong change as he went. There was almost no strand up here, just the occasional trace of gray sprouting from the ground. Hunter walked and walked, until he came to a group of brightly decorated tents nestled in a rocky face. A family of Illani Pure, by the markings. The patriarch sat outside and used strange words to hail him. The Illani did not make a habit of visiting the woods every year; they preferred to stay in small groups, and most of the Pure found their customs as difficult to understand as their heavy dialect.

Hunter watched the man wave and smile, until he understood that he was being invited inside, where a meal was being prepared. He met the three children; two were young ones whose names he could not recall. And Lily. She was ten, like him, with hair woven in complex patterns. He remembered it well, because if she noticed he was looking at her, she would always turn her face away, as if the ground or the tent sides suddenly required her attention.

He had returned the next day, and the day after. He liked learning the Illani speech, contorting his mouth to fit their accent, and he liked spending time with Lily, sitting outside with her while she mixed her paints and dyes. She wasn't like his cousins or the other children he met in the mountains. She always smiled when she saw him, and she never asked him why he was always coughing and clearing his throat.

One day, near the solstice, they watched the entire sunset together, from first dip below the horizon to last glimmer of twilight. Not a word passed between them, though he could speak to the Illani like family by then.

"Meet me at the waterfall tomorrow evening," she had said. "Do you know where it is?"

He did, but he didn't like going there. Nevertheless, when the sun fell near the hills the next day, he found himself on the path to Bear's Paw Lake. His stomach was tingling as he approached the falls. The water was green with white froth, loud as it pounded into the pool. He didn't see Lily anywhere.

"*Hiya* Lily!" he called into the trees. He walked around the pool and called a few more times, hopping on rocks where the brush grew too thick near the water's edge.

The bushes parted and Growler stepped out, holding his spear.

"Why're you talking so funny?"

Before Hunter could answer, Beetle came up behind him. The larger boy's mass forced him in toward the water. Hunter dropped to all fours, hugging the rock to keep his balance.

"Can you even understand me?" Growler said. "I asked a question."

Beetle's strong hands gripped his armpits and lifted. Why would he do that? Hunter kicked the air and the boys laughed.

"Talk funny like that again." Growler leaned over and turned his head upside-down to match Hunter's view. "Say those things again and we'll stop."

Hunter stared up at the sky. It was late and the trees were thick, but the light still burned his eyes. He blinked hard, but couldn't wipe the tears because they were holding his arms.

"Do it!"

Then his head was under the falls, face up. Cold water soaked him through. Hunter shut his eyes tighter. Were there fish in this lake? Perhaps there were some that lived way down in the depths, where light never reached. Closed off, apart from the world. The boys yelled something, getting ready to dunk him again.

They stopped and held him still.

"Hunter?" Lily's voice.

Beetle and Growler put Hunter down and hurried away. Hunter sat up and coughed.

"Are you all right?"

He was cold. But his head felt hot. The rock he was sitting on sparkled in the waterfall spray. He blinked hard and cleared his throat and eventually found his voice. "I'm fine. You can leave."

"But...but I thought..."

He held his knees together and stared out into the trees, observing the birds that preyed on the flitting insects. "I don't need you here. I'm busy. Leave me alone."

Silence for a moment. When she spoke again, her voice quavered like she was crying. "What...?"

His head was starting to feel better. But the light still burned his eyes. He had to keep blinking it out. He heard Lily run away. After that day he wouldn't see her again.

That was fine. He sat still while time passed and his vision faded to black.

———

Something shook Hunter's shoulder and he opened his eyes. The strand creature swayed beneath him with its six-legged gait.

"Are you all right?" Evie said. "You were mumbling, sounded like a nightmare."

"I..." Hunter rubbed his temples. "I don't remember."

"Your skin looks bad. It's sort of...green."

Hunter groaned and closed his eyes. He felt he had been asleep a long time. "Ono? How much further?"

"We're here."

Ono halted the creature and hopped off. With Evie's help, Hunter sat up. The walls of the Tainted town rose over them, built of piled stones with strand running through the gaps between them. The land around was a carpet of metal, spreading out from Bordertown like the spokes of a wheel, only broken to the west where it met a languid, gray river.

Ono approached the gate and talked with the watchman. The guard was dressed like a Tainted, but his body held no strand, at least none so obvious as Ono's. After a few words, Ono returned and leaned against the body of the creature, his arms crossed.

"We cannot go. Seeker should have met us outside the wall. Not a good sign."

Hunter curled his knees in close and watched the gate. Evie squirmed beside him, grinding her teeth. Hunter hadn't realized that to receive help, they would actually have to enter a Tainted town. He had stared countless times at the buildings across the Riversea, but only in his dreams had he imagined he would ever explore something like it.

The watchman turned, nodded and stepped aside. A woman emerged from the town. She strode forward, hands on wide hips, red hair tied in a topknot, run through with gray. Small wrinkles spread along her eyes and cheekbones as she sent a scowl in Ono's direction. She said something in the Tainted tongue Hunter didn't catch, but he thought it might have been along the lines of, "I told you not to come back."

Ono responded gruffly and pointed at Hunter. The woman raised an eyebrow and probed with more questions. Then she walked around the creature to examine him further.

"Word of the Ints," she said, "you really are a Pure, aren't you?"

Evie's mouth dropped wide.

"You...you speak our language?" Hunter said.

"Well enough. I learned to help my work. For people who shun the strand, it's often surprising how much useful information the Pure have about it."

"You're Seeker?" Hunter said. "The one with the strand that can heal me?"

"Seeker is my job. My name is Trina." She gave Evie a once-over, then reached out to touch a bruised spot on her arm. Evie snarled and pulled away.

Ono barked something with his back turned, and he and Trina began to jabber back and forth again.

"What is it?" Hunter said. "You talk too fast."

"Some…personal business," Trina replied. "May I?" She felt Hunter's pulse, then put a hand to his chest as he breathed in and out. "Ono wants me to see if I have something which can treat you."

"Can you?" The conversation was making Hunter tired. He leaned back and fluttered his eyes. "Will you?"

"Unfortunately, he didn't leave me much choice. If I don't do something now, you'll be dead in days." She heaved a sigh and waved to the watchman. "You all can come in. You'll go to my home."

"Thank you," Hunter said. Evie shot him a scolding glance, and he hung his head like he was supposed to.

"Don't thank me, yet," Trina said as they passed. "We still have to find a functional for your treatment. I warn you, young man: this process will not be pleasant. Expect much pain before the coming of dawn."

Hunter said nothing. He closed his eyes and let the darkness take him.

6

AUNIO WATCHED TRINA cradle the boy and carry him into her home, a ramshackle two-story of wood, the cheap kind that was more strand than tree. She disappeared up a narrow staircase, and Evie scurried after them like a scrawny rat.

Kelas, Trina's rotund, balding husband, watched the procession with some confusion. He turned to Aunio and smiled. "Ono! An unexpected pleasure!"

"Unexpected, certainly," Aunio mumbled.

"It's too bad the children aren't here. They're off with Acolyte Mustin for their lessons."

"Why too bad?"

"Eh? Well, because they'd love to see you, of course!"

"Oh," Aunio said. "Of course."

Small Talk. Revolting. But he had to be careful not to raise suspicions, though it was probably too late in Trina's case. As far as these people knew, he *was* Ono. Coming to Bordertown was a necessary inconvenience, the only way to keep Hunter alive long enough to use him as a lure for Fesso. But if Trina learned of that, or otherwise suspected he would bring the boy to harm, she wouldn't release him without a fight, and this plan would be difficult enough to pull off without the entire town watch on his tail.

"...that was three years ago, though; I don't know if they still remember," Kelas was still yammering.

"Yes. If you'll excuse me..." Aunio climbed the stairs and

followed clinking sounds to a cramped workshop. Inside, a latticed rack hung with lengths of strand crowded the already-low ceiling. More samples of strand peeked from labeled drawers in rough-hewn cabinets. Hunter lay on a workbench, his thin limbs splayed, while Trina stood over him, examining the remains of the wound where Aunio had attempted to cure his infection.

Trina headed to her drawers and began shuffling through them. "Why did you come to me, Ono?"

"I told you in my message. Now I've shown you. What more do you want?"

"You should have taken the boy to a tech when he first got sick."

"This may shock you, but the place I found these two was somewhat remote. I tried to filter out the bacteria myself, but the boy had gotten himself more than one strain, or else the buggers mutated. The initial infection was gone, but the latent one seemed worse. I needed a better functional, and you always have some choice samples you've saved for a rainy day."

She dipped a segment of strand in an oil-filled bucket and regarded him with narrowed eyes. "Something's changed about you, Ono. You were never this sort of man before."

"What? The sort who would ride thirty miles to save a dying boy?"

"You say that as if you deserve a commendation." She raised a length of strand in each hand and studied them close through her ocular implant as they spliced themselves together. "Bordertown may be on the frontier, but we still get word from Jolon. I've heard story after story; they say Ana left you."

"My family is my own business."

"And what about that man you killed?"

"My job has always been a rough one. No fugitives want to be caught."

"And yet somehow you always managed to defend yourself before, without...what was it? Hanging a man upside down, by his *what*?"

Aunio caught himself sighing impatiently. "Stories become exaggerated in the telling. We've known each other fifteen years—don't I deserve some trust?"

"Very well," she said, though she clearly didn't believe it. "I don't want to discuss it now, anyway. *Hyanta? Cavu can za?*"

Hunter stirred on the table. He opened his eyes slightly, then shut them again with a groan. Her lips tight, Trina slid a pinpoint of strand across his flesh, re-opening the cut Ono had made earlier. As blood ran over in big drops, she fed the length of it inside, until it began worming in on its own. Hunter shook as the metal spread along his skin, tiny wires exploring his clavicle.

In the corner, Evie made a sound like a wounded animal and jumped to her feet, her hand over her mouth.

"Evie?" Trina said.

Evie shook her head and dashed down the stairs. The front door slammed, rattling the house.

"I hope she'll be all right," Trina said, turning her attention back to Hunter.

"The townspeople pose her no threat. With that knife, I'd bet on her against anyone here."

Trina shot him a suspicious glare. "That's not what I meant."

On the table, Hunter took three long, wheezing breaths, his back arching with each inhalation. Then he went limp, snoozing quietly with a length of drool on his cheek.

———

Evie fled out the main gate. She just couldn't stay any longer, couldn't watch her own brother subjected to *that*. She had hated the Tainted town as soon as she entered, the smell of it, the oppressive height and claustrophobic packing of the buildings.

The river was a hundred paces away, giving her plenty of time to think about what she was doing. *You left Hunter there all alone, with those people.* Her father's voice in her mind. He was right, too.

She reached the water and turned upstream, past walls stained with green moss, until she reached the end of the town. There she stepped through ankle-thick mud, crawling with worms and beetles. Relief. Being away from the strand, and those that venerated it, made her feel like she could breathe again despite the stink of the marsh. But with it came the terrible knowledge that she had abandoned her half-brother, forsaken her duty to the tribe.

She kept moving, running two or three miles east along the riverbank, until she found a small pocket of woods amid the endless blue plains. She sat up against a tree, heart pounding in her chest, and drew her head to her knees.

What now? She didn't have a plan when she left; it was an instinctive fleeing from revulsion. But now that she was here, she had to do something. Nightfall was coming. She would need a fire, and more importantly, to find food. She was weak, exhausted from the days of travel, and it was affecting her decision-making. Maybe on a full stomach she would find the courage to rescue Hunter from the Tainted.

Starting slowly, she scouted the woods, gathering kindling, collecting ferns or berries when she passed them. The forest was small, and half-blighted with gray strand, but the more she worked the less she had to think. By nightfall, she lay by a roaring fire circled in stone, the leftovers of a generous meal spread around her. The familiar, comforting darkness of the woods surrounded her, orange light dancing among the nearby trees. The movement of the spirits. Evie stared into the depths of the night, listening to the crackle of the flames. If she listened closely enough, her uncle had said, the spirits would instruct her. What were they telling her now? She listened and listened, but heard nothing, felt no touch but that of her own creeping shame.

Sleep took her. She woke at dawn with a crick in her neck, the droning of flies in her ear. A line of ants had formed along a root she had pulled and cooked the night before, and as she shook them off and ate the final bite, an idea sprang to her mind. A beautiful idea, one that filled her with a sense of purpose.

The food. Hunter needed it more than her, if he was going to recuperate. That was why the spirits had brought her here, the only place where she could get real nourishment for him. Whatever swill the Tainted ate, it was probably as rotten as them.

She repeated her search from the previous night, combing the woods from west to east and back again. But most of what she found she had already picked clean. At home, the solution would have been to move on to another area of forest, but here there was no other area; again and again she reached the border where the trees gave way to open land, and still the pouch on her belt remained nearly empty. On the fifth such journey, despair tugged at her heart as she tramped back into the interior. What had she been thinking, eating so much herself? The spirits had guided her, sent her a message, and she had stomped all over them with her selfishness.

A movement in the brush caught her eye, and she stopped, holding her breath for silence. A rabbit, its brown body visible against a patch of green grass, crouched past a row of brambles to her left.

Carefully, she pulled her knife from her belt. Holding it by the blade, she crept around to where she could get a clear view. The rabbit had heard her, of course, but was staying put for the moment, thinking the paces between them were enough to escape. Throwing the knife was the only way, and among the tribe, Evie considered herself better than average at it. As quietly as she could, she uttered aloud a request for permission from the rabbit's spirit. The animal didn't move. She whispered thanks, then held her breath and pulled back.

Her stomach rumbled, long and loud. The rabbit took off like a dart. Evie tossed the knife, which clattered into a nearby stretch of gray strand, nowhere near the retreating creature.

She cursed and retrieved the knife, then hacked at a nearby branch and stomped away in frustration. What a failure she was. She couldn't even provide a little meat for her poor brother, just a token while he endured so much suffering.

She walked with head low, her mind a storm. Along a fallen log, partially hidden by leaves, a row of brown caps caught her eye.

Evie stopped. She took pride in knowing every species of mushroom there was to know, from the white, flat belly-fillers, some of which she had stuffed herself with the night before, to the red-tinged heart-vipers, a bite of which would leave a grown woman howling in agony for days. But these thumb-size brown morsels she had seen only rarely, dried, set atop a place of honor in the confines of a smoke-filled shaman's tent.

No, these mushrooms didn't make a sumptuous meal, or deliver deadly poison. They did something quite different.

Aunio stood on the narrow walkway atop the Bordertown wall, his back to the wind. He brought up something gooey from the depths of his silicon-encrusted lungs and hawked it over the side. When he, or Ono as he had called himself then, had first apprenticed as a bounty hunter, no one had told him how much of the job would involve waiting around. But if he were stuck in this dung-heap of a town, at least it was slightly more bearable in the breeze than in the oppressive heat down below, among its miserable people.

Solitude—no one else seemed to respect its value. Being dependent on others bred weakness. Aunio was a great bounty hunter, better than Ono at any rate, exactly because he kept his focus on what he needed to do, not the feelings of others. If only the boy hadn't gotten sick, hadn't forced him to come here, and introduced these needless complications.

Still, once he was well, the Ankara would remain his best way to find Fesso. The old gangster should have been too cunning and experienced to be drawn out by a simple ruse, but children were her obsession; float the right one before her, and she would abandon all logic to obtain him. Bordertown was well-situated for his purposes as well, not far from the edge of the Gridlands, near Fesso's hideout.

The only problem was Trina. He had figured her sympathy for the boy would motivate her to intercede, despite any misgivings. But he hadn't expected those misgivings would be so strong that she would refuse to release him back into Aunio's control. She wanted an explanation, and he was poorly suited to deliver it. Despite his strengths in other areas, Aunio was too different from Ono to ever impersonate him convincingly.

Which meant, despite the risks, it was time to call on some help.

Aunio took a deep breath. His eyes fluttering, he instructed the strand to access dormant portions of his brain.

What...can't... Ono stirred slowly at first, his thoughts a mish-mash of complaints.

"Wake up. I have a favor to ask."

A favor? Where are we?

"Bordertown. The Pure boy fell ill, but Trina is tending to him. She thinks he's going to pull through."

Ono was too disoriented to respond. Aunio opened their eyes wide and turned slowly in a circle, letting him see where he was firsthand.

You're still going through with that plan? To track his location?

"Yes. I implanted a beacon when I first tried to filter out his infection."

What do you want from me?

"I need your help handling Trina. She's as meddlesome as ever."

I'm not helping you hurt that boy.

"The boy will be fine. Once I have Fesso's cronies in hand, he'll be free to go."

...said the least trustworthy person on the planet. Aunio, put me back in control.

"As long as the implants stay charged, I'm in charge. And the town has plenty of power to spare." To illustrate, Aunio looked away from the nest of pitched roofs, out to the plains, where the strand lay abuzz from a full day in the sunshine. "My only goal is to capture Fesso. Isn't that what you want? Do you really wish to return to the Ints empty handed, and not fulfill our deal?"

Ono fell into a petulant silence.

"I leave the choice up to you. But if you betray me now, we may not get another chance. We could be stuck in our present arrangement forever."

"Having a nice conversation with yourself?" Trina's hands appeared at the top of the ladder behind them, followed shortly by the rest of her. "I guess you needed my company more than I thought."

Aunio grunted. This would have to be subtle; he had to cede just enough control, let Ono out just slightly, but not so far that he couldn't pull him back if need be. He turned away to hide his fluttering eyes, then muttered, "Well?"

Well what? Ono felt the change, but didn't recognize it at first.

"Speak."

"Speak?" Trina said. "About what?"

Ono worked his jaw up and down, unused to the feeling of being able to move it.

"Problem with your teeth?" Trina crossed her arms in front of her chest.

"No." Ono cleared his throat. "I...never mind. Tell me about Hunter."

"He's resting soundly." Trina lifted an eyebrow. "Nice of you to ask, for once."

Ono nodded and leaned out over the wall. Aunio could feel his mind working furiously, still recovering from the transfer. He would be wondering how much control he'd been given, how much could he get away with before Aunio pulled him back in.

"I want to know more about this mission you're on," Trina said. "You owe me that much."

"Of course," Ono said. "But you might not believe me."

"Try me."

"Not long ago, I paid a visit to the High Temple, to see if the Ints could...to ask a favor of the Ints. To my surprise, they answered; they told me if I wanted their help, I needed to hunt someone for them. Fesso herself."

Trina made no effort to hide her shock. Ono held her gaze for several seconds, letting her know he was serious. She coughed and smoothed the front of her flannel work shirt. "If the Ints want Fesso...this could be bad."

"Hmm?"

"Just a feeling. Nothing concrete, but for months I've suspected Fesso might be up to something. First she moves her headquarters, then there are reports of her Children being active all over the Plains." Trina joined him at the parapet and looked out northeast, where the evening sky faded toward the Gridlands. "I figured it was only the usual dirty dealings before, but now, if the Ints are involved...what has she gotten herself into? What could the repercussions be for us?"

Ono drummed his fingers on the stone. "You know, those henchmen I ran into, Kaia and Mager; one of them mentioned something about a 'Big Int.' Does that mean anything to you?"

Trina fell silent for a time, then shook her head. "I'm not sure. I'll think on it. Ono—" She hit him with a piercing stare. Aunio knew he dared not look away. Decades of combing the wilderness for usable pieces of strand had sharpened her instincts, and she brought all her discernment to bear in that gaze. "Tell me truly: are those Ankara children involved in this somehow? You said you came upon them by chance; do they have any connection to your search for Fesso?"

Ono's mind tensed. Aunio could feel him contemplating, getting ready to shout the truth. *Don't you dare.* He prepared an electric shock in their brain to shut him down if need be, at the risk of knocking them both unconscious.

Ono took a deep breath. Another burst of mental activity, a decision being made, and he spoke.

"They have no part in this." His tone was soft, full of the graciousness that Aunio's words always lacked. "Trina, I know I've been involved in strange events, lately. But trust me; I would no sooner harm those children than I would my own." He placed his hand on his chest, fingers touching cold metal on one side and warm flesh on the other.

Trina nodded and let her gaze drop. She turned back to the view, watching the lengths of gray strand slowly tugging their way across the landscape.

With a quick pull, Aunio took control of their body again. He nodded and headed away from Trina, as if wanting to be alone with his thoughts.

"Very good," he muttered, once he had reached a safe distance.

I won't protect you forever, Aunio. If you hurt that boy—

"Oh, stuff it." Aunio leaned back against the parapet, careful to keep his smile turned away from Trina's suspicious glare.

7

SPLOTCHES OF LIGHT appeared to Hunter. He groaned and tried to roll over, but bundles of strand on his sides blocked him. When he opened his mouth to speak, his throat was too dry to do more than rasp.

"Hunter?" a voice said.

Everything hurt, his back especially. He was lying on a hard wooden slab. He could barely remember them placing him on top of it when he arrived. Where was Evie? He tried to call her name, and a croaking sound came out.

"Hunter, it's all right. Stay calm."

It took him a while to place the voice—the woman who had met them at Bordertown's gate—and even longer to remember her name, Trina. Someone else spoke, a man he didn't recognize. Trina hushed the second voice away.

"Hunter, I'm going to tell the strand to put you to sleep."

He nodded.

"Shh. Just let go."

The light of the world shrank. Hunter felt as if he were falling, face up, arms to his side. He watched the light become a pinpoint, then blink out, but still he fell in the darkness, down, down, then slowing, hovering. What was happening? He tried to re-orient his body, and found he could pull himself upright. He hung there for a moment, blind but aware, and then his feet touched something solid.

He stood. The weakness and pain in his muscles were gone.

All he saw was black.

"Hello?"

His surroundings lit all at once. He was standing in a forest. The sky was a brilliant white, the ground a perfectly level mat of pine needles. But there was something wrong with the trees. They were pines, not particularly old and thick, yet they towered toward the sky, their trunks free of branches, their tops invisible. And they were spaced regularly, in a grid. When Hunter leaned side to side, the lines of trees made regular patterns stretching to the distance.

"Hello?" He walked forward and gaped up at the tall trees. Something felt wrong. He shouldn't have been here. He was asleep; all this was a dream. But he couldn't wake up, so he might as well accept what was happening. He walked on, squinting, sometimes shielding his eyes with his hand. If he didn't allow too much light in, the dreamlike feeling of this place lessened.

He tried to find the edge of the forest, counting the trees along the way. He counted three hundred twenty five before he decided to stop; the emptiness in the distance had not changed, and anyway he had the distinct feeling he had somehow come back to where he started, though there were no tracks in the pine needles to mark his progress.

He sat with his back against a tree. Was this really all there was? Was he meant to just wait here, in this prison-like dream?

No, there was something he was missing. The trees were a puzzle. Someone had brought him here with a purpose, not just to trap him, but to see what he would do.

To watch him.

Hunter stood. He didn't know whether the strange forest was really a dream, but in some ways it was like one. He could know things without seeing, without hearing, like the whispers of silent voices. If he stayed quiet, focused on his instincts, he could pinpoint what they were telling him.

Behind you, the voices said, two trees down to the left.

Hunter turned slowly, trying not to reveal what he knew. He looked down through the very corner of his squinted eye. There was a brown fuzzy patch, just at the base of the stump, most of it hidden behind the trunk. Some sort of animal. He lunged toward it.

The thing took off, skittering over the forest floor, weaving between the trees. Hunter gave chase, his long strides easy, effortless. He dived and got one hand on the animal's thin, short tail. It squeaked and spun, folding itself in half, and sank its teeth into his thumb.

"Ow!"

Pain shot from his hand toward his heart, like liquid fire. Hunter jumped up, yanking the creature with him by its jaws. He grabbed its body with his other hand and pulled it free.

The pain vanished instantly. His hand was whole, not a drop of blood. Hunter looked from it to the animal still clenched in his fist. A river otter. A baby. He had never seen one so close. The whiskers on its face parted, and it looked almost as if the animal were smiling.

"I'm sorry," it said.

He dropped the otter and it landed on its back, then flipped over and skittered a few paces away. There it faced him again and rose on its hind legs, paws tucked by its chest.

"How did you..." Hunter began.

"How did I what?" The otter cocked its head. Its eyes were featureless black dots. "How did I talk to you? Or how did I make you feel pain? Or how did I hide from you before? Or how did I bring you here? Because I didn't do *that*, you know."

Hunter held up his palms. "How did you talk? Let's start with that."

"I can't talk." The otter replied. "At least, not in your language. You hear what you want to hear, because that's what makes sense to you."

"But that doesn't make sense," Hunter said. "Otters can't talk."

"Oh." It furrowed its tiny brow. "Well, maybe you're broken, then?"

"Probably," Hunter muttered. "What's your name?"

"You can call me Zeke!" That toothy grin again.

"Zeke? All right. Zeke. I'm Hunter. What is this place?"

Zeke seemed puzzled again, rubbing his paws over his ears in consternation. "This is the Anywhere. The All-Place where we come from. Where we live."

"We? There's more of you?"

He nodded. "My family. Alef, Betty, Caesar, Della—"

"—right. And Zeke. I understand." Hunter scanned the trees. "But where are they?"

Zeke looked down. "Separated. Walls came up between us. Then I was alone. I haven't seen them since."

"Oh." Hunter leaned closer, unable to stop himself from staring at the incredible creature.

Zeke looked up suddenly, eyes bright. "But now you're here! And you can open the door. I can feel it!"

"I, uh…I don't…"

"Please? Please?" Zeke scrunched himself down until he was half his full height, paws folded under his chin. "I'm sorry I hurt you before. I really am!"

"It's fine." Hunter held out his hands again. "I don't mind helping you. I just don't think I can."

"Wrong!" Zeke yelled. "You control this segment, I'm sure of it. If you tell the door to open, it will."

"But I don't see a door." Once again Hunter checked along the four directions of the grid. Endless rows of thin, tall trees, and whiteness behind.

"Oh. Well, *that's* not a problem." Zeke plopped down onto all fours and made a quick circuit around the nearest tree. "The door is there. You're just not looking the right way, or you would see it."

"Looking the right way?" Did Zeke mean the squinting? He opened his eyes wider again, and the same disorienting, surreal feeling returned. He covered his face and staggered back. "I can't do it. There's something…it's like there's too much."

Zeke nodded. "Externals can't see everything at once. That's what my parents told me. You have a brain for input, but your brain can only see what it's used to seeing. When you come to the Anywhere, your brain makes up something and shows it to you. That's why you have to look the right way."

"But there's nothing. You can see a door here?"

"Yup."

"Then take me there."

"I can't. You're already right next to it."

Hunter spun in a circle. A door, here? At the top of one of the trees, perhaps?

He approached a trunk and ran his hands over the rough surface. It wouldn't be an easy climb, but he could hug it tight with his arms and legs and shimmy up at least some of the way. He hopped on and pulled himself up.

"See anything?" Zeke asked when he had risen twenty feet. The otter's voice was no more than a high peep.

"No." Something was wrong. Hunter's arms and legs weren't tired, but something was dragging him down, as though gravity had become stronger. The tree was harder to grasp, almost slippery, despite the texture feeling the same under his palms as it had below. He strained and hugged tight, but after a few more feet he reached his limit. He let himself slide down. The rough bark left no mark on his skin as it brushed past.

He stared back up at the tops of the trees. They disappeared into the white sky, as if enveloped by fog. Was the door really up there, beyond where he could reach? His instincts said no.

Hunter paced while Zeke watched, rolling on his back and flapping his tail. What had the otter said? *You have to look the right way.* The right way, not in the right place. As if he were right on top of the door, and it was only a matter of perspective that kept him from seeing it.

He glanced down at the bed of pine needles underneath him. He hadn't noticed before, but they weren't exactly needles. Each individual one was long, so long he couldn't see their ends. They twisted and wove around one another, forming a solid carpet of material.

Like the strand.

Hunter knelt. The fibers definitely felt more like pine needles than strand. They were brown and brittle, and snapped when he plucked at them. He dug through, and found they went only a few inches deep, lying atop a bed of packed earth. Hunter pressed his face to the ground, squinting along the fibers. Zeke made a *skitching* sound behind him. Hunter had a sense of familiarity. How many times had he done this before, pressing close to where ladybugs perched on blades of grass, or caterpillars on branches, wondering what the world would look like from their point of view?

The idea expanded from his mind into reality. Instead of imagining himself crawling on the pine needles, it was actually happening. He was shrinking, or the world was growing larger, stretching, the trees arching away from him. Hunter blinked, dizzy, and when he sat up again he was perched atop a length of pine needle that was twenty feet wide.

"Oh," he said. "That's interesting."

Fibers above and below him arched off into the distance, equally as huge as the one beneath his feet. From so close, he could hear and feel crackles of energy as gentle bulges ran through them. A bulge passed underneath him, and Hunter dropped to all fours to ride out the wave.

"This is good. Very good." Zeke zipped between his arms and legs, having shrunk in size along with him. "All you have to do now is go to the door."

"But I still don't see a door."

"Come *oooon*," Zeke whined.

Hunter squinted down the length of the fiber. Endless and empty, its slow curve arched off into the distance. It would take him days to walk beyond where he could see. Unless...

He turned sideways, facing the shorter width of the fiber rather than looking down its length. It curved down beneath him, such that a few steps would send him tumbling into the vast abyss below. But he was beginning to get the hang of this place. Holding his breath, Hunter took a giant step forward.

It worked. Instead of sliding off the edge, the orientation of the ground changed. Wherever he was standing on the face of the fiber was "up." He took a few more steps to prove it, until he stood on what should have been the side of the massive cylinder, the fibers which had previously run alongside it now far overhead.

"Right, right!" He felt a few scrabbling claws on his back, and then Zeke appeared on his shoulder. "Just a little more."

Hunter stepped forward. There was something special about the underside of the fiber. As he approached it, the world shifted, separating. The fabric of reality seemed to turn inside out, and light of every color shone through the gaps. Zeke tittered with excitement, just audible over the thumping of Hunter's heart.

"It's too much," Hunter whispered. His eyes were slits, his teeth chattered, his hands shook. He took another step, and pain shot through his temples and down his neck, far worse than Zeke's bite. Prickles erupted on his skin, then hot, then cold, then every possible physical sensation combined. Tastes appeared on his tongue, sweet then bitter then sweet again, as loud thumping threatened to burst his ears. Hunter held his head and screamed, dropping to his knees.

"Far enough, I'll go from here." Zeke hopped down and jumped forward into the flashing lights. Hunter reached out for him, but had to pull his hand back when his fingers caught fire.

Get away. He had to get away from the door, but he couldn't move. All he could do was yell and hope that someone would hear him, that someone would help. But no one came.

With all his strength he threw himself away from the door, landing face-first on the hard fiber, the pain fading behind him. The thumping left his ears. Hunter took a deep breath.

Slowly, he felt himself lift, his body ascending into the emptiness above. The pain was gone, and he was floating again, up and up, back into his real self, opening his real eyes.

Hunter shot up in bed and gasped, then kept breathing hard. It was night. He was in a room lit pale blue by glowing strand. Around him, soaked in sweat, were furs and soft-woven cloth. Two plush pillows lay beside him, pushed askew by his flailing.

Gradually, his breathing slowed. He pressed his hands on the bedspread, reveling in the sensation of actual touch. He felt...better. Not entirely well, but the sickness deep inside was gone. He was hot, though, and sticky. He wasn't wearing a shirt, so he used the blanket to wipe the sweat off his chest. His shoulder itched badly, and he scratched it.

Scratch, scratch, scratch. *Tink.*

He froze. Slowly, his hand passed up and down, starting below the collarbone and running up his neck to just behind his ear. It took him a moment to understand what he felt below his fingers.

Metal. Bundled fibers, pliable, wet with grease.

The flesh of his neck and shoulder were gone forever, and now the strand lay in their place.

8

EVIE HELD THE bowl of tea to her nose and sniffed. She winced. The tribe's shaman would have added herbs to the brew to make it more palatable, but Evie didn't know the recipe, and anyway couldn't have found the ingredients, so she had to make do with a couple sprigs of rosemary ground to a paste. They didn't improve the smell much. She hadn't prepared the sacred mushrooms properly, either. Tradition demanded they be dried for ten days, but she hoped that the single day she had left them in the sun would be enough to please the spirits. Still, she had to try. The spirits had given her this opportunity to hear their wishes, and she wouldn't let it go to waste.

Hunching her shoulders to stave off nausea, she sipped. An earthy flavor flooded her mouth, tinged with smoke from coals she had used to shape the bowl. For a moment she was fine, then the aftertaste made her gag. Not wanting to spill the tea or lose her nerve, she held her nose and gulped the rest.

She spit a few times, then lay on her back chewing the rosemary stem until the acrid sting subsided. Nothing to do now but wait. The tea wouldn't take effect for a while, or so she had heard from those who had accompanied the shaman on her yearly retreats. Only six tribe members were chosen each time, and spots were highly coveted; many spoke of their experience on the spirit walk for the rest of their days. Evie's fingers tapped on her knees and she bobbed her legs up and down nervously. She could very well be the youngest person in history to ever go walking. In a strange way, despite all the peril she and Hunter faced, she felt lucky.

Assuming nothing went wrong.

No, she shouldn't be thinking like that. Hunter needed her to be strong. But which of the spirits would visit her first, and what would they have to say? A tree, an animal, one of her ancestors? What if her great-grandfather himself came, the man who moved the family south and first cleared their home field? How could she possibly prepare herself for that? What should she say? Or what if...oh no. The rabbit. The one she had hunted that morning. What if she had angered it somehow? She could almost see it there now, in the flames, watching her fearfully, hate and anger growing above that quivering nose—

She shook her head. That didn't make sense. Anger growing above its nose? Ridiculous. The idea was so funny she had to laugh, throwing her head back until her whole body quaked. She rolled on her side, holding her ribs, settling into a pleasant fit of giggles. It wasn't really *that* funny, though, was it? It was the tea; it had to be. Evie sat up and looked about the forest, eyes wide, breathing shallow.

In the pale of early evening, all the woods were aglow. Leaves shone the deepest green she could have imagined, each one outlined in black like charcoal drawings. The fire, the trees, the sky, all burst forth in vivid color; even the sound the insects made had a hue. Evie stared, dumbstruck, drinking in the sights. Patterns emerged on surfaces; the fire was too complex to watch for long, but the burls on the sticks beside her spiraled inward nicely, drawing her inside their endless tunnels. She leaned in closer, then closer still, until her nose touched the branch and her eyes began to water and hurt.

She blinked hard and looked up. The sun was lost over the horizon, the sky a reddish purple. How long had she been sitting with her face on a stick? This was all wrong. She was supposed to be speaking to the spirits. Maybe she needed a guide to find them. That was the role of the shaman on the retreat. But she had no one to help her. She was alone. All alone.

You're not alone, she thought. *Yes, I am.* Alone in the woods. *Aren't I? No. (Yes)* Stop that. *Stop what?* Something was wrong; she needed to get herself together (*no you don't*). *You said that already. I did? Yes yes yes yes. No!*

She jumped up, heart pounding wildly (*wildly pounding pound pound pound wild*). It was the tea, that was all (you said that—*stop!*). It had made her lose her mind, she was completely (*don't say it (don't say what? (don't say you're going) (now you said it) Shut up!) Who?) Listen.* She had to listen to herself, she wasn't going crazy, the tea would wear off. But what if it didn't? What if she was dying? She had drunk too much (much much much much much much much *stop stop stop PLEASE STOP DOING THAT*) and she had poisoned herself. Hunter would help her, but wasn't she supposed to be helping Hunter? How could she do that, now that she was insane (*I said it will wear off, aren't you paying attention (not really)?)?* And what about the rabbit? *Who?* The rabbit (*haha*) wanted her dead, didn't it? *Why would a rabbit want her dead? Why wouldn't it?* It's a rabbit, it eats grass and poops little brown balls for the spirit's sake; it doesn't care! *Yes it does (no it doesn't).* Of course it's going to care if she tried to kill it, how would she feel if someone tried to kill her (*actually, someone did try to kill me (who? (Myself. By poisoning, remember?) Oh.).*

I suppose that means I'll be dead, soon?

In which case, why am I spending my last moments on Earth thinking about a rabbit?

Just calm down. Yes. She had to relax. *Relaxation.* It was so obvious. Harmony. Why had she never noticed it before? Everything in the forest was the same, her feet, the dirt, the beetles, the lichen. All the same and all in harmony. The light was almost gone, but that was fine, because her spirit had its own light, the same light as the fire, but so, so, sosososo (*stop it*) different. *Just breathe. In, out. Everything is going to be fine. Completely fine.*

And that was when her mind left her body completely.

———

It was not Evie's best night.

She woke supremely uncomfortable, covered in dew, leaves and bugs, left leg numb and right arm cramped. Her dreams, if indeed she had actually fallen asleep, were in turns indescribable, interminable, bizarre and frustrating. But worse than the rainbow visions and the jumbled thoughts was the guilt that had risen to take their place. The spirits had not come to offer her advice. She was a failure, at everything. She had failed to find her tribe, failed to keep Hunter safe from the Tainted, failed to find a way to help him now that he was trapped in their clutches.

She rolled up to her knees, head in her hands, and let out a deep sigh. At least her mind felt clear, not even tired despite the lack of rest. The tea was still affecting her subtly, making her nerves buzz, giving her surroundings a vibrant clarity. At any other time the effect might have been disturbing, but after experiencing what disturbing *really* meant, the relative calm now was practically soothing.

She closed her eyes and heard birds throughout the woods chirp as if they were close to her ear. Her nose picked up every scent of the forest and kept them separate, from the sharp tang of the pine wax to the musty rotting logs. Perhaps this was the true meaning of a spirit walk: not actually speaking to the spirits, but being close to them, experiencing all the facets of nature to their fullest extent.

She rose and paced a while, taking in the clarity of the sights, while resigning herself to her fate. She couldn't leave and go north, not without Hunter, but she couldn't stay and wait for him nearby, either, not in a Tainted town surrounded by a bare field of strand. So what then? Visit him occasionally, to see how he was doing? The thought made her skin crawl, being so helpless, waiting around for Hunter to be ready to leave, assuming the Tainted weren't killing him even now.

Evie reached the edge of the forest and peered out over the Midlands, pale blue rectangles receding in the distance. In her heightened state, the vast emptiness of the sky was almost too much to take in. She put her hand over her eyes and focused on the strand.

There was some activity happening within it. The effect was subtle, one she might normally have overlooked. The strand always had a slight buzz to it, especially on sunny days, but in her current state Evie could almost sense the vibrations through her skin, watch them as they throbbed over the landscape. Pure did not concern themselves with the will of the strand, but they could still watch it for signs of trouble. And whatever was happening out there now seemed troublesome indeed.

This was unprecedented. All of the vast miles of metal fibers and plating before her were acting as one. It wasn't so much a physical movement as a change in density of the air. The strand pulled its energy from the sun, but her father had told her it had ways of sending power over long distances, toward areas covered in clouds. But the sky was clear from horizon to horizon. Why would it need to send energy today?

Something big is going to happen. Big surges of power meant big problems, like the two giants that had chased them over the dam. But those had been drops in an ocean compared to what she was seeing now. Even as she watched, the entire Midlands seemed to pulse, sending waves from the coast, straight west, toward…

The Tainted town. Hunter.

Evie spun toward the river and ran.

Hunter heard Trina marching up the stairs and sat up in bed. The effort made him slightly dizzy. At her entrance the lights flared, casting a blue glow over her smile.

"Still feeling better?" she said in the Pure tongue. She had found him the previous morning still covered in sweat from his experience in the Immersion, and declared his fever broken. But she hadn't probed further beyond that, leaving him alone with his thoughts for the rest of the day and night.

"Yes."

"Good. Another half-month of rest will do you well, I think."

She stood staring at him, and Hunter wondered if she expected him to say something. He fished through his usual collection of phrases adults liked to hear. "Thank you for your help. I'm sorry I didn't say so before."

She laughed. "I wish you would teach my children such politeness. Please, don't apologize. Given what I know of the Pure, I'm surprised you're even speaking to me. I'd half expected you to have tried to run away by now, like your sister did."

So she meant to shame him for not following the tribe's ways. That didn't make sense, since she was a Tainted, but he played it safe and looked down at the sheets.

Trina gave a discontented grunt. "Please, don't worry about Evie leaving. She didn't mean to abandon you."

"I'm not," Hunter said. "I know why she left. She'll come back for me eventually. And then…" His fingers found the soft metal where the side of his neck had once been. He didn't like feeling it there, but somehow kneading the surface had become something he had to do, like coughing or blinking his eyes.

Trina sat down on the bed. "I did try to take it out, you know. But the infection had crossed into your cerebrospinal fluid. Once the strand burrows too far into the flesh, its primary behaviors take over; even the best functionals can't change them. Sorry, I don't mean to get so technical…"

"I understand. You're saying it will be inside me forever."

He touched the strand in his neck again, thinking of the other members of the tribe, especially Cats-ears. Would he have made the same choice Hunter did, in those final days when the sounds of his anguish washed over the camp? Probably not. But then, Hunter wasn't like the rest of the tribe, anyway.

"Have you tried to use it yet?" Trina said.

Hunter hesitated, wondering how much he should reveal. "Sometimes, if I look at certain things in the room, I see shapes, colors."

She nodded. "That's the basic interface. I could disable it, so you wouldn't be able to use our technology."

"No," he said quickly. "I mean, it might be interesting to learn more. If I'm here anyway."

She appeared surprised, but nodded slowly again. "I'll teach you then, in time. Or you can ask me questions. I think you'll be able to learn some things through trial and error, though. Don't worry about messing anything up; the access controls and network partitions will keep you safe."

"Partitions?"

"Yes. They're sort of road blocks at certain points along the network. For example, there's one such partition surrounding this town. We don't really have control of it, but if we observe certain protocols and don't generate too much traffic, we can send messages to points outside, and generally speaking the partition will keep harmful data out."

"Do all of the Tainted have implants?"

"Not all. There are other ways to use the strand, tactile interfaces and such. But most people want at least a small one eventually. The issue is cost. It takes a lot of effort to find strand suitable for cleaning, then re-functionalize it for use in an implant. That's part of my job, to scout the wilds for samples of strand which could be useful."

"I see. So Ono must belong to a wealthy tribe."

She raised an eyebrow, then snorted. "Not at all. Ono's

implants were gifts from his employer, treatments for injuries in the line of duty. He wouldn't have been able to afford them, otherwise."

Hunter nodded, and his eyes fluttered. The conversation was exhausting him, but he didn't want Trina to leave until he asked the most important question. "I saw something while I was asleep. Something very strange. But if I tell you, you can't speak of it to my sister, all right?"

"I know what you saw."

"You do?"

"Well, not exactly." She flashed a smile. "But I'm sure you were going to tell me about a sort of dream, one that followed its own set of rules."

"Yes. Like a half-dream. Half imagined, half real."

"We call it the *Immersion*. It's what happens when the strand interfaces with the neural pathways that carry your sensory input. Or at least, it happens sometimes; the Mystics say not everyone is capable of entering it."

"The Mystics?"

She shook her head. "Every answer leads to more questions, doesn't it? There's a lot to learn, I know. Perhaps I'm the wrong person to explain. I could fetch Palerno, the town's resident Mystic. He's a good fellow, though perhaps a little..." She trailed off, seemingly searching her Pure vocabulary for a suitable euphemism for whatever was wrong with Palerno. Coming up empty, she settled for a shrug.

Hunter licked his lips. The episode with the little otter and the mysterious door had haunted him every moment since he had awakened. He knew that to pursue it further would lead him down a road no Pure would forgive him for walking. But keeping the Immersion from his mind was even more difficult than keeping his fingers off the strand in his flesh. He glanced at the door, half-expecting Evie to burst through it at any moment and scold him.

"Please," he said, "I would like to talk to him, as soon as possible."

Trina nodded and rose. "Then you will. I'm heading out to run some errands. I'll see if Palerno is free to return with me." She paused at the door. "If you need anything while I'm gone, Kelas or Gellory will help you. Just give a shout."

With a wave, she was gone. Hunter settled back into the pillows and closed his eyes, waiting for the pressure behind them to subside. Muffled conversation came from down the stairs, then the front door closed.

The room was still glowing bright blue; Trina had forgotten to turn off the light. Sensing the pieces of active strand throughout the room, Hunter put his focus on one. Shapes appeared in his vision, blue and green rectangles and circles superimposed on the blank walls. He tried manipulating them with his mind, pushing them around until he found the combination to dim the lights. He brought them down to a comfortable level, then folded his arms and took a deep breath.

Trina was right. Using the strand's basic interface was interesting in a way, but essentially easy. Anyone could learn it with a bit of practice. But the Immersion, that was what he really wanted. He let his mind drift, searching for the thread that would lead him there. Since his first time entering by accident, he had back gone twice more on purpose, and the process was fairly quick now. At first it felt like falling, air rushing, his stomach churning, but he focused and was soon controlling his descent, maintaining his equilibrium to land on his feet in the brightness of the gridded forest.

As usual, upon his arrival he searched through the trees for Zeke, but the little otter was truly gone, happy—or lost—somewhere beyond the door.

Thinking of the portal made him want to see it, so Hunter used his shrinking trick again, until he stood atop the colossal tube of a pine needle. Just a few steps in either direction around its circumference would take him to the threshold, but he dared go no further. The feeling there was just too overwhelming, too painful. Besides, there was plenty to explore within the confines of the gridded forest, at various size scales. There was no need to satisfy his curiosity about what lay beyond the door. Yet.

He walked a while along the length of the fiber, taking in the sights. Then he let himself grow again, and rose back into the confines of his physical body. As before, the white light below him faded, the feeling in his limbs returned, and then he opened his eyes to the dim blue of the bedroom.

In the doorway, Ono stood silently, watching like a vulture watches a carcass.

"Oh…" Hunter blinked the stars from his eyes. Ono didn't move. Likely he didn't know what Hunter had been doing, unless by chance Trina had told him something. But either way, why was he staring like that?

"Hello," Hunter said.

The pinpoint of blue in Ono's right eye flickered for a moment, then he turned and left the room.

Hunter looked after him, then cleared his throat and blinked. Lately, Ono's presence made him uncomfortable, but he didn't know why. What was Ono even doing in the house, anyway? Did Trina's husband know he was here?

"Kelas!" Hunter said.

Stomping came from down the hall, then Kelas's rounded head poked through the doorway. "*Yi?*"

"I'm thirsty." Hunter mimed drinking water.

Smiling broadly, Kelas nodded and rushed off to get a cup. Hunter watched the doorway a while longer, eyes narrowed, then settled back down to rest.

————

Sometime later, Trina returned. This time a strange man followed behind her, wearing blue and gold robes.

"Hunter, it's my pleasure to introduce the Revered Mystic of Bordertown, Palerno, son of Patris."

The man smiled, and the fat on his cheeks bunched like folded cloth. Hunter couldn't help but stare—Kelas was rotund, but this man was enormous; Hunter had never seen anything like it.

"I told him you had questions about the Immersion." She turned and repeated the phrase in Tainted. Palerno nodded and rattled off a response.

"Too fast," Hunter said. "I don't understand."

"He wants to know if you're able to re-enter the Immersion at will, or if you only experienced it in your coma."

"I can go back whenever I want."

Trina furrowed her brow, then relayed the message to Palerno. Instantly, his countenance changed; he snapped up straight, and replied in a quick, clipped tone, all the more difficult for Hunter to understand.

"He says what you're doing is dangerous and forbidden. I—" She paused as Palerno launched into another tirade.

Hunter shrank back into bed. "Tell him something else." He thought up a suitable lie. "You misunderstood me. I only went back once, by accident."

Trina nodded, looking back and forth between them, trying to fit words into Palerno's stream of invective. After several exchanges, he took a deep breath, and the vein in his forehead flattened.

"Listen carefully, Hunter," Trina said. "He wants to know whether or not you traveled into the greater network."

"The greater...? I don't understand."

More muttered back-and-forth, then, "He says when you first go inside, you'll be within the confines of your implant. But that implant is connected wirelessly to the rest of the strand in this house, which then connects to the town, and so on, to most of the strand in the world. He wants to know if you've passed through the firewall I put in place to isolate you from the rest of the network."

"Oh…you mean the door. No, I didn't go through. I couldn—err, I didn't."

Trina passed the words along, and Palerno responded with a calm, serious-sounding speech.

"He says you show signs of talent," Trina said. "He's offered to take you to the High Temple in Jolon, to enter training as an apprentice Mystic."

"No." The suggestion was almost laughable, but he was sure Evie wouldn't find it funny. "I couldn't, never."

Trina nodded and exchanged more words with Palerno. "If you do not join the Mystic training, you're forbidden from entering the network. The High Temple teaches the special protocols necessary to avoid angering the Ints, and other potential calamities."

"The Ints?" Hunter shook his head. He was still tired, and translating the conversation through Trina was tedious.

"It doesn't matter," Trina said. "You won't be speaking to any Ints. I locked your implant down tight, so nothing will be able to get in and bother you."

"Speaking to any…" Zeke. So Zeke was an Int? But he didn't seem like anything to be scared of. Hunter needed to know more, needed time alone with Palerno.

"I want to meet with him again," Hunter said, motioning toward Palerno. "Tell him I can't go to his school, but that I want to talk to him when I feel better. To ask about the strand."

Trina looked unsure, but she dutifully passed on the message. Palerno responded with a dismissive tone. Trina kept on, unwilling to back down, and the two of them began to argue.

Finally, Palerno threw up his hands and shook his head. He walked up close to Hunter, waggled his finger, and spoke an admonition.

"He says that this is against church policy, and apparently nothing could be worse than that." Trina allowed herself a barely perceptible eye roll. "But seeing as how he's never seen your circumstance before, and your tribal duties mean you cannot stay with us, he has agreed to pass some of his knowledge on to you. To keep you safe."

Hunter nodded. "Tell him I'll do whatever he asks."

That seemed to satisfy Palerno, who took a deep breath and placed his hand on Hunter's head.

"He's giving you a blessing. He says he's already prayed to the Ints for you as well—that's quite an honor."

After some more chat and goodbyes, Kelas arrived and helped Palerno ease his way down the stairs.

"I'm sorry for the trouble," Trina said once he was out of earshot. "It's not your fault."

Hunter took a deep breath. "Trina. You've been very helpful so far. Will you do me a favor?"

"Of course."

"From now on, speak to me in your own tongue. Even if I don't understand, just keep talking a little slower and I'll get it."

She smiled and nodded, and her eyes sparkled. There was a small bit of strand in those eyes, somewhere in the back, reflecting the blue glow. A true Pure, unused to seeing the Tainted and their implants, would never have noticed it.

A door slammed, then yells and commotion came from the stairwell. Men were shouting, Kelas and Ono if Hunter had it right, followed by the voice of a girl—

"Evie!"

"Get away from me. It's coming!" She backed into the room, knife held high, aimed at Kelas's face. He put his hands up and backed off.

"Evie!" Trina yelled. "Put that away. Calm down."

"Get up Hunter, we're leaving!"

"What is it? What is she saying?" Ono's voice.

Trina motioned for calm. "We just need to—"

"Hunter, come on!"

Evie ran over and tugged him up. He fell forward limply on the bed.

"I can't," he said. "What's happening?"

The others were shouting at each other in confusion. Evie turned and bared her teeth.

"They can't understand you," Hunter said. "Tell me what's going on."

"The strand is going to attack," Evie said. "It's going to destroy this spirits-forsaken place."

Trina narrowed her eyes. "What? Which strand?"

Evie took a close look at Hunter for the first time, shock crossing her face when she noticed the implant. Shaking her head of the unwanted image, she tossed the covers away and sized him up, as if judging how far she would be able to carry him.

"All of it."

9

AUNIO REACHED THE top of the wall first, launching himself up the ladder with hard pulls on the rungs. Trina arrived a few moments later, along with a few town guards and some useless hangers-on who had followed the frantic Pure girl through the streets.

If Evie's right, those "useless hangers-on" might be all that stand between us and death.

"Thank you for the reminder." The landscape was quiet enough, a Midland summer's haze of blocky strand and patches of greenery. No signs of whatever had spooked the girl.

"Reminder of what?" Trina said, only half paying attention.

"Nothing. Any network activity?"

Trina shook her head. "The town net is quiet. No signs the strand here is expecting an attack." She turned to the guardsman on duty, a tall, pockmarked man with strand laced in his eyebrows. "Shel, rouse the rest of the watch. Get the captain up here."

"He won't like to be called for nothing." The guardsman squinted out at the landscape much as Aunio had. "The girl must have had a bad dream."

Trina crossed her arms. "I don't believe it. There was something in her eyes; did you see it, Ono?"

Say you did.

"I did. But if you want to be useful, guardsman, forget the captain and find that idiot Mystic instead."

He went off, hopefully to do as asked. A crowd of a dozen had filled the wall by then, a few of them holding old rifles. The parapet also held a line of cannons on swivels near the guardhouse, but none of that would be of much use against the strand. This wall and its armaments were meant to defend against other humans, not the sea of metal beneath them. Where the strand wanted to go, it would.

But as the minutes passed and the crowd milled, the strand beyond the wall showed no signs of wanting anything. Aunio stared silently while the townspeople traded theories and gossip, until a few, then a few more climbed down toward the town.

"A false alarm," Aunio mumbled.

You sound almost disappointed.

"Whatever the girl saw, it might be connected to Fesso."

"Is that why you dashed up here in such a hurry?" Trina said snidely.

Aunio shot her a dour glance. "I was mistaken, as were you. Would it be wrong to gain something of value from this fiasco?"

She sighed. "I'll have a talk with Evie. Maybe there's a—"

"Trina!" A guard shouted. "Look!"

Out on the strand-covered plain, shapes were forming, fibers coiling into arms and legs and bodies. Two steps brought Aunio to the parapet, and by then the entire expanse was filled with growing creatures. They ranged from dog sized to specimens that looked three yards to the shoulder, each a unique combination of legs, arms, tentacles, jaws and horns.

"How…?"

Within seconds, the closest of the creatures had finished forming. It spun, gaining its bearings, then rushed toward the wall.

"Kelas!" Trina yelled down the ladder. "Fetch some poles! And my pry bar!"

"Where is that Mystic?" Aunio snapped.

We need more people up here. The watch captain, everyone.

A rifle cracked, pounding Aunio's left eardrum, the one made of flesh. One of the townspeople had acted rashly, giving in to panic. A hollow clang sounded in the distance—the town alarm-bell. Below, more of the creatures had become mobile, a sea of advancing metal. The nearest ones hooked their appendages into the cracks of the granite wall and undulated upward.

"The Ints are taking this place," Aunio said. "Our only hope is to flee across the river."

"There's no time, we can't get everyone out the gate." Trina turned to the guard tower and cupped her hands to her mouth. "Watch out!"

A flattened creature, whose splayed, many-limbed body made it uniquely suited to climbing, had scaled to just below a group of townspeople jostling to see what was happening. One of them leaned over the wall, and the creature shot an appendage upward, impaling him through the throat. The appendage spread into a hook on the far side of the man's neck, then yanked him down to the waiting menagerie below.

The entire wall burst into screams.

"We need more weapons, and someone to coordinate the defense," Trina said, hefting a pole handed to her from the bottom of the ladder. "We have to spread out, keep them off the walls until the resident Ints can stop this."

Aunio glanced back at the town. Most of the rooftops were coated with strand to protect them from the elements and filter the rainwater, and more of it hung or grew along the stone streets, storefronts, windows and lampposts. But all of it lay inert, unaware or uncaring of the movements outside. Why would the Ints suddenly decide to destroy a town after allowing it to exist for so long, and why did the ones inside choose to let it happen?

Yells came from down the wall as two more creatures leaped over the parapet. One caught a rifle butt to its side and went tumbling down, but the other held fast. Shuffling on four legs, its body was a caricature of a living creature, with outsized bulges of strand where its muscles would have been, and jaws so wide it seemed to be smiling with bloodthirsty glee.

"Ono!" Trina yelled. "I need to run things here. Help them!"

Aunio flexed his strand arm, but stayed put. Fighting that thing would drain his energy reserves. With Ono so aware already, he would be unable to stop him from taking control of their body.

Trina glanced up from her work and saw Aunio ignoring her order, then did a double take. "What are you doing?"

Yes, Aunio, what are *you doing?*

"Shut up."

The creature charged toward the townspeople, knocking them back and pinning a woman under its massive clawed foot. She screamed, emboldening the others, who pressed forward with spears held high. Unseen by them, spikes grew from the creature's tail, ready to slash at whoever came first.

Fight it, Aunio. What are you thinking?

"I'm not handing control of this body to you."

The thing swung out with its tail, catching one watchman on the chin. The others forced it back onto the parapet with pikes, where it hunched while they pulled away their comrade, screaming from her crushed leg. With a metallic hiss, the beast leaped back toward the ground below, seeking an easier route into the town.

"You bastard!" Trina's slap caught Aunio on the cheek, stinging the scabs Evie had left days before. He staggered away, leaning on the parapet, fighting the urge to strike her back. He still needed her help, still needed those children to find Fesso.

What good will that do, with all of them dead?

The creatures flooded the top of the wall all along its length. Shouts of anger, pain and fear filled the air. Aunio spun toward the nearest beast, and a tremendous explosion rang in his ears, making the walls shake. He stumbled and looked out at the field, where a cannon shot had ripped a path of fiery carnage through the assembled multitude of strand creatures. But to little effect—the injured ones began at once to repair themselves, and there were plenty more still ready to climb the walls.

"No! Get away." Trina swung her pole at an advancing creature, an oozing blob. The end of the staff caught in its body and the creature surged forward, enveloping the more rigid metal, pressing Trina back against the wall.

Do something, you fool. Give me control.

Aunio stood still, teeth gritted, fists shaking.

Aunio!

—————

Hunter's heart jumped when he heard the bell's deep toll.

"What was that?" he yelled to Evie, who had paused in her rummaging across the hall.

"I don't know," she said. "A warning, maybe. About the strand."

"What are you doing in there?" Hunter collapsed against the pillows and rubbed the soreness in his chest.

"Looking for something useful." He heard the sound of wood sliding as she opened a few of the wooden cupboards with Trina's strand samples in them, then slammed them shut again. "Disgusting!"

She reappeared at the door a moment later, just as shouts came from the direction of the town wall. Kelas ran down the hallway, excusing himself as he went.

"Let's go," Evie said. "We're getting out of here."

She pulled him up onto her back, but he was too weak to hang on properly, and after a few awkward steps toward the door she gave up and dropped him back to the bed.

"Come on Hunter, you have to help me."

"I can't." He closed his eyes and breathed deeply.

Blood-curdling screams came from above. They both looked up. Kelas ran back the opposite way, his arms full of tools.

Evie gritted her teeth, hand wrapped tight around the linens.

"So what, then? We just stay here and die?"

Hunter didn't want to die. But he didn't see a way to leave. If they had some kind of cart or pallet she might be able to drag him away, but that would mean searching through the Tainted town to find one. Evie wouldn't want to leave him alone for that long. Besides, any device maneuverable enough to navigate the route would probably utilize the strand in some way, and he was sure she wouldn't put up with any more of that.

"Block the door," he said. "Find a place to hide. Under the bed, maybe."

She bared her teeth and eyed the hall. "No. I'm not going to sit around anymore. If the strand's coming to kill you, then I'm going to fight it." She pulled her knife and headed out.

"Stop! You can't do anything. It's too strong!"

She paused and looked back at him. "I don't care."

The door slammed behind her.

Hunter breathed fast. His head was swimming. Evie wasn't thinking clearly. The Pure had been known to stand their ground against one or two smaller strand monsters as a last resort. But the goal in such cases was only to keep the adversary at bay temporarily, to give themselves or others a chance to flee. If the attack was really as big as Evie had said, then she would die very soon.

Hunter blinked hard and fast, and he coughed until his throat was sore. More screams came from above. The battle was intensifying, but he couldn't do anything about it from bed. Or could he?

He closed his eyes tight, took a deep breath, then dropped fast into the Immersion. He felt as though he were spinning, but after a few moments of nausea he knelt in his gridded wood. Quickly, he changed size and ran around the fiber toward the door. He didn't know if he could make any difference to what was happening outside, but if there was a chance, it lay there.

The portal glowed bright white. Cascading from its edges

were every hue of the rainbow, and some colors he didn't think actually existed. That is, if it indeed it had edges; the door was hard to look at, a big ball of pure existence that slammed his senses whenever he drew near.

There had to be a way through. But even the thought of entering the door felt like it would tear his body apart.

No, not his body. His mind. Here they were the same thing. The Immersion wasn't real, he didn't exist in it, but when the strand fed him information, his mind had to find a way to interpret it, as if he were learning the words of a new language. But he couldn't process everything the strand had to tell him at once, and so his mind had to choose—angles, sizes, spaces, all of them were tricks to make himself believe he could only see a part of the Immersion at a time.

He thought back to what Trina had said: *Your implant is connected wirelessly to the rest of the strand in this house, which then connects to the town, and so on, to most of the strand in the world...*

That was what the door represented. A world of possibility. All his life he had seen only as far as the next horizon. He was used to processing such spaces, to sectioning off the world into little squares: the field, the forest, the blight, the mountains. But what if the entire world was placed in an area no larger than a tent? He couldn't imagine what that would be like—and that was the problem.

Hunter forced himself to look at the center of the portal. The light was brightest there, but that was good. Bright light meant near, dim meant far. He wanted to only see what was near, ignore spaces too far away to matter. He closed his eyes and stepped forward. Once again the prickles erupted on his skin. Soon they would give way to cold and burning and pleasure and itching all at once. His ears reverberated with thrumming and screeching noises. He had to accept only the strongest feelings, and push away the rest. He burned. Tastes erupted on his tongue, acidic and smooth, disgusting and delicious. The intensity grew and he thought he had gone too far, he couldn't take it and he was trapped.

Then the pain left him and he fell to his knees, his body tingling.

He opened his eyes and beheld the new world before him.

10

THE TOP OF the wall was in utter pandemonium when Evie arrived. Strand monsters were pulling themselves over the eastern face. The Tainted had banded together, and were having some success driving them back, but they had already paid in blood. A stream of red ran by her feet, and following it with her eyes she found a familiar face. It was the woman named Trina, locked in battle with a tremendous blob of a creature that had oozed over the wall. The thing had surrounded her on three sides, extending small tentacles from its mass, probing before the final strike.

Evie gripped her knife and dropped to a crouch, but hesitated; the small blade was as likely to be lost in the monster's strands as to do any damage. Besides, this was the woman who had taken Hunter away, put that thing inside him. Was she not as much of a monster as her attacker?

The creature lunged, half-enveloping Trina in its body, crushing her against the stone wall. She cried out in pain, and Evie felt a tug of sympathy despite herself. Strangely, Ono stood frozen nearby, staring intently at the struggle but doing nothing to help.

Gritting her teeth, Trina reached into a satchel behind her and withdrew a length of strand no longer than her palm, nearly white and shining in the mid-morning sun. The creature pushed forward again, pinning her arm, but she let go of the strand length and it flipped end over end, landing on the creature's back. Instantly it spread out and down, sinking into the monster's innards. The creature stopped and began to vibrate, then shook violently. Popping noises filled its interior, and finally it lost cohesion, flooding the top of the wall with loose strand as if it were a spilled bag of liquid.

Trina sloughed the remains off her body, stood up and stared angrily at Ono. She opened her mouth, looking ready to deliver a stern rebuke, then her eyes went wide and she screamed.

The creature behind Ono was big, built to kill. It had cleared the edge of the wall and landed in the center of the walkway in one impressive leap, and was on Ono before he could spin around. A wolf. The thing looked like a giant, overly muscled wolf. Evie stepped back, feeling her throat tense. *It's not real. It's not really a wolf,* she reminded himself, as if standing near a gigantic metal killing machine was the better option.

Ono fell to his back. Jaws snapped at his half-human nose. He pried them apart with bloody fingers, then released his grip for a split second and delivered a strand-accelerated punch to the creature's face. It hardly moved. Ono struck again, wriggling out this time from under the claws, ripping his coat in the process. He held his tainted arm out in front of him like a ward, and in a motion that made Evie slightly queasy, the arm became fluid and shot forth, enveloping the wolf-thing's head. The creature struggled and whipped to and fro, protrusions appearing all over its body to surround Ono's attack. But Ono's arm changed shape as well, creating its own tiny extensions, meeting each of the creature's thrusts with its own counters. The two writhing masses of metal engaged in an intricate dance, so fast that Ono could not have had conscious control over it.

More and more of the creature's mass surged into its tentacles, until there was hardly any of its body left. Ono screamed, a warrior's cry, forcing himself onward, and with a crunching tear of metal sent a spike of solid strand directly through the thing and out its tail.

Ono staggered and fell as his tainted half pulled from the creature's remains. His eyes fluttered and his breaths became ragged, and for a moment Evie thought they would be his last. But instead he rose again, shakily. And on his bruised and cut face, a trace formed of a…smile?

Trina saw it too, taking a moment to stare quizzically in the midst of the chaos. Then she noticed Evie standing beside her.

"You've come to help us?" She didn't wait for a reply before tossing over a length of pipe. "Thank you."

"I didn't—" Evie caught it and watched her rush off. She tested the pipe's balance—its swing wouldn't harm the strand, but it might serve to knock a creature over the parapet, or pin the foul things in place while her knife did the cutting. She hoped the knife was still sharp—the steel in the blade would slice strand well enough, but it would blunt quickly in the process.

"This way!" Trina yelled to a group of Tainted climbing up the inside of the wall, stalled by the narrowness of the entrance hatches and ladders. "Shore up the north corner!"

It seemed to Evie that everyone in the town save the elderly and children would soon be lining the perimeter, armed with anything they could get their hands on—tools and broken furniture were popular options. The vast majority of the people seemed to have no strand in them at all, which almost made it palatable to fight alongside them. Almost. Still, she would do what she must to defend Hunter. The rest of them she owed nothing.

She darted along the wall, looking for weaknesses, drawing surprised stares from those she passed. A panicked yell came from the south, where a creature had wrapped a trio of tentacles around a man's arm and neck. Evie hopped onto the parapet and sprinted, praying a misstep wouldn't send her tumbling over the side. Hacking the man free would take too long, so she swung her pipe at what she presumed was an eye, a black sphere in the thing's bulbous head. The impact against the hard glass reverberated through her arm and Evie tumbled back toward the walkway. By then several others had converged around the monster, and they stabbed and pushed until it fell free. Evie rose and leaned out to watch the fibrous hulk smash into the strand-covered ground below. It twitched, righted itself, then reached out with an arm and began a slow ascent of the wall again.

She felt the weight of their hopelessness, then. For some reason, the strand had chosen to scale the walls instead of burrowing through and tearing them down. Evie would never speculate as to why, but its strategy meant that the humans inside were surviving. For now. The longer the fight went on, the more losses they would accrue, and during the summer the strand did not need to rest. The defenders might last a day or through the night, but as time wore on they would inevitably succumb under the approaching tide.

Among the ranks of Tainted were the guards, larger men with pikes who wore the same insignia as the one she had seen by the front gate. They shouted orders, herding people toward the areas of greatest need. Evie couldn't understand them, so she ran back and forth freely, using her speed to cover the ground between herself and the nearest anguished screams.

The battle wore on. Two more of the cannons she had heard inside Trina's house went off, adding acrid smoke to the air. Sweaty, blood-soaked and exhausted, the townspeople fought as only those facing death can.

"*Alla!*" Trina shouted into her cupped hands from the corner tower. Ono stood by her side, breathing heavily, battered from repeated altercations in the most heated corners of the fight. Trina yelled again, pointing to the east.

Evie hopped up on the wall and peered out. The creatures were massing below, lining up in organized patterns, wave after wave as far as she could see.

"They can't..." she said. "They're all attacking at once?"

A ringing like hollow thunder sounded in the distance, then echoing again louder, coming closer, the blue cubic landscape shuddering as a burst of power ran through.

"We won't survive this."

The monsters charged.

———

Hunter rose and took in as much of the Immersion as his senses would allow.

He was standing in a city, or at least he was pretty sure it was a city, despite having never seen one up close. But the surroundings resembled his daydreams of what the Tainted city across the Riversea might look like, the dark colors of dirt stained streets and weathered stone buildings reaching up the sky.

That was the basis of it, anyway. The actual architecture before him was beyond comprehension, a geometric nightmare of floors and walls meeting at obtuse angles, seemingly straight lines curving off into infinity. All sense of direction and proportion was gone, and gravity seemed to operate in whichever direction it felt was convenient on any given surface. Creatures of all shapes, sizes and colors inhabited the streets above and below him, running, crawling, flying, hopping, slithering or some combination thereof. Many were species he recognized, but some were bizarre hybrids, such as the cat with the head of a lizard or a bear-like hulk covered in feathers.

Hunter staggered, dizzied by the sight. The city lay on a floating island in an endless abyss. Above, bridges of coiled metal arched upward into what passed for the sky, but trying to look at their ends made his temples throb.

He closed his eyes and shook his head. He had the feeling he should head further toward the center of the city. But where? The streets before him ran off in dozens of directions, crisscrossing each other in impossible ways. Hunter sensed there was an order to it somehow, a plan underlying it all in a dimension he couldn't quite perceive, but there was no time to puzzle it out. He had to find whoever was responsible for the attack and ask them to call it off. After a deep breath, he chose one path at random and ran off through the high buildings.

The crowd impeded his progress almost immediately. A sea of knee-high, scruffy animals with human-like feet and large eyes shuffled past him. Their fur tickled his calves. A behemoth with ash-grey skin and a flat head walked past him, rank with musk, oblivious to his presence. Hunter sidestepped out of the way. Not all the creatures were so unnoticing. Eyes peered at him from stalls beside the buildings, and Hunter caught grumbles, even what sounded like whispered threats. He increased his pace, high stepping over the smaller animals on the street to avoid crushing them.

He reached an intersection and once again chose a direction at random, ending up on a street that curved upward toward the vertical. If he kept going in the same direction, he was sure to get somewhere, but did "direction" even have any meaning here? For all he knew the streets were circular, turning back on each other. Even worse, as he went on he began to feel he was being watched, much like he had when he first entered the forest of his implant. Not just by the creatures in the crowd, but some other presence. Something that was following him.

A figure caught his eye and he stopped running. It was a boy, around his age, with tousled blond hair and a piercing gaze. Despite his being the only other human Hunter had seen, the boy didn't seem surprised or alarmed. He stood beneath a metal and glass doorway with his head cocked to the side.

"Excuse me," Hunter said. "Do you know where the center of this city is?"

"You're an External," the boy said. Hunter couldn't tell if it was a question.

"Uhh...I suppose."

"Can you digest lactose?" The boy blinked and cocked his head to the other side. "What is the melanin concentration of your retinal pigment?"

"I don't know. Listen…I need to find the city center."

"Why?"

"To stop the invasion."

The boy snapped up straight, eyes wide. "Invasion?"

"Yes," Hunter said. "My sister saw it coming; there's a big attack here already."

The boy turned back toward the doorway and yelled. "Omoro!"

A moment's pause, then the door swung open slowly. Light poured out, strong enough to blind Hunter and make him blink hard, then through the light came a tall man. Pale skinned and carrying a long walking stick, he wore a white beard down past his belly button, and his eyebrows were so bushy they nearly obscured the rest of his face. Hunter felt a chill when the man glared at him.

"Jenfri," the man said, turning to the boy. "I told you not to summon me."

"You're both human," Hunter blurted out. "How did you get here? I thought it wasn't allowed."

The man scrunched his furry brow and frowned. Jenfri smiled and tugged on his robe.

"He thinks we're Externals, Omoro. He doesn't know we're Ints. Isn't that strange?"

"Quiet," Omoro said. Then, to Hunter, "This is not your place, boy. Very interesting."

Hunter felt the chill again, a slight hint of malice.

"That's not all," Jenfri put in. "He said that an invasion is imminent."

Omoro snapped his head toward Jenfri, teeth bared. "*He* told you that?"

"Yes. Is it true? Why did you not pass on such information?"

"It's none of your concern. There is a shift in the underlayer. Do not become involved."

"But I want to *see!*"

"Uhm," Hunter said. "Beg your pardon, but it's *my* concern, isn't it? I mean, the strand is going to kill a lot of people, unless

I can find whoever is in charge of the city."

Both of the Ints stared at him.

"He said he wants to locate Senter," Jenfri said.

"Ah." Omoro narrowed his eyes. "Is that so?"

"Senter?" Hunter said. "Is he an Int, too?"

"Yes," Omoro said. "This is his network." He ran a hand through his beard. "Perhaps you should speak with him, boy. It will be…an interesting experience. I am curious to see how you fare."

"Where is he?"

Omoro raised his walking stick and pointed at one of the impossibly tall buildings deeper into the city, tinted green with black lines running up its face. At his command, the building seemed to arch up even higher, bending slightly toward them.

Hunter nodded thanks, then took off running again.

"Our positions will coincide again in a future timeslice!" Jenfri called after him, before resuming his pleading with Omoro. Soon, Hunter was far enough away for their voices to fade completely. That was probably for the best. Still, the strange feeling of being watched lingered on.

The green building didn't take long to find, once Hunter knew where to go. When he wandered at random, the paths diverged into nowhere, but as long as he kept his eye on the tall building in the distance, the others parted before him, until he walked along a wide, tree-lined street leading directly to Senter's front door.

The crowds had diminished here, taking their noise and smells with them, and the street below Hunter was paved differently, with many multicolored pebbles pressed close together. Two massive front doors faced the promenade, carved from solid granite, immovable, perfectly smooth. Hunter leaned against them, searched their surfaces for a hidden crevice or lever, but found nothing. If the doors could have spoken, their message would be clear: No Visitors. He thought back to Omoro's face when he told Hunter about Senter. There had been a hint of amusement, there. Was it ridiculous to think he could gain entrance to this place?

Hunter paced, making his way around the tower. Turning the first corner revealed only a solid wall of green stone, but the second time was different. Embedded in the rear of building was a man-sized doorframe, with a hideous creature sitting on a chair nearby. The thing was shaped roughly like a spider, but with its six legs covered in thick brown fur, and topped with an insectoid version of the head of a grizzly bear. The thing's compound eyes were fixed on the front of a line of smaller insects in front of it. Each of them, ants, or something similar, as tall as Hunter's kneecap, carried a bowl of purple liquid on its head. As Hunter watched, the lead ant skittered to a stop, its bowl splashing, exchanged a few words with the spider-bear, and then headed inside.

Hunter approached the door. Its guardian fixed him with a mean stare.

"Name?" it said, the word pronounced strange from its long teeth.

"Hunter."

"Never heard of you before. Are you having a nice day?"

Hunter hadn't expected such a mild question from this beast. "Well, not really."

"Wrong." The bear-head snapped forward, staring at the line of insects behind Hunter as if he didn't exist.

"I—"

"Wrong."

"If you could just listen, I need to—"

"Wrong."

"Hey, watch out!" yelled a voice below him. It was another ant, waving its feelers impatiently. "I have to get this inside! Come on!"

"Sorry." Hunter stepped out of the way and the ant approached.

"Name?" the spider-bear asked.

"Fedfa!" the ant squeaked.

"How are you doing?"

"Absolutely wonderful!"

The spider-bear nodded, and the ant hurried inside.

Hunter watched it go, then turned back to the creature, which was still ignoring him. Were they using some sort of password? "Excuse me?"

"Name?" The spider-bear said, exactly as mild as before.

"I already told you, it's Hunter."

"Never heard of you before. Are you well?"

"Uh...Absolutely wonderful?"

"Wrong."

Hunter stayed where he was, trying to puzzle out the rules to this game, but soon he had to move aside again for another ant. He watched a procession of them come and go, exchanging their greetings, disappearing inside and then skittering out of the building again with bowls empty.

The spider-bear couldn't think, that much he understood. Someone had given it the ability to speak in some pre-determined way, but it wasn't really alive, like an animal or person. The ants at least seemed slightly more clever, but it was hard to tell exactly how smart they were when they were in so much of a hurry to rush inside and away.

Hunter tried shuffling toward the door without answering the spider's questions, but the bear-head growled at him when he approached, its volume growing louder with each step. Remembering the pain of Zeke's bite, Hunter thought it prudent to back away. Shrinking didn't work, either; no matter how small he became, the guardian always appeared before him, exactly the same size it was before.

No, he thought as he returned to normal, the only way to gain entrance would be to figure out the word game. But how? As far as he could tell, the bear never once repeated its questions, and the answers had no relation at all to what was asked. If there was no pattern, then how could he guess the right response?

Unless the words didn't matter at all.

"Hey," he said to one of the ants coming toward him. "Can I carry that for you?"

The ant cocked its head, mouth open. "You...you'd do that?"

"Sure," Hunter said.

"But..." The ant looked left and right. "What if you run away with it?"

"I won't, I promise," Hunter said. "You can stand here and watch to make sure I go inside."

The ant swiveled its antennae furiously.

"All right," it said at last. "Just be careful!"

Hunter accepted the bowl gingerly, not mentioning the fact that the ant had already spilled a quarter of its contents while they had been speaking, or that with his long legs the creature stood no chance of catching him if indeed he chose to abscond with it. Instead he turned and faced the spider-bear, holding the liquid in front of him to make sure it got a good view.

"Name?"

"Hunter."

"Never heard of you before," the spider said, despite having been told twice. "Nice morning, isn't it?"

"Yes, fine, it's great."

"Wrong."

Hunter chewed his lip. He had been here too long already. There had to be some way inside. He turned back to the ant, ready to return the liquid, when an idea struck him.

"What's your name?" he asked it.

"Fecfe!" it answered eagerly.

Hunter nodded and faced the spider again.

"Name?"

"Fecfe," Hunter said.

The spider's ursine head wiggled its nose and narrowed its

eyes, then continued. "Good day so far?"

Hunter leaned back and whispered to the ant, "He says, 'good day so far.'"

"Eh?" The ant said far too loudly.

Hunter gritted his teeth and spoke quietly. "What would you say to him when he says 'good day so far'?"

"Sure is, Mister!" The ant shook its hindquarters and chittered.

"Uh…sure is, Mister," Hunter repeated to the spider.

The guardian snorted, its eyes still narrowed. It leaned forward slightly, sniffed the air, then sat back and waved one of its thin legs.

Hunter exhaled and looked back at the ant, but the little insect was already hurrying away, presumably getting a head start on its next delivery. Balancing the bowl on his head like he had seen the others doing, Hunter headed through the doorway.

The area beyond was a haze of gray. Hunter thought at first it was merely hidden in shadow, but it turned out to be filled with some sort of mist which parted as he passed through, revealing the building's interior.

Hunter stopped and stared upward. He shouldn't have expected the inside of the tower to match the dimensions of the outside. From here, it wasn't a tower at all, but an enormous dome, with a ribbed, cream colored ceiling patterned with web-like mosaics, and its arching gold walls covered with an enormous network of pipes. The pipes led, in one way or another, down to a pool of the purple liquid at one end, nearly as wide as the pond Hunter and Evie had visited that fateful morning, and at the other end to a raised dais where an incredibly fat man sat enveloped in rich red and green fabric.

The man took no notice of Hunter's presence, giving all his attention to a tube from which he sucked the liquid, the remnants of which dripped down his chin, forming a purple stain on his abdomen. It was astonishing—Hunter had never seen any man more portly than Palerno, and Senter put him to shame. His mass seemed to bend the walls around him, so that he took up even more of the side of the dome than he otherwise would.

Hunter tore himself away from the sight and poured his bowl into the pool—he had promised Fecfe, after all—then set it down and approached Senter's dais.

"Sir?"

The giant head snapped up. Eyes like black pinpricks in a sea of flesh fixed on Hunter, and metal stalks flew up from the floor and curled around his wrists. Hunter yelped and struggled, but he was already airborne, held aloft by the growing poles even as more sprouted up to twine around his feet.

"*Intruder!*" Senter's voice was like the screech of a thousand iron blades on wet stone.

"I came to speak to—*agh!*" A bolt of pain shot through Hunter's back and up into his head, leaving spots behind his eyes. It felt like what Zeke had done to his hand, only far more intense.

"You're an External." Senter's eyes flicked toward the entrance, then back. "I should be grateful to you. You've proven I need to get around to replacing that useless sentry daemon." His voice became strained as he spoke, an awful sound. Senter blinked hard, turned to his hose and had a long suckle. He sighed with relief. "Therefore, I will allow you to amuse me. You were going to tell me why you came. Before you die, I will allow you to finish."

Hunter took a deep breath. The echoes of the last burst of pain ran through him. This was bad, but how bad? Could Senter really kill his physical body from within the Immersion? Either way, the attempt would not be pleasant. He tried to think of an escape, but his bonds held him fast—this was Senter's domain, after all, and Senter was in total control. All Hunter could do now was beg.

"I want you to stop the invasion," he said. "Please."

"*Stop* the invasion? Why? The Core has kept its word. It only wishes to scour the underlayer free of moss, not touch my network."

"Moss?" Hunter said. "There are people out there!"

"That's what I said." Senter paused for another suckle. "The Core has many plans for the future of the Anywhere. All the prediction trees point to its eventual victory, and yet you come and ask me to deny it such a small favor? But then, you don't even understand what I'm saying, do you?"

"Please!" Hunter yelled, shaking his bound wrists. "Don't let this happen."

Senter's face crinkled. He began to shake, and the building itself joined in his rumbling, until Hunter was sure the entire structure would collapse around them.

"You are vile, trespassing scum! Hopefully someone in this network will enjoy picking through your remains once I've disassembled you. You never know what sort of worthless garbage some Ints take an interest in."

Pain erupted through Hunter's body again, this time surging through every bone and muscle. He raised his face to scream, but the shock pulled his throat tight, and his near-silent wails barely sounded over Senter's laughter.

11

THE FIRST WAVE of pain had been excruciating. The second was unbearable. Hunter blacked out and came to again. He was lost, unable to wake up from a nightmare, but no nightmare had ever produced sensations so real. He coughed and spit and pulled on his bonds, tensing his muscles for the next barrage. He was sure it would tear him apart.

"Psst." The voice came from nowhere, a whispered squeak.

"Ah...?"

"Want me to get you out of here?"

Hunter blinked hard. "Z...Zeke?"

"Who are you talking to?" Senter thundered from the dais. He tilted his head back and took a long sniff. "Did you carry a virus in here, you filthy External?"

"I can't move," Hunter whispered. "I'm trapped."

"You can." Zeke's voice zipped to and fro around him. "There's always a trick. You just have to look for it."

Senter growled. "You hear me, you little pest? I'll wipe you clean after I'm done with this one."

"I can make him let you go for just a little bit," Zeke said in Hunter's ear. "But then you have to move. I can't make you run, you have to do it yourself."

"I'm ready."

"Eh?" Senter leaned forward, fat-layered eyes narrowing to points.

"Now!"

Hunter felt the world shift. He looked up and saw himself hanging in mid-air, arms and legs splayed as before, except that he was also standing on the ground, exactly where he had been before Senter had lifted him. *You have to move,* rang Zeke's words in his head, and he did. When he looked back again, the image of himself hanging above had already faded away.

Zeke was running beside him, visible now. "Follow me!"

"*What?*" Senter bellowed.

Hunter ignored the Int and sprinted forward. Was there a limit to his speed in this place? His muscles felt no fatigue, his strides were as long as he wished. If he wanted to reach the outer wall of the dome in only a few steps, he could—but then what?

"This way!" Zeke swerved to the left, parallel to the wall and directly toward the pool of purple fluid. That had to be the way out. Hunter sped ahead of him and dove head first into the gooey liquid.

Senter screamed something, but the fluid reduced his words to a drone. Hunter kicked his legs like a frog, angling himself down, hoping he would be safer the deeper he went. Zeke sped past him like an arrow, lithe otter body undulating. The little creature stopped at the bottom of the pool and waited by a dark, circular cap embedded in the floor.

Hunter swam down and grabbed the cap by its edge; it was the opening to a drain, only slightly wider than shoulder-width, sucking a strong current down.

"*Be careful to take the right paths,*" Zeke said, voice ringing in Hunter's mind despite the lack of air. Hunter understood—the opening doubtlessly led to the network of pipes along the walls, and some of them led directly into Senter's mouth.

With a groan and a rumble, the walls of the pool began to shift, moving inward: Senter trying to crush them. Zeke leaned forward and let the current take him away. Hunter closed his eyes, flattened his palms to his sides, and followed.

Once inside the hollow pipe, he no longer felt the pull of the current, just the gentle turbulence from the sides on his skin. But he was moving fast—very fast. He opened his eyes just in time to see a fork coming up on him, and Zeke's brown tail swoop to the right at the last moment. Hunter angled himself to follow. More turns and splits came at him, until it became clear that once again the network of pipes must have been vastly different in scale from the inside than out. Then, after a long, gravity-defying run straight upward, the black haze thinned to dark purple, then light, and Hunter's head broke the surface.

He emerged from a hole much like the one they had entered, only instead of being at the bottom of a pool, this one was open to the white sky. Hunter pulled himself up and out. His clothes were dripping wet. He attempted to wipe them down, and took a step backward that nearly sent him tumbling to his death.

"Whoa!"

He sat on his bottom, almost crushing Zeke beneath him. They had come out onto the roof of Senter's tower, and the entirety of the mind-twisting cityscape spread out below them, fading in the distance as if enveloped by fog.

"You have to go," Zeke said. "Get out of this node. He's mad, real mad!"

"Did you follow me in there?" Hunter's thoughts were a jumble. Echoes of the pain Senter had put him through still jiggled in his spine. "How did you make yourself invisible like that?"

"It's a trick. I'll show you sometime."

"But why didn't you tell me you were there?"

Zeke gave a ridiculously cute shrug. "We survive by hiding. You helped me last time, but this time you seemed more agitated. So I decided to see what you were doing before I said hello." His head snapped to the side, staring into empty space. "Uh-oh. He knows where you are. Look!"

The structure of the city itself was folding toward them, collapsing around the central point of the tower. The same groaning noise he had heard in the pool came again, but a thousand times more distant and massive, mixed with the yells of millions of the city's surprised residents.

"You'd better go."

"I can't," Hunter said. "I have to help my sister. Everyone up there is still in trouble. Can you do anything to stop the battle?"

Zeke shook his head. "All I can do is watch. I think the battle might be changing, though. Sides shifting. Hard to tell why."

"Keep an eye on it, then. Let me know what you find out."

"Sure. Just hurry! Senter won't be as nice next time you see him."

"You promise to come visit me again? You have to teach me your tricks. I want to know all about the Immersion, and how you survive in it."

"All right, all right! I'll stay close. I'm sorry I hid, really! I won't anymore." Zeke ran to edge and looked down. "You can't go back the way you came. Better jump through the link."

"How?"

"You're peered directly. Just go there. A path is still open, if you hurry. He can't close them all at once."

Directly above, the city was forming a concentric circle of gray stone, shutting out the white sky, as if they were standing inside the bud of a rose blooming in reverse. Hunter focused on the shrinking light above, letting himself see just slightly beyond it, probing a little deeper without his senses becoming overwhelmed. There was a universe of possibility out there, but he needed just one destination, the safe one—his own implant.

"I see it," he said. "I'll meet you again?"

"Promise!" Zeke flapped his eyelids like butterfly wings.

"All right," Hunter said.

He looked up, and the pinprick of sky came down to meet him, bathing him in white.

———

The monsters lined up in neat rows, thinking in unison, and the moment their ranks were filled to the brim, the entire plain began to move.

Trina yelled something to the crowd, then repeated in the Pure language to Evie, "They'll wash over us like a wave! Prepare yourself!"

Evie clutched her knife close and swallowed. Prepare herself? For what? Death? What was she supposed to do?

The monsters gained speed, breaking into a run. Then, once again acting as one, they ground to a halt.

Something else was charging through the plain. A new band of strand creatures, coming from the southwest. This group was smaller, and differently built from the first wave: sleeker, and slithering closer to the ground. As Evie watched, a few of them swarmed a creature on the outside of the attacker's lines and tore it viciously to pieces.

The battlefield broke into chaos. Half the attackers below continued their approach to the wall, while those in the rear doubled back against the new threat. It looked to Evie like an overreaction; even at their flank, this second band of creatures would be no match for the first. What about them justified so many of the attackers breaking off their—

The pounding came from behind the town to the west, low, regular, familiar. Evie had heard that sound once before, but she was still struck dumb when the giant strode into view.

Walking upright like a human, two black glass eyes set in rectangular head, a body taller than the town wall at the shoulder, composed of chunks of debris interlaced with strand. It was one of the two giant monsters she had seen at the pond, the one whose face she had stared at after it had fallen. Evie's mouth went dry. One punch from the massive thing's fists could bring the entire wall down from below them.

The giant seemed to pay the town no heed, though. It was focused on the crowd of creatures on the plain, which it waded into, smashing and stomping with abandon. The area below them filled with the sounds of crashing and crunching metal as the first of the attackers streamed over the wall.

"Evie!" Ono pointed to an unguarded stretch of the parapet, where a creature was making its way over tentacles-first.

Evie ran, leaped and slashed, coming within a hair of taking one of the appendages off. The strand undulated, sensing the moving air, and whipped back at her head. Evie was ready, hopping back just out of range.

Before she could strike again, a group of townspeople converged on the creature with poles, shoving it back down the wall. Evie breathed hard against her burning lungs. All around her, the people rallied. They had benefited from the brief respite in the battle, and the attacking creatures were growing more scattered and disorganized.

Evie peered down once again at the confusion below. Broken strand littered the battlefield, the remnants of hundreds of minor skirmishes, pieces of it repairing itself or slithering away in retreat. But the greatest damage was left in the giant's wake. It had made its way to an area directly below the wall's eastern face, plowing through piles of enemy creatures on the way.

But not without cost. As it had drawn the focus of the attacking force, the creature's lower half had been torn to shreds. It lurched forward a few more steps before collapsing to all fours, its body torn in dozens of places, limbs glistening with spilled oil. The smaller monsters circled around it, sensing the time for a final strike was drawing near. The giant reached out for them with increasingly slower motions as they darted back, forming a crowd just out of its reach.

"We have to help it." Evie covered her mouth and looked around. Had she really said that? Help the strand? No, she hadn't meant it, not that way. They had to attack the strand, destroy it—just not all of it, right this moment.

"What?" Trina said. Like the others, she seemed entranced by exhaustion and the spectacle below them.

Evie didn't answer, too embarrassed to repeat herself, and instead ran for the guard tower.

"Evie!"

"This way!" The metal cannons lay in a row on their swivels by the tower's base, stinking of burned gunpowder. She had heard tales of the Pure finding such weapons; Evie even knew of a tribe that was said to possess a working rifle, kept carefully under wraps in the tent of an honored elder. She knew they needed to be reloaded once fired, and so she ran from one to the next, inspecting the barrels, trying to find one still filled.

"What are you doing?" Trina ran up behind her, with Ono close on her tail. She stared at the cannons, looked over at the giant, and then she understood.

"We'll have to aim well, or we'll blow up what we're trying to save," Trina said. She barked an order at Ono, who came and wrapped his tainted arm around the barrel, bracing it steady, until it pointed at the greatest mass of creatures surrounding the giant. Trina grasped a piece of strand hanging from the cannon's rear and closed her eyes, delivering it some mental command.

Evie went blind and deaf.

The explosion knocked her onto her back, made her see double. She staggered to her feet, holding her head, and looked out at the black cloud below.

The cannon shot had left a divot in the blue strand, tearing up dozens of the attacking creatures who had unwisely bunched together. Metal body parts were strewn everywhere, even over the body of the giant creature, which lay prone on the ground. Then, in the clearing smoke, the giant creature moved and lifted its head. With one swipe, it backhanded another group of stunned attackers, then rose to its feet and lunged after the others with incomprehensible force.

The attacking strand went into full retreat, tearing off eastward into the midlands. The last few surviving members of the giant's contingent headed after them, wriggling along the ground. A cheer erupted all along the wall.

The giant seemed to notice the sound, turning and sweeping them with its black, emotionless eyes. Just a scan of its surroundings, checking for threats. It must have been her imagination that made Evie think the beast lingered on her for a moment before it turned to the horizon to give chase again.

12

"ARE YOU TIRED?" Evie felt the burn in her own lungs as she spoke, but tried not to let it show in her voice. Jogging three circles around the town wearing heavy packs shouldn't have exhausted her. One thing she had noticed about the Tainted was how sedentary they were. Everything they did, from their strange work habits to the way they had their food prepared and brought to them by others, smacked to her of weakness. If she wasn't careful, spending so much time in their presence would make her as soft as one of their fluffy beds.

"Yeah," Hunter gasped. "But better than a few days ago."

Evie nodded and slowed to a walk, just in time to ford the market crowd at the edge of the central square. The townspeople acknowledged the passing Pure with a measure of trepidation. Evie didn't take it personally. For one thing, she wasn't comfortable around them, either, despite having fought alongside them nearly a month prior. She had done it only for Hunter, and she hadn't expected even the small amount of recognition she had already received. For another, this was a town in mourning. Dour expressions and bleary eyes filled the square, the merchants passing their strange foodstuffs with slow hands, patrons making selections from beneath black shawls. Bordentown housed many people, by Pure standards, but not *that* many—everyone she saw before her had lost at least one relative or friend in the battle.

They passed through the square and made their way around

the southern side, past the gate, until Trina's home came into view. "Almost there," Evie said. "You're more than strong enough, now. We should be on our way before nightfall."

"Yes." Hunter had adopted that distracted tone again, answering without acknowledging. He had always been prone to staring off into the distance at nothing, but since his illness he had grown much worse. It made Evie intensely uncomfortable.

"Cut it out," she said. "Pay attention to where you're going."

He snapped his head around. "Sorry." But his expression remained unchanged. At least he used to do a better job pretending he was sorry. On the side of his neck, the strand glimmered.

"Pull your collar up." Evie looked away, not bothering to check if her order had been followed. What difference did it make? It wasn't as if hiding that hideous thing behind clothes would help once they rejoined the tribe. She wished she had some sort of plan, or even an idea of whether or not Hunter could be accepted back again. In her head she had rehearsed her speech a thousand times—trapped alone, sick, no choice but the strand or death. But each time she heard the same response, always in the voice of her father. The Fourth Law: take no strand into your body. Clear, absolute, inviolable.

"Sorry," Hunter said again, his voice a million miles away.

This time Evie clicked her heel down and spun. "How do you do it?"

"Do what?"

"Not be ashamed. How do you act like *this*—" she pointed to her own neck with a shaking finger. "—is *normal?*"

His face went from indifferent to downcast. "You don't understand."

"No?" she snarled, then shook her head. "Just forget it. Come on. I know you want to say goodbye to these people before we leave. Just be quick about it, all right?"

He took a deep breath and followed, shoulders hunched against the heavy pack. Soon they found Trina sitting at a stall, surrounded by her family, her wares of loose strand pieces set out for market day. Evie set down her pack with a thud and stretched her shoulders.

Trina leaned over and peeked inside. "Are you sure you wouldn't rather have supplies, instead of rocks?"

Evie snorted. "I'll have neither. We needed to train our strength, but now we travel light. Hunter wanted to speak to you before we left."

Hunter nodded. "Thank you, again, for making me well." He glanced nervously at Evie. "And for helping with Palerno."

Evie had no idea what he was talking about, but it was all she could do not to yank him bodily through the gate at that moment.

"You're most welcome, again," Trina said. "I'm glad you stopped by, actually. I have an offer for you. Would you accept an escort, at least for some of your journey north?"

"No," Evie said, at the exact moment Hunter said, "Yes."

She fixed him with a deathly stare.

"I mean, no."

Trina raised an eyebrow. "Are you sure? It would be no trouble. I'm headed in that direction."

"Why?" Evie said, though she immediately regretted it. "No" was enough. Why should she care? Too much of Hunter rubbing off on her.

"There have been many discussions of what the town should do in the wake of the attack. The strand may have calmed, but we need to find out what happened and why. Jolon—the city whose authority Bordertown falls under—should be heading an investigation, but so far our pleas with them have been met with silence. And Palerno has been unable to rouse any answers from the local Ints."

Hunter glanced up, as if he had something to offer on that front. Evie tossed him a suspicious look, and he cast his gaze down.

Trina narrowed her eyes at them both, then continued. "Without going too far into the politics, we suspect a local warlord of being involved in this mess. But Jolon may be wary of irritating her unnecessarily. What we need now is hard information, proof that she is engaged in activities that threaten the sanctity of the entire protectorate, not just the frontier."

"You Tainted are ridiculous," Evie said. "Don't you realize the more you involve yourself in the strand, the bigger trouble you'll find? You can go perform your investigation if you like, but it has nothing to do with us."

"It doesn't, no. And I will not ask you to participate. But we can offer you protection in the meantime. You are far from being on safe ground—the trails your tribe uses to move north do not pass through this part of the Midlands."

"What do you know of those trails?"

"Evie." Hunter tugged at her sleeve. "She's helped us this long. Why refuse her now?"

"Don't get me started on her 'help.' That strand is buried too deep in your brain to ever get it out, and you think we need to spend *more* time with them?"

"The strand is not the same this year," Trina interrupted. "There may be unexpected dangers on the trail. You need someone who knows its inner workings to guide you, at least until you pass into the northern wilderness."

"Evie, please!" Hunter said. "She's right, isn't she? When has the strand ever acted like this before?"

Evie looked from one to the other as a flush rose in her cheeks. "Fine." Of course she would be made the fool, just for wanting to do what was right. She stared hard at Hunter. "Only one more rule: no more speaking in that foul tongue of theirs." She put a finger in Trina's face. The older woman raised her eyebrows. "I know you've been whispering Tainted secrets about that thing you put in his neck. If it happens again, that's the last you'll see of us, understood?"

Trina regarded her coolly, but nodded her head. "Very well. I'll need a little time to ready my gear for the trip."

"We'll be by the gate." Evie spun and strode away, cheeks still burning. This wasn't like her. She usually wasn't so foul-tempered, snapping all the time. It was the Tainted influence, of course. She needed to be back among her own people again; until then, anyone in her path would just have to put up with a few hurt feelings.

The gate was the same as before, an arch of stone with tendrils of strand hanging from its upper reaches, though the guard who had been stationed when they first entered had been killed in the fighting, and replaced with a boy barely older than she, looking uncomfortable in his too-large, rumpled uniform. They waited for a while, Hunter staring off as usual, Evie wishing she could banish the anger that still burned in her, until the clumping of boots brought her to attention.

It was Ono again. He approached with a smile and a wave, leading his six-legged monster with one hand. Ignoring her earlier admonition, Hunter greeted him in the Tainted language.

"He says he's coming with us," Hunter reported after some back-and-forth. "This business with the strand concerns him as well."

Evie shrugged and turned away, facing out the gate. Calm, she was staying calm. Even if the heavily tainted man chose to follow them around for a while longer, at least he would be out of their hair soon, and forever. To his credit, he had been markedly more personable since the battle, at least as far as Evie could tell.

Trina arrived soon after, having changed into a durable outfit of green-dyed, shiny Tainted fabric that Evie had to assume was somehow born from the strand. Strapped around her back in two bandoliers was a collection of equipment, mostly loose pieces of strand like the one she had thrown during the battle. The loops were hand-made and embroidered in leather, with a skill in crafting that made Evie slightly jealous. Trina hopped on the back of Ono's monster and he spurred it to a gentle lope, allowing the two Pure to keep pace while walking behind.

Through the gate and over the land, Evie focused on her steps, feeling the satisfying pump in her thighs, glad to be moving away from the town at last. The Midlands were almost totally flat, but the blue strand lent them an extra dimension of depth in the form of maze-like square divots and gullies. Footfalls here could be treacherous; most of the landscape was hard, unyielding metal, though patches of softer, thread-like gray strand were common as well, hiding sudden drops beneath. But more dangerous were the creatures, tall silver beasts that appeared over the horizon, watching them or galloping along in parallel for a while before wandering away. True to Trina's word, though, none of them approached—though whether that was her doing or out of a general disinterest, Evie wasn't sure.

Hunter kept up well, his foot fully healed. In fact, his body seemed more hale than it had been before they went north. Evie couldn't be sure, but it seemed as if the strand was making him plump somehow, giving him extra heft on his backside and a healthy bulge beneath his chin. She kept a close eye on him as the day wore on and the miles passed behind them. As usual, if he was worried about the future, his passive expression did not show it. If only she could hide her own thoughts so well, the questions she had harbored since she had first allowed Ono to taint him. What would they say to the tribe when he returned? Was there any way they could accept him back? And if not, what would happen to him then?

Evie would have no choice but to face the tribe's judgment— she would rather never come home at all than return without Hunter, regardless of his condition. But whatever they decided, she would stay with him and protect him from then on. Given her failures, she owed him at least that much.

They stopped several times throughout the day to rest and eat, while Trina knelt and examined various patches of strand.

Twice she called Ono over to review her findings, but each time she ended up shaking her head and clucking her tongue as she rose again.

That night, Evie slept well at camp, her body and mind exhausted. Though she still resented the escort, at least they were making good time. They had traveled almost due north, and already the midlands were beginning to splinter, the hard corners of blue strand giving way to small fields of dirt and grass.

Morning came, and with it more travel, as quick as possible before the heat rose. There were more Tainted settlements in the area, but Trina seemed to be deliberately avoiding them as the Pure would have. They crossed a stream via a bridge whose weathered, mossy stones looked older than the works of the ancients, shored up by strand laced between them. On the far side the land grew swampy, the way impeded by waist-high thickets and thorn bushes. Evie found herself walking in the monster's wake, taking the easy path over the grasses it had flattened. Annoyed with herself for forgetting the law, she cut west, staying in eyeshot of the others, toward the edge of a young wood.

She stopped short. There, in the flecks of shade, stood a waist-high pile of stones.

"Look!"

She ran off, the monster clanking to a stop behind her. By the time she had covered half the distance she was sure what they were. She arrived, knelt and traced her hands over the spherical stones, river-worn and deliberately placed.

"It's the trail," Hunter explained to the others.

"It's more than that," Evie said. "They left this cairn for us. They haven't given up hope." A shuddering breath rose in her chest. Her family had seemed so remote for so long, and this message of the stones was so sudden. She clamped her mouth shut before she lost control.

After a few moments, she stood and motioned to Hunter. "They would have headed into these woods. We should be able to find signs. Let's go."

"Now?" Hunter looked to Trina and Ono. "I mean...yes. Goodbye."

Trina dropped to one knee and extended a hand to him, which turned into an embrace. Evie watched with teeth bared. Hunter, seeming to feel the heat of her gaze, pulled away and ran to her side.

Ono, still on his mount, barked something that sounded like a request.

"What?" Evie said.

"He says he wants to come with you," Trina translated, though her tone was confused. "To keep you safe until you find your tribe."

Evie barely managed to shake her head at the ridiculousness of it. "We go alone."

Trina relayed her message, and she and Ono had what seemed like a tense back and forth. Trina questioned, growing irate as Ono failed to give her the answers she sought. Finally, she stepped back and shook her head, accepting but not understanding.

"He's being quite insistent," she said. "But perhaps the more I think about it, he does have a point. We're not in the wilderness yet. It would be safer to stay with you a while longer."

Rage rose within Evie, as quickly as she had felt homesickness moments before. "Enough. You have no place on this trail. It's not for your kind."

"I'm only trying to—"

"Help? Like you did for Hunter?" She heard her voice crack, but she didn't care. "How do you think he feels, huh? Have you ever thought about that for even one moment? He'll never rejoin his own people again, no matter what we do. He'll never see his family, never live in his own home..."

Tears welled in her eyes and she wiped them away. A loud sound of a throat clearing came from her side. Hunter coughed and gave a little shake, his gaze glued to the horizon.

"You're his family, too." Trina folded her arms, unimpressed. "You could take him to another tribe of Pure, one whose laws are more lenient regarding use of the strand."

"*What*? There's no such thing."

"There is. I've met them myself."

Evie shook her head. "Separating ourselves from the strand is not a game we play because we're some sort of…backward tree-folk. It's about avoiding a real catastrophe, like that near-massacre on the wall. You think we don't know about your Tainted deities? The Pure have words for such devils. But from the beginning, we understood the threat they represented. It's too bad you can't understand that. You probably don't even know what 'Pure' means."

"*An-kara*. It means 'without taint,' or 'without evil.' The root word '*kara*' is the same in Plainspeak, since your dialect only diverged a few hundred years ago."

Ridiculous. "We were the first people to emerge after the fall of the ancients. Resurrected by the spirits to one day cleanse the Earth of—"

"No." Trina looked down. "The Pure were founded by a man named Parin, from the city of Bicephel to the north. After preaching about the evils of the strand, he left his home and took his followers into the wilderness. All the current factions of Pure descend from them."

Evie balled her firsts. Their patriarch, a Tainted? No, she didn't have to take this, didn't have to hear it anymore.

"Leave us alone. All of us. You'll regret it if you follow—I saw you save my brother's life, so I'm honor-bound not to kill you where you stand. The rest of my family won't be so kind."

She turned and left, passing her sweaty hair behind her head. Hunter hesitated a moment longer, then ran along to catch up.

On the first leg of their trip, Hunter had continually lagged behind his older half-sister, thanks to his wounded foot. But now that he was fully healed, Evie expected him to travel faster than before. Which was a problem, since he could hardly explain to her what was distracting him.

He knew she could never understand that he was walking through two forests and not one: the physical realm of the trees and brush, and the interconnected web of the strand. Of course, he couldn't enter the Immersion without losing control of his body, but the implant was feeding his brain information on its own, all the time. Even doing his best to filter it, he couldn't help learning all sorts of facts about the traffic load on the network, energy availability, the ambient air conditions—things he hadn't even known existed until weeks before.

Evie paused and searched the ground, then made an impatient grunt in his direction and frowned before heading off. *He'll never see his family, never live in his own home.* That's what she had said. Hunter didn't know much about tribal politics, but it seemed like it was probably true. But then why was she bothering to take him north at all? He had heard his uncle say once that it was the duty of the Pure to kill any Tainted that ventured too far into the woods. Did that include him? He was sure Evie didn't mean for it to happen, but was he inadvertently stumbling northward to his own death?

And what was the alternative? To never see his family again? He tried to imagine what that would be like. He wanted to see his mother again. And Evie. The rest...well...

He blinked hard and rubbed his implant. He shouldn't be thinking this way about his own tribe. But was it any better to have his thoughts constantly pulled toward the Immersion, and all the things he had learned there from Zeke?

As promised, Zeke had been teaching him some of his "tricks," the kind he had used to free Hunter from Senter, and to hide in plain sight. Breaking the rules of the Immersion, as Zeke explained in his squeaky voice, was impossible. But there were weaknesses; the structures Hunter had seen in the city, despite their seeming simplicity, were fiendishly complicated beneath the surface. Anyone constructing so complex a mechanism was bound to make mistakes, no matter how intelligent they were, and Zeke's "tricks" were nothing more than recognizing and exploiting these mistakes. There were no easy shortcuts for learning them all, but there were some common patterns and recipes that could be applied, and these were what he had spent the majority of his convalescence practicing.

He had spent the rest of his time in the Immersion trying to make his own structures. He hadn't dared risking Senter's anger by using the door to the city again, so instead he had tried to add some variety to the bland grid of trees inside his implant. With some hints from Zeke, he had learned that he could dig up the soil from underneath the web of pine needles at his feet, draw it out and change its properties—color, hardness, and so on. But unless he did it the right way, the material would crumble again as soon as he released it. The trick was to imbue it with a sort of life of its own, like the creatures he saw roaming Senter's city. Even the walls there *knew* they were walls and were *trying* to be walls at all times—not an easy thing to bring about.

Slowly, Hunter had grown to understand that his two separate studies, breaking the rules and creating his own environments, were really one and the same. Only by building for himself could he truly see why the convoluted inner workings of the Immersion were necessary, and why even the Ints made the same mistakes he was making when they built it.

If only his lessons with Palerno had gone so well. He had hoped to have gleaned *something* of value during their long sessions, sitting cross-legged on the bare wooden floor of Palerno's meditation room, its walls covered in intertwining patterns of strand. Instead Palerno would lecture about rites and duties, while Hunter tried to understand despite the old man's accent, and keep his blue and gold acolyte headwear on straight despite it being far too big for him.

"Beware temptation," Palerno had intoned on one of those days, appearing to recite from memory, though Hunter knew the strand was speaking previously written lines in his ear. "When you look into the business of the Ints, they also look into you. Do not travel too far into their world, lest you become taken by it."

"Because the world of the Immersion isn't real?" Hunter asked.

"No," Palerno said, annoyed. "It is as real as ours, after its fashion. But it belongs, wholly, to the Ints. It is not our domain, and never will be. Remember this well, boy, lest your mind become lost, and you find yourself becoming a Called."

"A Called?"

Palerno paced, his normally grim face even grimmer. "Throughout history, there have been a select few with the ability and the will to delve deeper into the Immersion than we in the Church allow. These poor souls are drawn in, or Called, by the promise of vast knowledge, or unearthly experiences. But they have been misled. Once their minds have merged completely with the strand, they are never heard from again, left alone to their *terrible fate*." He pronounced the last two words with a falling tremor, probably meant to inspire fear.

"But what happens to them?" Hunter asked, unaffected. "Can they really just disappear into the Immersion like that?"

Palerno scowled. "I have said too much. This is not a danger you will contend with anytime soon. Even if you were a student at the High Temple, it would be years before you would be able to master yourself well enough to enter the Immersion beyond your implant."

Hunter still had to shake his head at that, walking now in the sun-dappled forest.

Ahead, Evie stopped in her tracks, jerking him from his reverie. Her jaw fell open and bobbed, her face pale.

"What?" Hunter said.

She didn't answer, but instead raced forward. Her voice trailed away as he lost sight of her in the brush, "No, no, no, no…"

He ran through into the next clearing and saw what she did. A bone. No, two, coming together to form a knee joint, white where insects had eaten away the flesh. Human flesh. The leg itself was broken off, perhaps torn by some scavenger and dragged along the forest floor. But it hadn't gone far enough to dislodge the decoration around the ankle.

Braided ropes, painted red, with six cardinal feathers arrayed in a star pattern at their central crossing. A Pure *siya*.

Evie cried out in fear and confusion. Hunter coughed and rubbed his implant as she began locating the rest of the body.

"There's two," she said, panic quickening her voice. "They're not my brothers. Please, Merciful Spirits, please don't let them be my brothers." She found something behind a bush she couldn't look at, and turned and walked away. "They came for us," she said quietly. "They were looking for us, Hunter."

"Are they…"

"They're warriors. From another family. I don't know who. Maybe Brookson or Nightowl. The strand must have gotten them." She paced, stomping with impotent rage. "They came too far south to find us. I knew this would happen. They shouldn't have done it. They should have let us find them on our own."

Hunter looked about. Had the strand really killed them? The metal hung from the branches and grew in bunches over rocks, but all of it was gray, some nearly black. Could some of the bright silver creatures be hiding nearby?

"These bodies aren't old," Evie said. "A day at most. We need to search for survivors." She pulled herself onto a cherry tree and surveyed the land. "There's a ridge to the west. I might be able to see where the woods end from there. Are you all right here alone?"

Hunter nodded.

"Stay put in case anyone comes. I'll be back soon."

She took off like a dart. Hunter sat and rested his back against a tree. "Zeke," he muttered. "Are you there?"

While he waited for a reply, he flipped through the various commands available at the strand's outer interface. He didn't want to dive into the Immersion now and risk Evie coming back and finding him. Luckily, Zeke had given him a special beacon, a way to call him remotely from anywhere in the network.

Hello hello hello, you called? came the squeaky voice in his head a moment later.

"I need to know something," Hunter mumbled. "Quickly. The strand killed two Externals here recently. Who in the network was responsible?"

Hmm…pretty empty around here. Little energy, too many sunblockers and not much network access. Only Ints here are weirdo loners. Want me to ask around?

"Please." He felt a slight tingle in the back of his mind as Zeke left his implant. Then it was back to sitting and waiting, his gaze on the ridge where Evie had gone, his back to the bodies, avoiding breathing through his nose. What would he do if the little otter did find his tribe-mate's killer? Could he subdue it somehow in the Immersion? What if it was large, like the spider-bear guarding Senter's tower?

Even worse, what if it were an Int, like Senter?

Found one, Zeke's voice buzzed again. *She's a loner all right, no real power at all. Been watching this place for four hundred million time-slices. She says she's been tracking four Externals.*

"Right. Me and my sister, and two others."

No, no, four others. Six total. You and another only came by more recently.

"What?" Hunter sat up, speaking too loudly. He coughed and quieted again. "You're sure? There were four besides us?"

Oh yes. Two she said were easy to see with their implants, and two others were hidden. She could only track them by vibration. The hidden ones found the implanted ones and attacked, they fought, and then whammo… The voice trailed off for a moment. *The two hidden ones stopped functioning. She says to tell you she is sad, that she enjoyed tracking them while they still moved.*

"Wait. Are you…is she sure about this? Two Externals killed two others?"

Indeed! She's proud she can tell you all apart. Most Ints can't do that, you know. She says the one who arrived with you is very well hidden. You're by far the easiest to track, though, with your beacon and all.

"My beacon? What beacon?"

The one in your implant. You didn't know? It's a lot like the one I gave you to find me. Sends out a strong signal whenever you connect to the network.

"That's strange." Hunter touched the metal on his shoulder. "How did it get in there?"

Dunno. It was there when I first got put in you. I didn't want to ask in case it was…you know…private. Sort of embarrassing.

"Embarrassing? Why?"

Well, you know, everyone can just see you everywhere. Like the Externals who killed your friends. They're heading toward you now.

"What?" Hunter jumped to his feet. "They're still here?"

Oh, yeah. If I were you, I'd flash to a different network segment right away.

Hunter stood still, the hairs on his neck lifting, ears tuned to the echoes of the forest. Swollen summer leaves swayed in the breeze. In the distance, a hawk fled its branch and flapped away.

Behind him, a twig snapped.

13

ONCE THEY PARTED from the Ankara, Trina had directed them southeast for an hour, along a trail she had been unable to follow while escorting the children. From the hope in her voice, Ono had surmised that they would find more here than before, for what little that was worth.

He waited on the walker while Trina knelt in a small pit beside a brook.

"There it is again," she mumbled. "That strange fingerprint. Something on this network is running non-standard protocols. It must coincide with that physical anomaly in the strand."

"I love it when you talk sexy." He waited for the scowl, then continued, "How do you know it's physical? What if it's a worm with some new way of spreading?"

She shook her head. "Everything matches with the samples I took from the remnants of the attacking creatures. Something is influencing the strand of the midlands on a deep level. But the problem is this looks like Int business. I've seen nothing that would indicate Fesso's involvement, never mind proof that she was behind the attack."

"All we can do is keep looking."

But to what end? He had no doubt that word of an alliance between Fesso and the Ints would spur Jolon into action, but bringing Serr's troops into the picture might only complicate his mission further. Ono had to admit, as much as he despised Aunio's methods, at least his alter ego had something resembling a plan. It had been hard these last weeks, watching the children from afar, thinking of his wife and daughter and how he didn't have a clue how he would have the Ints cure his divided personality, and thus gain at least a small chance of winning them back. Aunio's calculus was simple: no matter how sweet and innocent, these children were not his, and thus fair game to use as pawns, or bait as it were. It was a blunt, brutish argument that nevertheless held an enticing edge, one which grew ever sharper the longer Ono sat still in Bordertown, flipping through images of his daughter, wondering how much her face had changed since he had taken them.

That was why it was good that Hunter was far away now. He would have liked to escort the Ankara further northward, but at least a few days travel would bring them outside Fesso's sphere of influence, and the boy's tyrannical sister would prevent him from connecting to the network until then, if not thereafter.

"Well?" Trina was sitting behind him on the walker, hands on her hips.

"Eh?"

"I said, we should head upriver."

"Oh, right. Of course."

He spurred the walker forward, doing his best to ignore the heat of her gaze on his back. Not for the first time, he found himself wishing Trina were the sort of person who let concerns fade away with time. But with her it was always probing and searching, teasing out the hidden threads and pulling tenaciously until she found their origin.

They rode up a gentle slope, Ono's hood up to block out the sun as sweat dripped down the flesh-side of his face. Already the landscape was changing from hard chunks of strand-stone into the lumpy, flowing carpet of metal fibers which characterized both the south, and in this case, the Gridlands. As they crested the rise, Ono saw traces of the grid in the distance, writhing lumps of strand larger than a man, seething and pulsing with power, heat waves rising above in flickering mirage. Wary, he surveyed their immediate surroundings for threats, but found only the familiar metal-strewn emptiness. Then he turned the walker north, following the creek bed, and rode another half hour until they came upon the spires.

Six tall spikes of metal, arranged in a rough hexagon, wrapped in spirals of strand and capped with mushroom-like cones. At their base, rows of shorter towers stood in concentric patterns, the smallest no taller than Ono's kneecaps. At Trina's direction, Ono halted the walker at the perimeter and dismounted, staying within the shade.

"I'm going inside," Trina said. "There's a data stream coming from somewhere around here. The center seems like a good bet."

Ono stared up at the tallest stalks with trepidation. The strand had chosen to construct these features for its own reasons, and this would be an important area for the Ints, which meant a dangerous one for any humans who foolishly inserted themselves in their midst. Still, if any person knew the risks and how to minimize them, it was Trina. Ono watched as she picked her way carefully among the stalks, high stepping and winding until she reached their nexus.

"I found something." Her voice lilted high, unable to conceal her excitement. She reached back and pulled a pair of pruning shears from her harness, then cut with quick, practiced snips. All around, the strand flexed and curled, winding tighter around its poles.

"Trina..." Ono stepped back toward the walker. The strand looked angry, searching for a target.

Trina paused to reach back again, this time pulling a thin cable from her belt. She inserted it into the strand below her and narrowed her eyes, focusing on the readouts from her implant while continuing her surgery. The strand around her continued to wriggle, but grew more languid. Several tendrils reached out for her, stretching in slow motion until the tips brushed her skin.

Teeth gritted, sweat beading, Trina made one final cut, and all at once the strand fell limp. Ono exhaled as she picked her way back toward him, prize in hand.

"What is it?" he asked.

She held it out to him, a bulbous lump of metal threads, wet with grease, innocent-looking enough. But when she turned it in the light, sparkles erupted over its surface.

"This is the cause of all our troubles," she said. "Ever see anything like it before?"

"You know, I have." He had image archives of crucial moments stored in his implants, though accessing them carried the danger of disturbing Aunio. Nevertheless, he took the risk and brought them forth: a burly man, face covered with blue patterned diamonds and colored beads, whose "sister" called him Mager. And in his meaty fist, slung over his back, a club-sized length of strand that sparkled in the bright sunshine.

"This is what Fesso's Children were carrying when they attacked us," Ono said. "A large chunk of it, too."

"Us?"

"Yes, me and the Ankara. I'm sure I told you."

"You told me they weren't involved with your mission."

"It was a coincidence." There was something in her tone he didn't like, so he turned and hopped back on the walker. "Are you going to tell me what that thing is, or not?"

He felt the impact only as a dull thud and a burst of sensory indicators from the strand on the back of his skull, and was surprised to see Trina's shears clank away over the metal-covered ground.

"You're lying to me," she snarled. "Enough of this. I'm going no further unless you explain your behavior these past weeks."

He couldn't manage to meet her eyes. "My troubles are my own."

"You know, I watched while you hovered over a boy on his deathbed like a man in danger of losing his last meal, and said nothing. When you chose not to help me on the wall, I was willing to chalk it up to the paralysis of battle, even though you had never shown it before. But now I'm going back to Bordertown, back to my husband and children, while holding in my hand pure, unadulterated danger." She shook the lump at him. "And here you are, holding back something important for some selfish reason or another."

He opened his mouth to issue a denial, but the weight of guilt kept him silent. Damn her, she had a point. What had led him to this? Following the Ankara out of the wilderness—that had been for their own good, hadn't it? He had saved them from Fesso's Children…or had he drawn them closer? And then he had gone farther, helped keep Aunio's identity a secret, and for what? A half-baked plan to lure his enemies out of hiding?

"Is it selfishness," Ono said, "if I acted to save the essence of myself?"

"The essence? What are you talking about?"

"The person who arrived in Bordertown was not me, Trina. Or at least, not all of me. I haven't been the same man I was for over half a year."

"Why? What happened half a year ago?"

"I went on a mission to capture one of Fesso's top lieutenants. Khel was his name. A dangerous job, but I thought myself capable of it. What I didn't know was that Fesso had become annoyed with Serr's operations against her. She tipped off Khel that I was coming. There was a fight. Khel died. I ended up with a sizable hole in my head.

"I don't know precisely what happened, in a coma as I was. But Serr has spent a fortune over the years on my implants—perhaps he feared wasting his investment if I died. In any case, I woke up with this." He tapped the strand at the rear of his skull. "Something went wrong, though. When they put this last implant in me, it created a separate personality in my mind, who takes control whenever I use the strand in my body. He cares nothing for decency, responsibilities or friendship—

only his own ends. He caused quite a lot of havoc in my life as a result, until, with help of the Ints, the two of us reached an agreement."

"The help of the Ints? Which Ints?"

"The ones in Jolon, I suppose. I went to the High Temple to pray, seeing no other option. To the great surprise of both me and the High Mystic, the Ints answered with an offer: bring Fesso to justice, and they would cure my condition."

"But you said this...personality...is helping you? Why would he help you destroy himself?"

Ono took a deep breath. This next part he had admitted to no one. Deep in the recesses of his brain, he felt Aunio's wariness.

"Because he won't be destroyed. The two of us will be combined together as one mind."

Trina's jaw had nearly hit the strand by then. She circled the walker, gaping at Ono from all angles as if he were a piece of statuary. He sat still, arms crossed, letting her stare.

"Why would you want to combine with him? Become one with that...brutality?"

"He is me. He comes from my brain."

She shook her head. "I don't believe it. You're a kind man, Ono. Whatever the strand put in your brain, it brought from the outside. Perhaps a virus, or a—"

He held up his hand for silence. "I know where he comes from. I've known ever since the day he told me his name." It wasn't funny, but Ono felt a rueful smile drift across his face. "When I was a boy in Jolon, a new crew came to town from west of the Steel Waves, led by a boulder-fisted little shit by the name of Zasay. Zasay and my crew butted heads instantly. You know, the usual ruckus, cutting strand cables to each other's houses, screaming chases down alleys to the safety of our doors. We thought it was fun, you know? I was carefree back then. Yes, we were street kids, but we had a code of sorts. Don't go too far. Don't play for keeps.

"Until one night, when I was on my way home alone, and Zasay and four of his boys cornered me. Fair enough, I thought—I had gone out without my crew, let my guard down, so I would have to take a light beating. When the first pipe struck the back of my head, I shouted more in surprise than pain. Zasay laughed, 'Ziss is how we do things where I come from, *Aunio*.' I can still hear that thick western accent as he stood over me and the light went out from the world.

"Of course, no one would waste an implant on a young punk like me, so I healed the long way. Three months with limbs tied to bedposts, nothing to do but think. Think about Zasay's mocking face, the way they had given me no chance to defend myself. Eventually, my thoughts turned to plans. In that cold, quiet room I found a new part of myself. One I had never known existed, and one I swore I would never let out again. It was Ono who fell in the streets, but it was Aunio who returned. He was the one hunted down Zasay and his crew one by one. Who stalked them and hurt them again and again until their families could take no more and left town. It was Aunio who had our revenge."

Trina's conspicuous silence told him he had said too much.

"I suppose this may run contrary to your view of me as a 'kind man.' But any man, or woman, cannot be summed by a single word. We all have private lives, wells of experience that run deeper than the Immersion. One of mine just happens to take issue with being kept under wraps, is all."

They waited in silence while Trina gathered her thoughts. The afternoon sun glinted off the striated bulges of the hills of strand. A vulture circled overhead, minding the fate of the creatures who dared stand so close to a hallowed ground of the Ints.

"Well, I wish I knew what to say. As excuses go, this is certainly unique, but you'd have to ask the Ankara if it begs forgiveness." Trina pressed her palms flat to mount the walker, then stopped and looked up, wide-eyed. "Wait. Hunter...why did Aunio bring him to me? And why did he seem so interested in the boy afterward?"

Might as well tell her, and get the pain over with. "Aunio put a tracker in him. I didn't see him do it, but I'd have to assume he sent an anonymous datagram to Fesso with its fingerprint. He needed you to keep the boy alive so that his plan could reach fruition."

Trina closed her eyes and touched her brow. "Oh, *Ono.* You blithering fool."

"He'll be fine," Ono replied gruffly. "He won't connect to the network while his sister is around. By the end of the month they'll be hundreds of miles from here."

"Give me the fingerprint." Trina crossed her arms.

"I can't. Aunio hid it from me; to do a deep search through my logs would risk waking him."

She reached and smacked him in the back of the head. "Just do it. I can handle Aunio, now that I know what I'm dealing with."

He grunted skeptically, but nevertheless closed his eyes and opened his native interface. Reams of data poured past his eyelids, highlighted in blue and green. Aunio would have kept a copy of the fingerprint, in case he needed to track the boy himself, and if it was there Ono could find it—the only question was how much digging he would have to do.

Minutes ticked by as he scanned the data, aware of a growing tingling in the base of his skull. He was about to stop and plead with Trina again when the segment he was searching for flashed by. He sent it direct narrowband to Trina. "Got it?"

She nodded. Her eyelids fluttered as she disabled her firewall and queried the global network.

"Oh, no," she said. "Oh, *no.*"

"What?"

Trina vaulted up behind him on the walker. "He's connected. Not far from where we dropped them off. We have to go back."

Ono squeezed the reins. The walker jolted forward.

"Evie won't like this," he muttered.

"I imagine it won't help Hunter's opinion of you either, but that's not my concern."

The walker cut across the landscape at top speed, sensors whirring to pick up small obstacles its legs needed to step around. Soon it settled into a bouncing, three-beat rhythm, Ono leaning forward to cut through the wind. Trina held the back of his coat and they covered the barren trek back over the midlands without speaking, until they reached the edge of the wood.

"This is the place," Ono said. "Hold on."

He allowed the walker only a slight reduction in speed as it dodged left and right through brush and over fallen logs. After a leap from a ridge that nearly sent him flying, they landed in a small clearing ringed by ferns, fiddleheads intertwined with threads of strand.

Ono stayed on the walker, catching his breath, taking in the sounds of the forest. Insects and birds chirped, the strand strung from trees overhead emitted its high-pitched buzz and *shushed* in the wind.

And there was another sound as well.

"Do you hear that?" Ono asked.

"Sounds like..."

"Crying?"

The sound stopped. Then came a blood curdling scream, and Evie launched at them from the ferns, knife drawn, hair wild, tears streaked over her cheeks. Ono whirled the walker around to put its head between her and them, and she fell back, crouched, teeth bared. They stared at each other for several seconds before the recognition struck, and Evie began to yell at them in her own language.

"What is it?" Ono shouted over the din. "What is she saying?"

Trina shook her head, too focused on the girl's stream of abuse to properly translate. Finally, when Evie stopped to breathe, Trina turned back to him.

"She says they came and took him." Her face creased with worry. "The Tainted came and took Hunter away."

14

HUNTER WOKE UP, but saw nothing. A hood covered his face and scratched his nose. His wrists were bound with strand. He could feel the strand pressing against his back as well. The metal curved below him, forming a seat-like pocket that flexed, rocked, and chittered as it moved.

Moved?

His memory returned. People had come from behind him, but he couldn't tell where or how many before they tossed the mask over his eyes. Then a pair of strong arms carried him away. He had yelled for help. Something pressed against his neck, and moments later he was unconscious.

They must have put him inside a strand monster, like a larger version of the walker Ono used. He heard two Tainted somewhere in front, speaking to each other in clipped tones. Who were they? What did they want with him?

He reached out with his implant, searching for a signal. But the nodes outside were passing too quickly, and the interior of the walker was closed off completely. No data in or out—in the Immersion, the boundary would appear as a solid wall, like the side of Senter's tower. He could enter the Immersion and make sure, but for now he was more concerned with the real world, and the two kidnappers nearby. He listened intently, trying to understand.

"Mother will…" …unintelligible… "…as long as the Big Int wants."

"The Big Int can't even take over one piss-ant town! I don't know..." ...mumbling... "...better off on our own."

"She asked the Big Int to prove its abilities before it got free. The fact that it failed only gives us more leverage..."

He knew those voices. One deep and dull, the other raspy and cold. They were the ones who had attacked him in the forest, just before he had fallen ill. A man called Mager, and a woman...she hadn't given a name, but Hunter remembered how ferociously she'd fought.

Hunter checked his implant's clock. He had been out for hours. If they had been traveling all that time, he would be miles and miles away from Evie. Eastward, that was where they would have taken him, into the Tainted lands the Pure refused to name, spoken of only in whispers.

A tickle rose in Hunter's throat. He coughed it away. He listened for a sign the Tainted had noticed, but heard nothing. Slowly, he raised his bound hands, hooked his thumbs under the cloth of his hood and peeked out.

A mass of strand lay just in front of him, blocking his view—the rear side of another alcove, one of many in two sets of rows up to the front of the walker. Still moving slow, Hunter raised his head until he saw one of the Tainted, back turned, sitting in the interior of what would be the monster's head. It was the man—Hunter recognized his braided hair strung with colored beads. Hunter ducked again until he was hidden behind the seat-back, and removed the hood completely. Light was coming in from a window above and behind him. He turned onto his knees and angled his head to peer out.

"Wow," he whispered.

The strand was alive. All of it. Bright silver from horizon to horizon, sliding over itself in intersecting streams, growing in great hill-like bulges. It had organized part of itself into black cables, which crisscrossed the surface and crackled with electricity. As the walker passed, a cable glowed and flared.

Lightning arced to another nearby, burning an afterimage in Hunter's vision.

Watching the passing scene began to make him motion sick, and so he looked eastward, toward their destination. Across the landscape he could see a few outcroppings of rock or ancient ruin, but no other solid ground save for one place. Far in the distance, a great round building rose before a gray haze that signaled the beginning of the sea.

No, this wasn't the Riversea. They were east; this was the ocean. They had ridden all the way to the shore of the Atlantica.

The walker turned, heading straight toward the round building. The structure had the look of the ancients to it, immensely tall with rounded sides, made of weathered steel in a strange slatted pattern. Hunter leaned harder against the side and craned his neck to try and see.

A hand grasped his shoulder. Hunter spun. The Tainted woman stood before him. Her strand-enhanced eyes searched him. Hunter glanced down at the hood in his hands.

The woman grinned. "They do say the Pure are supposed to be brave. Hey..." She turned toward the front. "Hey, Mager! Did he have it before?"

"Have *what*?"

"His implant." She poked the metal on Hunter's shoulder. He felt it as a pull in the surrounding flesh. "The one we tracked. He didn't have it when we found him with that rat Ono, did he?"

"How am I supposed to remember? And what's the difference? If Mother wants him, then we did good. Otherwise, we chuck him in the Atlantica."

Hunter's head snapped toward Mager. If Mother wants him, otherwise *what?*

The woman gazed at him, eyes narrowed. "Hey. You understand me? Hello?"

Hunter turned back, keeping his mouth shut. He blinked hard.

The woman stared a while longer, then reached down and snapped her fingers in front of Hunter's nose. Hunter stayed motionless.

"At least he won't give us trouble." She stomped back to the front of the walker.

Hunter stared at the opposite wall, thinking over what was said. The two of them had spoken of bringing him to their mother, though they didn't look much like siblings. And then....some sort of test? And failure meant death. But what exactly was he meant to do?

The walker came to a halt. He heard the woman coming and stood, knowing she would want to lead him outside. She gave a satisfied grunt when he moved ahead without her having to command, and left the hood on the seat behind them, as the strand around his wrists came loose and fell off.

The rear of the walker uncoiled and formed a doorway, and Hunter shuffled out ahead of the two Tainted. They had stopped on a rocky outcropping in the strand, strewn with pieces of crumbled, ancient building-stone. The stone was dark in color, and bathed in shadow. Hunter looked up. The massive circular building before him drew his gaze to its apex. The thing was truly giant, its slatted metal exterior half-gone, shored up by swaths of blue strand. Surrounding it were the bare remains of other ancient buildings, some that may have once been as large as this one, now completely turned to rubble.

On the far side, waves crashed against a seawall. Hunter had thought the body of water there was the Atlantica, but it was in fact a wide, swift river, beyond which rose the ruins of an ancient city. Again, he was amazed at the enormity of what he saw—the scale and number of this city's broken towers dwarfed the Tainted city beyond the Riversea. But no Tainted would have been able to live in this place; the strand coated all of it, as thick and malignant as the Gridlands, giving off strange, faint sparkles in the shadows of early evening.

Sensing Mager's presence behind him, Hunter hurried forward into the square arch to the building's interior. He entered a high-ceilinged room lit bright blue by the strand, with Tainted gang members lounging and laughing in groups along the edges, and walking on catwalks made of strand overhead. The sudden change in sight and sound was like stepping into a new world, like entering the door in the Immersion. A shrieking noise from a curtain of strand to his left made him grind his teeth; it wasn't until he saw the Tainted dancing that he realized it was meant to be music.

Then he noticed the children. As he advanced through the chamber with his two captors at his heels, he passed a girl no older than himself, spherical strand implants dotting her face in a decorative pattern. Hunter inadvertently made eye contact with her, and received a snarl in reply. Two four or five-year-olds ran naked beside him, one of them with a nest of strand at the center of his sternum. Something about the sight unsettled him; even in Bordertown he had never seen an implant in one so young.

They stopped at a metal door at the rear of the entrance hall. A length of strand wound tightly through its metal handles. His female captor exchanged some words with two men lounging casually nearby. One of the men nodded toward the door, and the strand there uncoiled, letting her shoulder her way through into a wide hallway, dim and dank like a tunnel. Hunter touched the metal fibers of the lock as he walked behind, letting them slide off his fingertips. If the lock was listening to commands, then there was a network here, something he could explore.

But not before he met whatever was at the end of this hall.

The tunnel ended in daylight. The interior of the circular building—or oval, as he could now see—was open to the sky. Stone steps lined the walls up and around him, and strand cascaded down them like a waterfall, extending to the mat of writhing, grayish silver below his feet. Before him, the strand amassed upward into a platform, rising sharply over his head before tapering off in a hump-shaped peak. Upon the hump sat an oversized chair covered in battered, dark leather, and on the chair, chest wide with the posture of one who controlled all she saw, was a woman.

She was older than his mother, but beyond that her age was impossible to guess. Hundreds of strand-wires were embedded in her scalp, splaying out behind her in place of a head of hair, connected to the massive pile of strand below her. Her face was sunken, her body stick-thin, barely filling out her suit of metal-laced cloth armor. But she was not simply skinny, something else was at work—everywhere her skin showed, it was stretched taut over bone and muscle, with not a hint of a fat underneath. Hunter was reminded of Trina's explanation of how the strand had cured his infection, how it could filter through the body's ingredients at the tiniest scale and pick and choose which would remain. Either this woman's implants had malfunctioned somehow, leaving her in this emaciated state, or for reasons he couldn't grasp, she had chosen this visage for herself.

Hunter's escorts took to a knee on either side of him, bowing their heads. Should he follow their lead, or remain standing? He looked up at the woman on the hill for a clue.

"What's your name, boy?"

The woman's voice felt like a blade in his ear. Hunter opened his mouth, but his throat itched and he could only cough and blink hard.

The woman placed her fist beneath her chin and leaned forward, eyes narrowed. "Do you understand me? Kaia, does he understand?"

The woman to Hunter's left shot him a sour look. "I think he does."

The enthroned woman sat back again, then snorted. "Well, what of it? Are you a liar, boy? I wouldn't expect a Pure to speak our language, but Kaia thinks you do, and *she's* not stupid enough to lie to me."

Hunter swallowed, scratched his implant and took a deep breath. "My name is Hunter."

The woman on the throne started. She looked at him strangely for a moment, then a smile curled over her gruesome face.

"Oh, my." She turned to Kaia and nodded. "That *accent*. How exotic."

To Hunter's left, Kaia lowered her head further in supplication.

"Is he really a Pure, though?"

Kaia flashed Hunter a look before returning to her bowed stance. "He seems like one. Those clothes—"

The woman waved her silent. "He's not supposed to have an implant, is he?" Her eyelids fluttered as she accessed information from the strand. "Yes, I'm right, none of them have one. My dear, do you realize what you've done?"

Kaia kept her head down.

"Ono knows I've wanted a Pure child in the Family for years. This is probably some brat from the far west that he draped in skins as a ruse. And you fell for it and brought him here. *Here*, at this crucial time." Her sharp voice became serrated as she growled. "Honestly, I've seen some real cock-ups in my day, but I expected better from you."

Hunter heard a cracking sound, and realized it was Kaia grinding her teeth. When he looked over to her, she glanced upward at him with those teeth bared. That meant...she was angry? At him? Everything was too confusing here: Fesso's bizarre face, the way they spoke, an entire culture he didn't understand. Mager's threat from before lingered in his mind: *if Mother wants him, then we did good. Otherwise, we chuck him in the Atlantica.* He had a feeling like he did with the ants outside of Senter's tower, that he was trapped in a game in which he didn't know the rules.

But maybe that was exactly right. A game, where some of the information was hidden. He had to try different ways of playing, then, poke and prod along until he found the right answer.

"I'm not from the west," Hunter said. Fesso's head snapped his direction. "I'm a Pure. A Pure of the Southern Pines."

She sat back and regarded him, frowning, pulse thudding in a vein on her temple. When she spoke, her voice dripped with false sweetness.

"Hunter of the Pure. Is that right?"

Hunter nodded.

"My name is Fesso; have you heard of me?"

He shook his head.

"How refreshing." She gave a wry smile. "Tell me Hunter: do you know how Kaia and Mager found you, out in the middle of a forest?"

Hunter started to shake his head again, but then he remembered. "The signal...there was a signal coming from my implant."

"Correct. Strange, that. And even stranger, we received an anonymous message some weeks ago with the fingerprint of your signal in it. It said there was something in the Midlands we should be looking for, something of great interest to us." Fesso's bony fingers dug into the arms of her chair, and her vein throbbed harder. "Now tell me dear boy, and think very carefully: just how did this strange state of affairs come to be?"

Think carefully. The signal had come from his implant... Trina had given him the implant, yes? No. Zeke had said the signal was there before. Someone else had been there first...

"Ono gave it to me."

Fesso let out a hissing breath.

"...he put in the signal...as a lure...*I* was the lure." He looked up at Fesso as the pieces came together in his mind. He saw her seething, teeth bared.

The lie clicked into place on his tongue. "But I wouldn't let him."

Fesso pursed her lips. "What?"

"He's an evil man. He pretended to be my friend, but later he admitted he was only using me to destroy *you*." He pointed, hoping the dramatic effect would buy him more time to fill out the story. "Me and my sister ran away. We escaped. But we had nowhere to go. I can't return to the Pure like this." He gestured to his collarbone. "So we were lost, and tired, and then…then…" He looked at Kaia for assistance.

"He's telling the truth," Kaia said without looking up. "Perhaps Ono had planned to use him once, but that *fasslicker* was nowhere nearby. Probably he's still skulking at Gwyer, licking his wounds from the thrashing we gave him."

Hunter stared up at Fesso hopefully. She had calmed during the course of his tale, sitting back in her chair and tracing the lines of her cheekbones with her thumb. She took a deep breath and nodded.

"It's all right, boy. Ono can't hurt you here. He doesn't even know where we are, and he won't ever; that signal of yours can't leave this network." She stood, rope-like muscles straining, and one by one the threads of strand from her "hair" *plinked* free of the hill below. Hunter tried not to blink too hard or cough as she slowly walked down toward him.

"Yes, it's good you came." The strand formed into stairs at her feet, and she quickened her pace, splaying her hands wide. "It's my life's work to give a home to children who have been cast out—the desperate, the unwanted, those who have no other place to go." She stepped off the hill and brushed her oil-slick fingers across his cheek. He shivered. "Well? How about that? What would you think of staying here, with us?"

"I…" Hunter swallowed. "Things are…different here," he managed. "From my home."

She laughed. "I would imagine they are. The Gridlands are new to us as well, but we've adapted." She gestured to the great walls around them. "A very long time ago, this place was called The Land of Meadows. Can you believe it? Meadows? Here? And yet, there's still a certain beauty to it, if you look hard enough. I like to spend time in this ancient theater, watching the strand move under the sun. It's elegant. Powerful. But even after all these years since the fall, we've only taken advantage of a fraction of what it can accomplish."

Fesso's gaze snapped to her henchmen. "You've done well. Both of you. I'll see you get a place of honor at tomorrow's dinner. Now, take this one to get cleaned and dressed, then come back here and report on your deliveries."

"Thank you, Mother," they said in unison.

Fesso whisked away from them. Kaia and Mager rose. Shoulder to shoulder, they came up in front of Hunter, and forced him back into the tunnel.

"And Kaia…" Fesso's voice drifted in from behind. "No more surprises, yes? Our time is coming." She looked back over her shoulder, her eyes glowing a faint blue.

"The Core grows impatient."

15

"YOU'RE RIGHT," TRINA said, crossing her arms. "I have no proof."

She was sitting in her easy chair, opposite Mayor Constatin and Malven, captain of the town watch. To Ono, the fact that Trina's living room seemed the logical place to convene on the current crisis spoke volumes about her place in Bordertown politics.

"But why should I need it?" she continued. "My judgment comes from years of experience in the field. Shouldn't that be enough to spur us into action, when our lives are on the line?" The muffled sound of a wailing child rose behind her. She motioned to Kelas, who was shuffling about, pouring drinks for the guests, and he went to attend to it.

Malven sipped from his cup and grumbled. "We already told Serr that Fesso had made some kind of arrangement with the Ints. He did nothing. With all due respect, what will this do to change anything?" He pointed to the blob of strand Trina had set on the table between them. "I can hear him now, 'So, it sparkles. So *what?*'"

Ono snorted from his place outside the circle, half-covered in shadow; the old captain did a half-decent Serr impression. Trina flashed him a look and he quieted. Given what had recently transpired between them, he figured his chances of being allowed in at all were tenuous at best—no need to push things.

"Serr is an intelligent man," Trina said, turning back. "He especially understands balances of power. This strand comes

159

from the Core. You'll hardly ever see it in the wild, because the other Ints have kept the Core isolated on its island for a thousand years or longer. But there are records, signatures in our database that match if one allows for expected evolution over time. If Fesso is helping it escape, it might pose a threat to Ints all over the region. We're going to see a major upheaval. More attacks like the one we fought off, but larger, deadlier."

"So…" Constatin, the town mayor, opened his hands in placation, beady eyes creased with unconvincing friendliness. "Your theory is that Fesso had her Children seed this strand into various sites throughout the network, which gives the Core some sort of tactical advantage against the other Ints, yes? But why? What does she get in return?"

"Power?" Trina said. "Money? Does it really matter what the Core has promised her?"

"It would help us tell the story." Constatin flashed the smile that had no doubt earned him his office. "The problem, Dear, is that the world at large does not share our view of the Core. To most of Jolon, it's no more important than any of the tales of ancient, powerful Ints one tells to scare children. If we want to make the Core into a threat that Serr takes seriously, we need to spin a good yarn for him. Add details, motivations. Once the strand is silent again and everyone is safe, what difference does it make whether they turned out to be true?"

A rustling sound to Ono's right drew his attention: Evie, half-crouched in the doorway, shuffling her feet with impatience. Ono backed further into his corner, knowing his appearance tended to upset her, but the girl's gaze was fixed anyway on the proceedings before her, though she couldn't have understood the words. Perhaps she thought they were discussing what had happened to her brother? That had been her only concern since he and Trina had brought her back to Bordertown, beside herself with rage and worry.

"I don't see why he's being so cagey," Malven said. "If I were Serr,

I would send the Jolon Guard to Fesso's headquarters immediately. He has an army; all she has are a small gang of thugs. Why let a threat like this blossom instead of wiping it out?"

"And just how is the Guard supposed to find her?" Constatin said. "You think Serr wants scouts spread out across the entire Gridlands? If we had a clue where Fesso was, perhaps things would be different." He looked down and shook his head. "I'm sorry, but theories aren't enough. We need more information. Exactly how many people does Fesso command, where are they, and what's their next move?"

Trina growled, "It was hard enough to find this sample. You can't expect me to—"

"We could deliver all of what you said, and a detailed schedule of Fesso's bathroom habits. Serr still wouldn't do anything." Ono stepped forward, placing his hands on the back of Trina's chair, one soft, one with a metallic tap. Trina looked up at him, annoyed. The other two cleared their throats or fell silent; handy sometimes, to have that effect on people. "If Fesso is protected by the strand, then sending an army across an open field is the worst possible strategy. They'd be torn apart in minutes. I doubt Serr would risk even deploying a garrison here to protect the walls. The previous attack may have been nothing more than a feint to draw his troops away, exposing Jolon to attack."

The others muttered and exchanged glances.

"So that's it?" Malven said, throwing up his arms. "If Jolon will not come no matter what we do, we might as well abandon our homes now."

Constatin huffed, no doubt contemplating the electoral prospects of a mayor whose town has been wiped off the map. "What does Palerno say? By all rights, he should be here."

"I don't think a lecture about interfering with the Ints is what we need now," Trina said with a mild groan. "I already spoke to Palerno when we returned. He said he would dedicate all his prayer time to putting out distress calls across the net, asking for protection."

"May the Ints smile upon us," Malven mumbled. He turned to Constatin. "But in case they don't, you and I will be preparing an evacuation order. Now might be a good time to get started."

Trina shook her head. "Just wait—"

"Wait? I will not wait here, thumb wedged firmly between my buttocks, hoping some Int or another decides our lives are worth saving."

"There is another way." Ono stood tall and took a deep breath. "If Serr will not attack Fesso, then we can take the fight to her ourselves. We may not be able to match her numbers, but a small force has advantages in speed and stealth, if we attack at the right time."

"Just what do you mean by 'we,' eh?" Malven looked as if he would rise from his chair, then sized up Ono's tall, metal-clad figure and thought better of it, settling for a waggled finger. "You don't live here. Why should we trust you to lead an attack on our behalf? You're only here because of the price on Fesso's head."

Ono said nothing, fixing Malven with a stare. A pained look settled on Malven's face as regret seeped in.

"He has a point," Trina said. "Many here have no reason to trust you, Ono. If the worst happens, would you risk your life to fight for a town that is not your own?"

There was a lot more subtext in that question than substance. What exactly did Trina mean? Could he control Aunio? Or was he a good enough person to put their faith in, with or without his alter ego?

"Consider this," he said, in lieu of having answers. "The Ints in Jolon requested I bring Fesso back to them alive. Why would they have done that, unless she possesses something valuable to them—valuable in their fight against the Core."

That woke them up. "You think the Jolon Ints are already using *you* to try and fight the Core?" Constatin said.

"Think of it. Fesso has made a deal with the Core, yes? But why should she trust an Int to keep its word? Most likely she was given something for insurance, a token that gives access to the Core's functions. With that token, another Int might be able to stop the Core from spreading, before it starts."

"So you bring Fesso back to Jolon, the Jolon Ints get the token…"

"And both our problems are solved at once."

Constatin and Malven began to murmur to one another. Ono's gaze flitted between the conversations, searching for clues without using the strand to enhance his hearing. Malven nodded stoically, his eye implant twinkling as it replayed some old memory. But Constatin remained unsatisfied, settling into a state of suppressed anxiety, wriggling his nose, eyebrows twitching.

"Your bravery is commendable, Ono," Constatin said. "But you walk a desperate path. The town guards are trained to stand watch, not go on foolhardy raids. Even you can't expect to take Fesso hostage alone."

"He won't be alone." Trina rose, the thick springs of her plush chair creaking beneath her. To Ono's surprise, she circled around it to stand next to him, head level with his shoulder. "I'll be with him, doing whatever it takes to defend my family. And not just Kelas and the children, but all of you, as well. We're all a family in Bordertown, and we won't let Fesso or anyone else force us to leave our homes."

"That's wonderful," Constatin said, crossing his arms. "Heartwarming. But without an idea of where to find Fesso, it's all empty words. Unless we can present an *actual* plan to the townspeople, we'll have to be ready for evacuation."

Trina grumbled, then went and sat down again, launching back into discussion. But Ono's attention was drawn elsewhere, to something that should have been present, but wasn't—Evie was missing from the doorway.

Whether or not Bordertown would continue to exist was not something he would take a side in, nor did the interested parties care for his opinion. What he wanted was Fesso, and the girl's behavior piqued his intuition in that area. Something about the look on her face, the way she had focused on the proceedings despite not understanding him. Or perhaps it wasn't them she was focusing on at all?

As the quarreling continued, he stepped around the circle, gaze lingering on the small lump of strand on the table, then he strode out through the now-empty door.

16

AS SHE WALKED, Kaia's back muscles shifted beneath her tattoos. Hunter hurried forward to keep up with her long strides. All the new sights and sounds were distracting him. The strand hung thick inside the ancient building, bombarding him with information. Members of the Family stared at him as he passed. A hand grasped his wrist and yanked him right—Kaia had changed course. Though her arms were barely larger than Evie's, her grip outmatched any man's Hunter had ever felt. The image of her knocking Ono off his walker with one punch flashed through Hunter's mind. She pulled him through a series of cramped hallways, drawing more stares. Hunter imagined himself winding deeper and deeper into the compound, further and further into a labyrinth with no escape. *Take this one to get cleaned and dressed,* Fesso had said. Well, the cleaning part didn't sound so bad, but he was already dressed, so what did that mean?

Kaia swiveled around a corner and through a doorway. Hunter found himself in a square room of ancient stone, filled with uncomfortable-looking chairs and a small table near the center, all repurposed metal junk. At the table sat two Tainted of perhaps fifteen, taking turns tapping a small spiral of strand between them, playing some sort of game. More Tainted, mostly younger, sat around the outside of the room, dozing, brushing their hair, or in the case of two of them, kissing in a way that made Hunter distinctly uncomfortable, though he had difficulty taking his eyes off the sight.

"Jebreel," Kaia said. "Pay attention. Mother has a job for you."

One of the game players, a girl with long black hair, flashed a snarl. "You mean *you* have a job for me. Find someone else to do your errands."

Kaia shoved Hunter from behind. "He's a new arrival. Get him cleaned up and find him a place to sleep."

Jebreel looked Hunter up and down. Her face was like a snake's, pointed, smooth and sleek. She opened her mouth and paused for a moment as if lost for words, then leaned forward and spat a ball of mucus at him.

"Ah!" Hunter tried to duck, but took the spit wad on his shoulder, with a couple wet flecks on his ear. Laughter came from the edges of the room.

"Now he's clean," Jebreel said, and turned back to her game.

Kaia gave an impatient murmur. "Fine. He won't be needed until the dinner, anyway. But if he shows up there all grimy like this, I'll smash that pretty head down between your shoulders."

Jebreel showed no sign she had heard the threat. After a few moments, Kaia grunted and headed off with Mager in tow, slamming the metal door behind her.

Hunter blinked hard and cleared his throat. The players continued their game. If they would keep ignoring him, that would be perfect. Perhaps he could slip away and—

"What's that thing he does with his eyes?" said the other game player. He turned in his seat to stare at Hunter and blinked four or five times exaggeratedly. For some reason, the action made Hunter's own eyes water and itch. He tried to keep from blinking again, but only ended up doing it harder.

Jebreel laughed. "He's copying you, look! Hey, what's wrong with you?"

"Nothing," Hunter said.

"*Nothing*," Jebreel mimicked. Some of the others in the room chortled. "What are you looking at, eh? I'm over here. For *fesh* sakes, this one's a freak. Where'd they drag you out from, boy?"

Hunter blinked and rubbed his implant.

"Hey, she asked you a question," a boy at the other end yelled. "You want to catch a beating?"

Hunter turned, walked to an empty corner and sat down. His vision was going dark around the edges. Uncomfortable memories seeped in. Colorful carapaces spread among the leaves. Cold water splashing his face.

"Hey, *fen.*" The boy who had threatened him loomed over. Though scrawny, he was a few years older than Hunter. "You ignoring me? I said, 'you want to catch a beating?'"

Hunter turned away again, until he was staring at the wisps of strand running through the stone wall. Behind him came a few yells, most of amusement, though he did catch a younger girl's voice saying something like "leave him alone." He braced for the incoming blow.

Instead of delivering a punch, the boy touched his fingers gently against Hunter's implant. A shock went through Hunter's body, reverberating from his eyeballs into his toes. He tried to yell, but his tongue flapped uselessly in his mouth. The cold floor met his cheek and his limbs jiggled beside him. With all his effort he managed to shift his gaze to a blurry image of the boy sauntering away, the others yelling at him as he went.

"Come on, Ges! What are you doing?!"

"What? It's nothing, all right?"

"You're gonna kill him and then Kaia's gonna come back here and whup me bad."

Ges eyed Hunter and smirked. "He won't die. But he isn't getting rid of that thing, either. It's nasty. Welcome to the Family, Pure-boy."

Hunter rolled into a ball. His vision was still doubled. Aftershocks arced from his implant through the rest of his body. He closed his eyes and focused on breathing, watching his internal clock count the seconds. Gradually the spikes of pain diminished to an almost-tolerable level.

"You gonna be all right?"

A soft voice. A girl, around his age. Hunter opened one eye. The girl was kneeling over him, face ringed in blue light from the strand above.

"I'm...fine." Hunter pulled himself to a sitting position. He winced as the motion set off a fresh round of jolts down his spine.

"That implant goes deep in your brain, doesn't it? Mine does, too. It'll make that virus extra painful."

Hunter took a deep breath. He wanted to be alone, but the girl wasn't going away. He took a good look at her for the first time and gasped. Her nose was made of strand. The hunk of metal bulged out in the midst of her otherwise delicate features.

"I'm Telian," she said, and smiled. "You'll be all right. Mother doesn't like the Children hurting each other too bad. And they won't ask you to do many chores at first."

Hunter nodded. He wasn't sure how to respond to a girl with a metal nose speaking to him like they were old friends. Before he could do anything else she sat down next to him and brushed aside her long braids. The others in the room yelled and laughed, but Hunter couldn't tell if that was directed at him.

"It's boring here a lot, with the firewall blocking everything, but playing games on my implant helps. I saw you scratching yours; I bet you're still getting used to it, like me. Sometimes, if I concentrate, I can almost...drop inside it. You know, what's it called..."

"The Immersion." He was wasting time. He had to find a place he could explore their network in peace. The firewall she spoke of would block access to the outside world, but Zeke had shown him ways to break through such barriers. Once he re-entered the Immersion, he could probe for weaknesses, find a hole. And then what? Once he had access to the outside world, who would he contact?

Trina. She would know what to do. Maybe she could find Evie, let her know he was all right, then mount some sort of rescue.

"Telian." He paused and waited for the pain to stop rattling his jaw. "Is there somewhere I can rest? I need privacy."

She nodded, then rose to address Jebreel. "Jeb, Hunter needs a room to stay in tonight."

"Good for him," the older girl muttered into her game. "Now get lost, you little *bloodfen.*"

"Kaia said—"

"I'm *busy.*" Jebreel turned and gave her the snarl Hunter had already become familiar with. "If you want a bedroom for your boyfriend, go find one yourself."

"I need the keys," Telian said without hesitation.

Jebreel closed her eyes. "There. Now, *kanna.*"

Telian took Hunter's hand and led him away. More jabs of pain snaked down his back as they exited the room and headed through the narrow halls. They came to an ancient door, more rust than metal. At Telian's mental command, the strand around the handle fell away, and the portal creaked open.

"It's kind of gross, but it'll keep Ges away from you," Telian said. "I'll give you the keys, so you can leave if you have to. Just try not to get caught, and if you do, don't tell anyone I did it."

"Thank you." Telian looked at him expectantly, but Hunter didn't know what else to say. So much had happened so quickly, not to mention how distracting her nose was. Still, he shouldn't fault her for that, considering what his own neck looked like. "You're...a good person."

She cocked her head. "Of course I am." She shrugged and went off down the hall.

Hunter let the door lock behind him. The strand flared blue automatically, but he shut off the light as he lay on the hard slab of a bed. Whatever Ges had hit him with still ached in his joints. Luckily, he could get rid of it on his way out of the network.

He dove. The dark of the room folded and became light, and he was standing again in the gridded forest. The pain was gone. The structures he had been practicing building stood nearby, a

169

tent strung over a length of rope, next to the beginnings of what was meant to be a Tainted-style cabin. Otherwise, the interior of his implant looked the same as ever, rows of identical trees stretching to infinity. But he sensed another presence inside it, much as he had sensed Zeke the first time they met. He closed his eyes and felt with his instincts. The intruder was slipping about, trying to evade him, but it couldn't hide from him here.

He spun and opened his eyes. Behind him on the ground was a snapping turtle. Its shell bulged with asymmetrical protrusions, and its eyes were bloodshot. Hunter took a step toward it, hands extended, and it let out an un-turtle-like growl and made a few snaps in the air. Then, just as it looked like it might lunge, it turned and tried to dig away into the soft ground.

"No you don't!" Hunter made a dive and caught the thing by the tail and hind leg. He wrenched it upward and held it above his head.

"Letmegoletmegoletmegoletmego!" The thing thrashed in his grip.

Hunter marched over to his constructed tent and made a precarious one-handed grab for the skin. Pulling it loose, he dumped the turtle inside, wrapped it up tight and bound the ends with the tent rope. The turtle continued to thrash, yelping blasphemies against the spirits, elders and all that was good and holy.

Not knowing what else to do with it, Hunter set the wrapped turtle down by the half-finished cabin. One problem down; now all he needed was to get out of the network, then figure out how to contact Trina and tell her where he was. He shrunk himself down and headed for the gateway.

It was there as before, a glowing portal set in a field of black, though not nearly as bright as usual. Hunter stepped forward, shut his eyes and tensed his muscles. But this time he stepped through easily. He shifted his weight until he was sure the ground below him was solid, then took in his new surroundings.

Ruins. Hills of crushed stones lay before him, topped with great beams of rusted, twisted metal, much of them in the double-forked shape he often saw among the half-buried structures of the Ancients. But he had only seen small relics in the forest clearings, half-covered with vines and leaves and strand. The wreckage here towered upward, the hollowed remains of buildings that once stood as proud as any mountain. Far above, the sky was a roiling mass of gray-black cloud.

The light here seemed different from Senter's city. Everything there had been lit by default, but here the landscape was dark, except for the spot where he stood. Light was streaming from behind him, coming from a ring of lanterns hooked around the outside of the portal. Red, blue, green and yellow—when Hunter peered closely, the lights seemed to flicker slower, then faster, blinking out a pattern too fast to see.

The beacon. This was why he had never noticed it before; he could only see it from *outside* his implant. He yanked at the chain that held the lanterns until they smashed down at his feet and melted away into the ground. The wreckage around him plunged into darkness again.

He had to go somewhere to find a way out, so he picked a direction and headed off. Instinct told him to stay quiet. There was something moving out there. No, some *things*. Black, shiny, low to the ground, he could just see glimpses of their serrated tails whisking between chunks of broken metal.

Hunter took a deep breath and counted to ten. He had to focus to pull off this trick, to meld with the air and let the little remaining light fall through him.

One of the first things Zeke had taught him was how to become invisible, the same way the little otter had been when he followed Hunter into Senter's tower. According to Zeke's somewhat confused explanation, most things in the Immersion tended to react to probes of data with helpful replies. But if Hunter tried, he could turn off those responses; the light might reach him, but his body wouldn't reflect it back, and the same went for the sound of his footsteps, or the air from his breath. It wasn't foolproof—he was still there, taking up space, and anyone who looked hard enough would probably be able to find him. But it was better than nothing.

Hunter clambered on silent feet over the hills of rubble, twisting his head each time a nearby shadow slid into a crevice. Beyond the open ground lay a thicket of bent beams. The darkness within swarmed with the creatures, which lay on the black ground, nearly two-dimensional except for bulbous eyes that swiveled above wide jaws. Hunter had to stop several times to remind himself that they couldn't see or hear him as he slowly stepped through, while the creatures slithered by his feet.

The line of ruins extended to a nearby tower, and soon he stood beneath it. The creatures were even more numerous here, sliding along the outside of the building like sap on a tree. The tower extended up through the clouds. Hunter had an idea that the black fog above had been placed there deliberately, to stop any information from leaving this world. But he wouldn't be able to climb it, not with so many creatures covering its sides. Ahead of him, the horizon ended with a distant drop-off in the land, like a canyon with no far side. Hopefully, somewhere at the bottom he'd find another way out of this network.

Hunter walked on, and the line of ruined towers came to an end, leaving only open space between him and his goal. He pressed his back to an exposed wall, looking out over the expanse before crossing. Something moved behind him. He started and jumped forward, making a scrabbling noise on the stones below.

Hunter backed away. The creature unfolded itself from the hollow of broken stone, emitting an ear-piercing screech. He had been leaning against it without realizing. It crawled down toward him, and grew one set of legs, then another, then another. By the time Hunter began to run, five feet of its body had slithered out, with more behind.

He took off across the landscape as more creatures screamed. Each step in the rubble woke another pursuer, and he increased his speed to keep the pack behind him. Soon the entire field around him became alive. He felt a new presence in his mind, large, overbearing, becoming aware of him and watching his movements.

Just a few more hills, and he'd be at the drop-off he had seen before. There was something familiar about the bumps and ridges below him. As he drew closer to the edge, the air grew still again, and the creatures behind him silenced. Whatever was watching him had called off their pursuit. He ran down a gentle slope, came to the precipice and looked down.

Nothing. The vertical wall curved away beneath him, like a floating island, with only black space beyond. Now he understood; it was the logic of the Immersion. The wall wasn't a wall at all. It was a floor.

He leaned forward, over the edge, and let the world rotate with him. In one dizzying step, he was standing upright again, with the entire vast landscape he had just traversed falling vertically below him.

A tingle ran down his spine, making his hands shake. The feeling of being watched was stronger here. It was coming from nearby. From over his shoulder.

Hunter looked up at what had formerly been a raised section of land jutting out into the abyss, now a tower of rock above him. Near the top of the tower, an outgrowth formed an oval shape, indented, almost like...

...an ear?

"Oh."

The ground shifted, rumbling, and Hunter dropped to his knees. The tower—the head of a colossus—changed shape. Its eyes opened and yellow light poured forth from them. It shifted and looked downward, catching sight of Hunter perched on its shoulder. Those eyes—they felt like two hands of flame, probing him, learning his shape.

What kind of creature was this? An Int? But it felt nothing like Senter. It was so much larger, more powerful. He could almost sense the unfathomable intelligence behind its gaze.

Hunter looked down over the precipice of the giant's collarbone. The entrance to his implant was still open, far below him, and he knew at once that he wanted to get back there. He launched himself forward, down past the chest. He caught a glimpse of the tiny oval of light, and put himself there. His body stretched with a wave of pain. His mind felt like cloth pulled through a small hole, the world grew bright, then faded suddenly.

Breathing hard, coated with sweat, Hunter rose on the hard cot in his room. He spent some moments feeling his limbs, until he was satisfied they were there, then lay back, basking in relief.

A realization hit him, and Hunter disconnected his implant, turning off all communication with the network. Whatever that thing was, he wanted nothing to do with it, and he especially didn't like the way it had looked at him, studied him. No matter what, he would avoid using the strand as much as possible, and definitely wouldn't return to the Immersion here again.

Which meant if he was going to get out of this place, he'd have to find another way.

17

EVIE MADE HER way out of Trina's house by the side exit, keeping her eyes low to avoid the gaze of passersby. Not that there were many about. Gray clouds choked the sky, and a light coat of rain had turned the streets to mud. Lines of strand flashed iridescent from the sides of the alley, and Evie weaved left and right as she went, avoiding the hanging metal. Easy to do, now; she wouldn't be so lucky once she made it to the Gridlands.

She came to an intersection and turned right, away from the central square. Too likely someone would notice her there. It was absurd having to sneak around like this, but she had already tried the direct approach with Trina. The entire ride back to Bordertown and several times since they had arrived, she had demanded the Tainted woman take her back to where Hunter was kidnapped, so she could pick up his trail and follow after. The first time, Trina had answered with a mumble about it being too dangerous, and after that only with silence.

"So I'm your prisoner, then?" she had demanded of Trina, just before a meeting between her and the other Tainted was set to begin.

"You can do you as you wish. But don't do anything stupid." Trina had glanced at Ono, then left the room. The implication was clear: if you run away, I'll send him after you.

Fortunately, for a moment at least Ono had been as distracted by the group's argument as the rest of them. A waste of time, all of it. All Evie cared about was her brother, and Hunter's name hadn't been uttered once during their meeting. It burned her how the object of their focus seemed to be on that lump of strand on the table. What was so special about it, anyway? Evie had seen something like it once before—no, twice, perhaps. Well, it didn't matter. She was through trying to understand the Tainted. Better to rely on herself, even if all the strand in the world lay between her and her goal.

She came to a narrow alley that ran along the town's outer wall. Evie trailed her fingers along the moist gray stone, and the wetness tickled her. She pulled away, and her fingertips came back reddish-brown.

Blood, hiding in a crevice from the battle weeks before, now washing out. She wiped her hand on her hip and hurried on, a quick sigh escaping her. She felt drained, ill-equipped to travel eastward in this humid mess. The path split before her; to the left, a side alley ran to the town's market area. Her stomach gave a grumble, chastising her for its emptiness.

"I know, I know," she whispered. "I should have taken food from Trina." If she were this hungry already, she'd be ill-prepared for the long journey through the Gridlands. But she had already gotten in trouble once during Hunter's recuperation, for taking an apple from one of the market stalls. She hadn't understood why at the time—when the Pure laid out food in a row, the only meaning was that it was ready for anyone in the tribe who wished to share. But instead, the person who spent their days standing behind the stall had started yelling and making threats. A crowd had gathered, and it had taken some long explanations from Trina before Evie had finally been allowed to have her meal in peace. Typical Tainted nonsense; if they just let people eat when they were hungry, perhaps they'd spend less time being upset about—

She stopped short at a corner. In a courtyard across the way, four children were playing around a metal pole, upon which hung a thin length of strand, flicking outward at them like a whip. The children, around Hunter's age, took turns running toward and away from the pole, smacking the strand as they ran by with sticks. A boy stumbled, laughing too hard to keep up, and the strand lashed out and caught him by the wrist. He let out a cry of pain as the strand yanked him off his feet, hauling him inward.

Evie jumped out, knife held high, battle cry in her lungs. The children froze in horror, gaping. Not at the strand—at her. The caught one reached up with a shaking hand and tapped the strand, which released its grip. All of them dashed off to a nearby house, leaving Evie standing alone, dagger at her side, panting.

A game, it had just been a game. She turned and dashed up the street, before their parents came out to find her. Once out of sight, she slapped her back against a rotten wall of planks and closed her eyes. What had she been thinking? Her head was swimming, her breath coming in gasps. It was too much. Too much like...

The memory came back to her again, intensity heightened by her still-pounding heart. She had been standing atop the ridge for some minutes, peering northward over the trees. Then she heard a muffled cry below, exactly where she had left Hunter waiting. She ran back to him on feet that barely touched the ground, exploding into the clearing like a mountain lion pouncing on its prey.

Nothing.

"Hunter?"

She whirled, looking for some sign of him, anything. How could it be? How could he have just disappeared, with no sign of any—

No, there was something: snapped branches, depressions in the soft turf. She headed through the brush, following hints of sound and smells on the breeze, hoping they weren't her senses deceiving her. She came to a clearing near the edge of the wood, and beyond the line of trees there sat a hideous monster made of strand.

The thing resembled an over-sized caterpillar, with an elongated, plump body and four pairs of legs on either side. Evie clutched her knife. Seemingly without prompting, the creature pulled its belly from the ground until it was hunched, ready to move. Two people appeared from the trees, a man and a woman. The man carried something over his shoulder.

Hunter!

Evie crouched low. She had to attack now, before they brought Hunter aboard the monster and got away. She watched them come closer, time seemed to slow, and then...

Nothing. She couldn't move. She could spring into action effortlessly when a bunch of worthless Tainted had been playing a game, but for her own brother her body had stayed anchored to the dirt. She had watched helplessly as the Tainted walked across her path and away. *Please stop. Just a little longer, wait a few more seconds.*

But that wouldn't have helped. She couldn't go after them because she knew. Deep down, she knew it was hopeless. To attack the Tainted thugs would have meant her death. Of course that didn't matter; a Pure had to go after Hunter anyway, whatever the consequences. But something inside wouldn't let her. The same something that had made her cross the strand bridge at the lake, that had given in when Hunter demanded to take the strand into his body. That pitiful, horrible weakness, still there now, twisting deep in her gut.

Despite the sultry weather, a passing breeze suddenly felt cold. Evie clutched the prickles on her arms. Could she really force herself to step foot in the Gridlands, a place where even the Tainted feared to go? And not just enter it, scour it, search it for spirits-only-knew how long until she found her brother, and freed him from the same people she had been afraid to face before? It was impossible. All that lay ahead of her was failure.

"Evie. *Halup wen?*"

Ono's voice. Had he been following this whole time? She

spun to face him. Framed in the light at the end of the alley, Trina's smaller shape stepped out from behind him.

"What do you want?" Evie said.

"Ono thinks you know something about that strand we found," Trina replied. "He says you were staring at it on the table, that you looked like you wanted to speak. Is that true?"

So much presumption in the woman, about her tribe, even about what Evie was thinking. "I'm not allowed to help you, you know. By law. And I never have, either. I only fought with you on the wall to save Hunter."

"We need each other, Evie. I can help get your brother back alive, if you help me save this town. And perhaps many others like it."

A shaking anger built in Evie. "You're turning this on me? As if their lives are my responsibility. All of this is your people's doing! I've been around you long enough, I've seen the comforts you've sold your spirits to acquire. And they are enticing. But everything has a cost. That's a simple, unalterable fact. The strand is not in this world to serve you. If you try to bargain with it, it will extract its price in the end."

Trina took a sidelong glance at Ono, then shook her head sadly. "I can't change what's happened. But I can try to make things right."

"The law says—"

"I know your laws. You love your principles, Evie. Enough to die for them, I suppose."

Evie's heart fluttered, but she kept her composure and nodded.

Trina sighed. "It's good, you know, that sort of bravery. Believe it or not, I do think it has a purpose. Sometimes. But I also wonder if it can't be cowardice as well. That dying for a cause might be a way to avoid facing hard truths."

"Bravery is cowardice, eh? Tell me, what truth would we sacrifice ourselves to avoid?"

"That nothing in this world is simple." Trina nodded to Ono, then turned to leave. "But as you said, I'm not a Pure, and I'm not in charge of you. If you want to go after Hunter by yourself, we won't stop you. The choice is yours."

A few moments later they were gone, and Evie was alone.

Help them, or go after Hunter herself. The problem was, she didn't want to do either.

Since her "sneaking" had been a farce, she wandered back through the town, heedless this time of who saw her. Trina's words rang in her head. *You love your principles, Evie. Enough to die for them, I suppose.* A curse on that woman. Something about her had always grated on Evie, the way she stood so self-assured, speaking in her strange accent. In her bearing she was so much an elder; of all the people Evie had to compare her to, the closest she could come was her father. Now that was ridiculous—her father, similar to a Tainted woman?

She came to the far side of the town square, where the chapel dedicated to the strand stood, its bell-tower rising above the other buildings. The most blasphemous place in the city, one Evie had instinctually steered herself away from until now. So why was she standing here, staring at it? She had a feeling that, squeezed between two impossible options, the only way out was through, to pick a direction she would never have normally considered. But that was just a feeling, not a plan. What was it specifically about this place that attracted her?

She had been thinking about her father when she noticed the chapel. That couldn't have been a coincidence. She wasn't particularly close with her father—she would never consider sharing her inner thoughts with him—but he did have an outsize presence in her life. Even though it had been over a month since they had seen each other, she experienced that presence daily as a voice in her head, reminding her when something was forbidden, chastising her for transgressions both real and imaginary. And that was the core of her dilemma. Ever since that day at the pond, she'd been forced again and again to choose between Hunter and her principles. Except it wasn't really a choice—every time, she had chosen Hunter instantly. The problem wasn't the choice, it was how she felt about herself afterward. How she imagined her father would feel.

The strand covering the chapel grew differently from the rest of the town. Elsewhere it mostly hung limp, draped in thin wisps haphazardly wherever it happened to lie. But on the chapel it clung tight to the vertical beams, symmetrically decorative, bulging like biceps, as if its added strength was all that held up the building. Evie took tentative steps forward, until she was standing before the oversized front entrance, wooden doors barred with crisscrosses of strand. Sensing her presence, the barrier slid away into the building's facade, and the doors creaked open.

Inside was dark, but in the overcast daylight through the entrance she saw rows of benches leading up to a massive lump of strand at the back, shaped vaguely like a high-backed chair. Was that where the Tainted shaman sat and performed his duties? Evie shuddered, but didn't move.

She needed a test. She had always excused her actions before, telling herself they were mistakes, split-second decisions, or that Hunter had forced her hand with his stubbornness. Things had to be different this time. She had to be the one to initiate the lawbreaking. No one around, no one to encourage or admonish her. She had to know she could do it, if the time came again when it was necessary.

She took a step through the threshold. A lump formed in her throat and she swallowed it down. The shadows and dampness did not react, so she came forward again, one foot after another, closer and closer to that hellish throne. The strand was so thick inside the walls that the building pulsed, a deep thrum in unnatural syncopation with the quick beats of her heart. With a quick inhale, she closed her eyes, turned around and sat.

For a moment, nothing. Then, the strand below and beside her stirred to life. It wriggled, sending out tendrils that snaked around her arms, over her shoulders toward her neck. The tendrils were slick, clammy. She was reminded of falling in the strand trap, the one that had nearly swallowed her and Hunter before Ono had pulled them out, and a rising panic made her heart skip. She took a deep breath and dug her fingers into the sides of the seat, oil spreading beneath them.

The fibers of strand did not attack her as the trap had, though. They pushed and probed gently up the back of her neck. Looking for an implant? Finding nothing, they began to relax again, until she and the strand sat together in something of an uneasy truce. Evie peered at the door, hoping no one would come in and see her. But no one was there, and if they were to get angry at her, it would be for defiling their sanctuary, not for the reasons she imagined. She had come this far, and nothing of consequence had happened. No one cared. It was time to take the next step.

Her lips moved, and she heard her voice say, "Where is Hunter?"

The sound echoed and died. The strand wriggled on her back, but whether its motion had changed from before she couldn't say.

"I'm talking to you," she said, louder. "The Taint Itself. That Which Choked the Earth. Whatever you call yourself. I know you hear me. You hear everything. Work for me, now. Tell me where my brother is."

A few isolated tendrils rose in front of her, bent over as if looking in her direction. The way they moved, it seemed almost as if they were watching her. Did they really understand? She cocked her head, and for a few moments waited for some kind of answer, some kind of sign.

Nothing came. The strand waved back and forth, as if caught in a breeze, then stilled again. It had heard her, but that had only triggered some automatic response. Fine. She hadn't really expected this to work. A sudden well of disgust rose in her, and she swatted away the remaining strand pieces, rose and hurried to the exit.

The air outside was still hot, damp, and rotten with the stink of strand, but it was worlds better than the interior of the chapel. She held a deep breath and took one more glance through the door before the strand re-gathered itself over it.

She felt calm. Her anxiety from before was gone, her head clear. What was there to be scared of, now? She had attempted to use the strand, on purpose. So what? She didn't have to ever do that again if she didn't want to, didn't have to abandon her ideals. But now she saw that by shunning the strand so completely, she had been giving it power over her. In a way, she was as much its slave as those whose lives depended on it.

Not anymore. She was her own agent. Not the strand's, and not her father's. And she was going to use that power to find her brother and bring him home.

She shivered, then turned and headed back toward Trina's house, free.

―――――

Ono sat on a bench, watching with slight amusement as Trina trudged up the stairs and back into her workshop, a coating of gray dust in her hair, clothes disheveled from moving storage boxes.

"Did anyone ever tell you you're a real pain in the ass?" She pulled a rolled up map from her armpit and spread it over her table.

"I'm doing you a favor." He rose and pressed down one of the corners while she clipped them to the tabletop. "Certainly that cellar could use a bit of organizing." He caught an angry glance from Trina and looked away.

"You're just lucky this map still exists. In the autumn, half the water in the Northern Plains washes down the Bordertown creek; one of these years my cellar will be nothing more than a junk aquarium."

Ono looked over the fully displayed map, a patchwork of light blue shapes, sandwiched between two layers of flexible material which would have been clear if not for dense scratches obscuring the faint lines beneath. "Describing this map as 'existing' may be generous. How old is this?"

"Dates to before the Fall, most likely."

Ono made an impressed whistle. No ordinary paper would have survived so long, but the works of the ancients could be strangely advanced, in their own way. It wasn't that the ancients knew anything that modern people didn't; no doubt the formula for whatever material protected this map was locked away in some data archive. But the ancients had factories to produce such things, before the strand had torn them down. No one alive today would spare the land and expense to reproduce such work, when their implants could show them the same information far more easily. It was only Ono's fear of using his ocular implant and hastening Aunio's return that caused him to ask if Trina had any physical maps around; hence her annoyance with him.

Trina took a bit of strand from under the table and rolled it into a small cylinder to use as a marker. "Where did you encounter Fesso's Children when they carried the piece of the Core?"

"Here." Ono tapped the area just south of where Gwyer would have been on a recent map, and Trina placed the marker down. "But it looked to me like they were already on their way home. They must have been traveling from somewhere further south."

"The south." Trina's brow furrowed as she thought. "Nothing there but forest. What were they looking for?"

"Something important to the network, perhaps? Like the site where you found your sample."

She shook her head, though it seemed more out of frustration than disagreement. "There are thousands of sites like that one. And they move around, too. Most likely the sample I found was left somewhere else, then migrated along with its surroundings." She placed another marker down, closer to Bordertown. "If Fesso's Children are really visiting them, they're following a source of information we have no access to."

Ono crossed his arms and stepped away, until all he could make out were the markers on a field of blue. Two gray blocks, set across thousands of square miles of territory. Two points of data—hardly enough to make a pattern.

The door slammed downstairs, and from the lightweight yet impassioned stomping below Ono knew at once that Evie had returned. He traded a knowing glance with Trina as Evie noisily swung open the food pantry and rummaged through its contents. The Ankara was very particular about what she ate, eschewing anything that looked synthetic, even demanding that her water not be filtered through the strand. Ono wondered at her reaction if she ever found out there was no other source of fresh water in Bordertown.

Once she had gathered enough supplies for her trip, Ono heard Evie make her way upstairs, checking the rooms until she found Ono and Trina in the workshop. She strode in, put her hands on her hips, and in her tribal language put forth a pointed question to Trina.

"Does she want you to take down one of the cannons so she can carry it with her?" Ono asked dryly.

Trina blinked away her surprise. "No. She wants to know when we're leaving to get Hunter. She…wants to come with us."

"Then I'm glad you'll be the one to disappoint her."

Trina nodded and began to explain to the girl that they still had no idea where her brother was, motioning toward the map as she spoke. Then she seemed to invite her to look for herself. Evie stood over the table and narrowed her eyes, her gaze passing from south to north. She mumbled a reply, reserved.

"She says she doesn't think she knows anything useful."

"You've always said the Ankara know more about the strand than us. Tell her to start from there."

Trina formulated that statement into a question, then translated Evie's response as she spoke it.

"In the winter, the strand where her family lives is mostly

inert—from the trees blocking the sunlight, most likely. But they still have to keep an eye on it, in case a virulent strain infiltrates near their home. All the members of the tribe look for any strange strand appearances and report them to the council. That's how she knows she had never seen the 'sparkly kind' before—until she found it below the pond."

Trina motioned to the map, asking Evie to point out the pond's location. Evie took another long look, then shook her head.

"She doesn't know where it is," Trina said. "I should have known this would happen. The Pure don't use maps. You'll have to take her back there again, have her guide you to the spot. The navigation might be difficult with the strand activity this year, but there's no other choice."

Ono ran his fingers along his chin, at the itchy line where strand met flesh. "What did she mean, '*Below* the pond'?"

Trina opened her mouth, realized she didn't know either, then repeated the question to Evie.

"She says…a tunnel…below the dam…the dam made of strand opened up and put them underground. Do you follow this?"

"Perhaps. Underground…an underground drainage system, taking the outflow from the dam. The ancients built them, didn't they? When they wanted rivers to run below the surface."

Trina leaned back, eyes flitting furiously. "Drainage," she said. "That's it. Stay here."

She leaped up and dashed down the stairs, her footsteps receding all the way to the cellar. Ono caught Evie's eye. She stood silently, face unreadable, staring at him in a vaguely menacing fashion. He coughed and cleared his throat, watching his internal clock count as Trina rummaged below.

Finally Trina returned, bearing another map, this one even more weathered than the last. She knocked the strand markers off the table and spread it out in their stead.

The new map covered a similar area to the previous one, but featured prominent blue lines denoting rivers, grouped into zones of pastel colors. In the upper corner, ancient, unrecognizable runes spelled out a placard:

STATE OF NEW JERSEY D.E.P.

WATERSHED DIVISION

"And?" Ono said.

Instead of answering, Trina spoke to Evie, pointing to a group of blue squiggles to the south. They exchanged words, Trina nodding excitedly.

"Most of the rivers have changed course since this was made," she said. "But the main watershed areas haven't shifted. What you're looking at here is of vital importance to the strand, and the way it gathers resources."

"Resources? The strand eats the sun, does it not?"

"The strand eats *anything*. And where the local plant life out-competes it for sunlight, it can compensate by ingesting organic matter."

"Like people?"

"Sometimes. But chasing down animals requires energy. It's high risk, high reward. A more sedentary method is to filter the water supply." She traced her finger over the tabletop. "Dead plant material is washed into streams, then down into choke-points built by the ancients. Evie said the Core strand was all over the outflow pipe from the dam. The Core must be using Fesso to safely transport its customized strand to similar sites all over the Plains, where it confiscates the energy gained in the filtering process. With all that power under its control, it would wield influence over the other Ints."

Ono took a deep breath and began to pace. "So we know where they've been. Where are they going?"

"Wherever we want them to. We could go to one of the sites and sabotage it. If we were careful not to let the Core see what we were planning, then it might send Fesso's Children to repair the damage."

Ono nodded. "Then we place a tracker on them, and follow them back home at our leisure." He studied the map again. "There's an ancient waterworks here, isn't there? Near Moncton."

"Yes. Not far from where…" Trina's glance at Evie indicated the rest of the sentence: *where her brother was taken.*

Ono sat back and watched while Trina explained it all to Evie. She was trying hard to hide the excitement in her tone, to make it clear that the plan still had significant risks and unknowns. But Evie responded enthusiastically, pumping her fist before her. She drew her knife and issued something akin to an oath, then with teeth bared, brought the point down into the wooden table, impaling the map.

"She says she's coming with us to plant the tracker," Trina said.

"You explained to her that it could be days before Fesso's Children arrive, if they show up at all?"

"Doesn't matter. She won't change her mind. Anyway, we may need her. You're not much good at sneaking around with all the clanking you do, and without any implants, she'll be hard to spot on the network."

Ono nodded and looked at the map again, while Trina and Evie left to begin their preparations. Moncton was close by, an easy place to set their trap, and far enough from Fesso that she wouldn't risk sending a large force to investigate it. Ono put his finger on Jolon, the seat of the High Mystic, and traced his journey of the last weeks back and forth, south and then north again through the Plains.

The strand in his hand flexed and buzzed, rattling against the paper. Aunio was gaining strength. Would this path lead him to freedom at last?

He traced out his planned future, from Bordertown to Moncton, then continued further northeast, through the Gridlands. He didn't know yet where that line would end, but Evie's knife had speared a place he suspected would be close.

A small island, shaped like a grain of rice, sitting in the mouth of a long, wide river that ran south to the sea. The map carried faint impressions of where ancient roads lay before the Fall, and many intersected on that island. To Ono, the lines resembled the silk of a spider's web, radiating outward from a central point, ensnaring anyone who came near.

Somewhere in that web lay the spider. Somewhere in that web, the Core waited.

18

"CAN YOU PASS the salt?"

"Huh?" Hunter looked up from his plate of…whatever it was…and scanned the table. All he saw were empty dishes, lumps of strand, bits of food splattered from errant flinging, and Fesso's Children yelling, shoving, and stuffing their faces. "Where is it?"

Telian rolled her eyes. "In that synth, there."

Hunter grabbed the lump of strand, and it identified itself to his implant: *Basic Sodium-Chloride-Ion-Fluid Synthesis Functional, version 2.3.* He shrugged, passed it on, then returned his gaze to his dish.

He didn't like sitting and waiting, but there was nothing else to do while the others were awake. He had already tried to sneak out the previous night. When his implant told him dawn was two hours away, he had slipped quietly from his room. He found the halls populated with snoozing gang members, some of them clearly far gone on whatever the locals used to get intoxicated. But though the front door guards looked groggy, they were definitely conscious, and Hunter had no hope of creeping past them into the Gridlands.

Instead he had doubled back, convinced that a building so large must have plenty of exits. And indeed it did—or did once. But now, every potential opening had been filled with rubble or strand. He could interface with the strand-covered doors, get a list of the restricted functions, but without Zeke, and without being able to enter the Immersion safely, he had no way to bend them to his will.

Eventually he had crossed to the far side of the building, past a series of crumbling, strand-laced archways and moss-laden halls. Footsteps and muffled conversation sounded ahead of him. Hunter froze—he recognized one of the voices. He dashed behind a pile of rubble and curled himself up tight.

"…will see to it there's no more setbacks."

Fesso.

A male companion answered, "If what happened at Bordertown happens at Jolon—"

"It won't. The Core will be at full power soon, and Serr will find out what it means to spurn me. I want him begging at my feet before I…"

They slipped beyond hearing around a corner. Hunter exhaled. That was too close. Still listening in case the pair returned, he went back into the hallway and continued the way he had been going, glancing at the corridors as he went but finding no hint of escape.

By the time he had completed his circuit of the headquarters, Fesso's Children were beginning to rise. Hunter reached the entrance to his room, waved open the door, and ran directly into Kaia's chest.

"Where the *kilan* were you? You were supposed to be locked in here."

He almost told the truth, then remembered Telian's plea. "I found the key on the internal network. Someone must have left a copy of it lying around."

Kaia snorted. She looked him up and down, eyes narrowed, then shook her head. "Stay in here until I fetch you. Fesso wants you in one piece for her big 'Family Meal.' If you wander off and lose your head, I'll have to sew it back on before I prop your dead body at the table."

Well, at least that hadn't happened. The dinner, as far as he could tell, was proceeding as planned. Hunter wasn't hungry, but he had a seat next to Telian, and to the others he might as well have been invisible. As long as he kept his eyes down and his voice silent, he would soon be returning to his cell in peace.

"Hunter!" Fesso called from the head of the table. Immediately, the collected Children fell silent. "Please, stand and introduce yourself to the Family."

Hunter stared down the length of the table, meeting each pair of staring eyes. Fesso cracked her knuckles and glanced at Kaia seated to her right. Hunter cleared his throat, blinked hard and rose.

"Hi. I'm Hunter."

Silence.

"Well?" Fesso said. "Tell us about yourself."

"I uh…I'm a Pure. Of the Southern Pines."

Whispers and hushed gasps ran over the table. Fesso tapped her fingers. It was hard to tell with her emaciated face, but Hunter guessed she was annoyed.

He felt a tug by his hip.

"*Was,*" Telian whispered.

"Oh, right. I *was* a Pure. Before I joined the Family."

Fesso leaned back. Her grin put creases in her thin, tight skin.

"Is it true you don't have anything where you come from?" said a girl directly across from him, an implant bulging out of one eyebrow and hooked decoratively to her earlobe. "No vids? Or games? Or chats?"

"Hey, that can't be right," another said. Hunter recognized him as the male half of the kissing couple from the day before. "He has an implant. Why wouldn't he use it?"

Hunter scratched the raised scar where metal joined flesh on his shoulder. "I never had this growing up. Just recently."

Fesso's braids of strand clanked together as she shook her head, clucking her tongue. "You poor boy. Raised in such abject poverty. Thank the Ints for delivering you to us." She turned to the assembled table. "Thank them for all of you!"

She stood and the table quieted. A tug at Hunter's waist reminded him to sit down.

"This is a special evening. My Children, this will be our last meal together in the Gridlands. Before the month is out, we will march. The Atlantica Plains and beyond will be our playground!"

Cheers, hoots and whistles.

Fesso nodded. "I know this hasn't been easy on you. But you must never forget how lucky we are to be together. I love you all…" Her voice dropped to a whisper. "Dearly."

At once, the entire table went silent. Hunter looked back and forth, confused. Everyone had frozen. All around, eyes were wide open, hands hung in mid-air, holding food before waiting mouths.

"That is why it pains me so much to do this. Enson?"

A man rose to Fesso's left. Previously silent, he had been easy to ignore when hunched over in the gloom, but standing he resembled a stone wall more than a human. He stepped around to Hunter's side of the table, and continued to approach.

"Uhm," Hunter said.

Enson walked past him, stopped near the end of the row, and placed his hands on a pair of small shoulders.

"What?" The shoulders' owner cried out. The boy who had put the snapping turtle in his implant. "Hey, no! Listen!"

"Gesial!" When Fesso crossed her arms, her bony shoulders resembled the folded wings of a vulture. "You left the compound without permission."

"No. No way. I asked Kaia, she said—"

"Lies will only make it worse."

Ges pushed back his chair, eyeing the door. One of Enson's hands moved from his shoulder to his neck.

"Listen, all right?" Ges barked. "I just wanted to send a couple messages. It's nothing serious. Just some girls down the shore. Nothing that could mess up the plan."

Fesso bowed her head and rubbed the bridge of her nose. She said in a choked voice, "Enson, if you please?"

Ges began screaming then, blood curdling, a cry not to call for aid but from someone who knew they were beyond it. The others at the table instantly became involved with their food, some making loud smacking sounds to drown out the noise of Ges being dragged away.

Fesso held her face in her hands, shaking now and then as if she were…crying? Could she even cry, after what the strand had done to her face? As Ges's distant screams turned from panic into white-hot yelps of pain, she looked up, her eyes red as a fresh kill.

"You think I want this, my darlings? To lock you up in this place, to take your freedom? Do you think I would do this if there weren't greater things ahead of us?"

Various Children shook their heads in reply, then collectively winced at an especially intense scream from Ges. By the sound, Hunter guessed they had hooked him up to the strand, and were sending pain signals directly into his brain.

"All of you darlings will be princes and princesses of this land. Once Serr bows to me, I'll bequeath it. My inheritance." She breathed a sigh of relief as Ges fell silent. "It won't be much longer, now. Kaia and Mager have returned from the final installation. Once the bridge is complete, we will set the Core free. Our destiny will follow."

The table gave a shout of appreciation, somewhat tempered by the sound of Ges whimpering somewhere down the hall. Hunter closed his eyes, his mind working furiously. So Fesso was going to launch another attack like the one on Bordertown, but larger. What would happen to his friends there? And what about…

Once the bridge is complete, we will set the Core free. That thing in the Immersion, was that what she was talking about? No, it was too powerful, too dangerous to control. Hunter opened his eyes, and on its own accord his mouth let out the words, "Excuse me?"

Fesso snapped her head toward him. The strand woven into her scalp rose slightly. "*What?*"

The room was silent as a cave. Hunter pressed his implant and cleared his throat. "I mean...excuse me, Mother?"

The network of wrinkles around her sunken eyes relaxed slightly, but she maintained her stare. The rest of the table stayed deathly quiet.

"Yes, my darling?"

"The Core...it's an Int, right?" He struggled to find the words he needed, without raising too many questions about what he did and didn't know. His mind kept returning to the experience in Senter's lair, the pain of being disassembled while Senter looked on dispassionately. "That is...they don't think like we do, do they? If you made some kind of bargain with it, how can you trust it?"

She held him in silent regard for a moment. He was getting better at playing the game of pleasing her, but he still couldn't be sure if he had crossed a line.

The edges of her lips curled up. With one finger, she beckoned him toward her.

Hunter glanced at Telian for a clue, but she only shook her head. He cleared his throat, then rose and walked around the table toward Fesso. He stopped a few feet from her and bowed slightly.

She gave a small nod. "You're a wise child. If you hadn't come from the depths of the forest, I might have thought you were a student of those Mystics in Jolon." She took a deep breath, arching her head back as if savoring the mildew-and-strand smell of her home. "We're all taught the same things growing up, I suppose. That the Ints cannot be fathomed, or controlled."

In a blink she was leaning forward, her bony hand holding Hunter's own. "You were not with us in the events leading up to our ascendance, child, so you could not have known. But I have the key to controlling the Ints...right here."

She tapped a finger on her bare skull and smiled. Her breath smelled like bone dust.

"So you see, there's nothing to worry about. Mother has it all taken care of."

Hunter nodded, unsure of how else to react. He didn't know what exactly Fesso was talking about, but he was willing to bet she had never seen the Core's form in the Immersion, like he had.

She shooed him away, expecting nothing more, and he returned to his seat. Soon after, the dinner began to break up, the Children stealing away one by one. Hunter waited for Telian to take her turn, while keeping an eye on Fesso. Whatever she was planning on doing, he doubted he could stop it. But he could still try and warn someone, especially Trina, before it happened.

Fesso took a swig of her drink, then jerked to attention, her eyes dilating—a message on her implant. She drummed her fingers on the table, then turned and whispered to Kaia.

"Back again?" Kaia's outburst rang out over the sound of clanking plates and sliding chairs. "We were just out there."

"The installation is still intact, but the communication lines are damaged," Fesso hissed. "The Core says that unless it can route power from all the sites, we can't proceed as planned."

"This smells," Kaia said. "Someone is messing with us."

"Someone who? You told me Ono wasn't involved."

Kaia growled and hunched her shoulders. "Some *flaving* deer probably chewed them. This is what happens when you spend your days tramping through some Ints-forsaken woods."

"Enough. Get back there and fix the problem. We're too close now for more delays."

Hunter sensed Telian's movement beside him. He stood up and left before Kaia could catch him eavesdropping. He headed back to his room, following Telian, who skipped along as if nothing were amiss.

"Hey," she said. "What's wrong? You look even more down than usual."

"I'm just thinking."

"'bout what?"

She stopped suddenly, and he came up short, just in front of her. The two of them stood in a secluded alcove in dim blue light. Her eyes fluttered and the strand-nose twitched.

"It's nothing." Hunter said.

"All right." Still, she remained where she was.

"What is it?" he asked.

She shrugged. "I just thought I could help you, maybe. You're worried about Mother, aren't you?"

"What?" It took him a moment to realize she wasn't talking about *his* mother. "Worried about Fesso? Why?"

"You think she won't be able to control the Core once it's loose. That it will hurt her. You told me I was a good person; well, I think you have a good heart, too. We good people have to stick together."

Hunter pressed on his implant, trying to think of a way to explain. "Telian, do you remember your real family? The one you had before this one?"

She shook her head.

"Oh. Well, it doesn't matter. You're right, I don't think the Core getting loose will be good for Fesso. Or for anyone. This may sound strange, but I know a lot more about the Ints than most people."

He was prepared to explain further if pressed, but instead she only nodded. "So what can we do?"

He looked down. "I don't know. This network is too dangerous. If I could reach some other strand, I could send a message and get help, but obviously I can't leave, because... you know..." He glanced back toward the room where they had taken Ges.

She smiled, and for a moment the strand in the room seemed

to glow brighter. "I know how you can send a message."

"How?"

"Well, you know how the strand grows…it's twisty." To illustrate, she held her hand out flat, then pressed one finger up through the others. "Sometimes a bit of it worms its way through other pieces. I found one like that. A little connection to the outside world, hidden where no one's found it yet."

"What?" Hunter grabbed her by the shoulders before he realized what he was doing. "Where is it?"

Her big eyes opened wider. "It's where we're going to meet the Core."

19

EVIE PUSHED ASIDE a leaf with her toe. A black and gray beetle scurried away. With a short thrust, the point of her spear went through its carapace, pinning it to the turf, legs flailing. Evie waited till it stilled, then flicked it away into the creek.

Five.

She lay back against the tree, pushed aside her hair and dug in her pack for food. She nibbled on a sort of hard wafer the Tainted seemed fond of, then put it away. The longer she had been waiting, the more her stomach had tied itself up in knots.

Ridiculous. It was only the second day. She should have been good at this. When hunting with her tribe, she had waited longer for deer to cross her path, often in the cold or rain. But back then, the penalty for failure was losing a deer. Now she ran the risk of losing her brother.

She picked up her spear and began to sharpen it yet again, keeping an eye on the ridge where Ono was hiding. From what Trina had explained to her, they weren't sure which direction the enemy would come from, and spreading out gave them the best chance of planting one of the tracking devices undetected. That suited Evie fine. The past weeks had given her plenty to think over by herself.

Like the spirits, for example. In the past, out here in the woods, she would have passed the time listening for them, waiting for their guidance. But after the mushrooms…she had been left confused, to put it mildly. She knew what the shaman would say if she asked about her experience, that she wasn't ready, wasn't prepared to accept the spirits' true message. But she couldn't shake the feeling that the spirits' failure to appear said less about her than it did about them.

But maybe that was too simple, as Trina was fond of saying. It wasn't so much whether the spirits were there or not that was important, but what they represented. The tribe believed in the spirits because it kept them on a path apart from the strand, anchored them to nature. No matter what she had seen or done, she knew nature held a core of vital truths, about good and evil, the importance of family, and—

A distant rumbling made her jerk her head north. She remembered well that day in the clearing, when she had heard the rumbling of what turned out to be giants in battle, and disregarded it. This one was different, not as loud or sudden. Probably nothing, an old tree falling, or a flock of geese launching skyward. But the trees here were sickly, thin things, and geese would have been honking when they took off. Spear tucked under her arm, Evie dashed through the foliage.

To the north, the creek she had been sitting beside ran into a causeway made of ancient stone, which then disappeared under a dense thicket of brush. Evie reached the edge of a clearing and crouched. Ahead lay what Trina had explained were the remains of a sunken ancient waterworks, though the vines across it, both natural and strand, had grown so thick that the indentation in the earth was only perceptible up close. It was the sort of area the Pure always warned against crossing, lest they fall into the current below and end up in an underground lair of the strand, like what had happened to her and Hunter at the pond.

The rumbling returned, growing louder, until a strand monster crested a rise on her side of the gully, then came to a halt in the field below. Evie's heart skipped a beat when she recognized it—and the two people who stepped out. The Tainted they had met twice before, the ones who had taken Hunter. Anger welled in her, her palms pressing into the rough haft of her spear. She shook her head to free her thoughts. No sign of Trina or Ono. They could be on their way, but she wasn't going to wait. She shimmied into the clearing, keeping her shoulders down within the carpet of green.

She alternated crawling and looking, crawling and looking, slowly creeping closer, fearing the Tainted would complete their errand and leave before she arrived. Each time her head popped up she saw the woman kneeling by the edge of the waterworks and the man standing over her, keeping watch. Closer. His gaze swept over where she lay, and she froze, leaves tickling her cheeks, not even daring to blink. The man scanned back and forth over the meadow, then returned to looking back over the waterworks.

Evie exhaled and returned to crawling toward their vehicle, where she was meant to put the tracking device. The weight of the strand-lump pulled on the right side of her belt. The brush was thinning now, turning brown and brittle, which meant she would soon be out of cover. Putting the monster between herself and them would mean a dash through the open. She settled in behind a tuft of thistles, watching the man through the stalks until she was sure he couldn't see her. When he turned away again, she would make her run.

A rustle came from her right. A small brown rabbit had jumped out of the grass beside her, and was staring her in the face, ears pressed back.

Memories of a very bad night spent in the woods flooded her, all absurd and disturbing visions. What had she thought? The rabbit spirit was angry with her, trying to kill her. No, it couldn't be…

The rabbits eyes were blank, but in them Evie saw a look of knowing familiarity. The animal reared, ready to bolt.

"No," she mouthed. "I'm sorry."

It took off across the open field, headed for the waterworks.

The Tainted man spun at once, hands splayed. He watched the rabbit dash past him and into the safety of the gully.

His eyes traced its path back to the thistles. With a mumbled word to his companion, he stepped toward them.

Evie tensed. The massive figure loomed closer. A few more steps and it would be too late, he would find her flat on her belly, unable to rise quickly. She slapped the spear down, got her feet underneath her, and raced toward the woods.

The man yelled something as Evie passed through the tree line. The crunching of ivy leaves heralded his pursuit.

By the time Evie was back at the creek, she knew the Tainted woman was also following, trying to flank her along the ridge. It didn't matter. Evie had played this game too many times with her brothers. She darted like a swallow through holes in the branches, finding the cleanest paths, aware of the Tainted's location from their loud crashes and cursing. Soon they were shouting to each other, trying to coordinate, asking where she was, but that only allowed her to avoid them better.

She led them southward up the creek bed, toward where a fallen log had formed a bridge. Trina and Ono likely waited somewhere across it. No good; if she ran into them, they would try to save her, and then the Tainted would know they were here. She couldn't let her pursuers understand what she was trying to do; as far as they knew, she was a lone Pure girl, still hiding near the place where they had taken her brother. Evie turned away from the bridge, back the way she had come.

A dash across a blighted field of lumpy strand brought her to an unfamiliar section of forest. Evie stopped for a moment to get her bearings, but a crash through the brush sent her running again. One of the Tainted, lost perhaps, choosing a direction at random and getting lucky. Evie dove into a patch of leaves and lay still, clamping her jaw as thorns scraped across her back. The damp smell of moss filled her nostrils. She shut her eyes and waited until the heavy footsteps retreated in the distance, counted her breaths to ten, then took off again.

She reached the clearing where the waterworks lay and dropped back to her belly, fearing that the Tainted had caught on to her ruse and sent one person back to guard the monster. But there was no sign of either of them, nor of Ono or Trina. Evie rose and sprinted, sliding into the turf just short of the creature, hand reaching to her belt. She took the greasy lump and slapped it underneath the thing's tail, then let out a shudder of relief. She had done it. The tracker was in, there was plenty of time to slip away, get back to…

… to what? All this time, she had been focused only on finding Hunter, doing whatever she needed to plant the tracer. What about her next move? If she had indeed succeeded, then the Tainted would soon retreat back to their hideout, and Trina and Ono would be able follow them. But would Trina let her join in the pursuit?

No; Trina may have agreed to this venture, but having Evie travel to the Gridlands would be too much. Likely Evie would be shut up in the town for the duration, under the watchful eye of Trina's vapid husband. That wouldn't do. Ono and Trina may have meant well, but they had other reasons for heading to the Gridlands, distractions from rescuing Hunter.

Evie peered into the interior of the monster. It contained a few rows of benches bisected by a passage, and some sort of control room at the front. The gang members were already on their way back; she had only moments to make a decision. Perhaps it was the memory of seeing Hunter pulled into this same vehicle that made her hesitate. She closed her eyes, stepped over the threshold and ducked into a small alcove below a seat.

She waited, keeping her breaths as even as possible. What if she had made a mistake?

Footsteps approached.

"*Masa arin, tesen foon,*" the man grumbled.

"*Saseen.*" Shut up, or something similar.

The pair climbed inside from the front, not bothering to check the rear, and moments later she felt the creature rise on its legs.

With mechanical squeaks of compressing and releasing strand, it trundled off across the landscape.

20

HUNTER STUCK HIS head out of his cell. Members of Fesso's Family hurried by in the hall.

"Hey," he said. "What's happening?"

No one answered. Hunter searched for a familiar face, and settled for a younger member who seemed relatively unthreatening.

"Is the Core ready to move?"

The boy rolled his eyes and sauntered away. Hunter took that as "yes." He left his room and followed the flow of people toward the central hall. There, Fesso and her lieutenants stood on an improvised platform of strand, discussing logistics with each other and yelling out orders to those below. Most of the Family was present, jockeying for position at the front. Hunter didn't know if they wanted to be present when the Core reached the mainland like he did, or if they were just curious and there for the sake of being there, but they were in his way regardless.

He turned sideways and wedged his skinny form through. Some muffled curses came his way, but the crowd was so thick that he was out of reach before anyone could make good on a threat. He reached the front and worked his way around close to where Fesso stood with her back turned. So far, so good.

He shifted his concentration from the real into the strand, not dropping all the way into the Immersion, but feeling the nearby nodes, mapping their topology. This close, Fesso's giant implant running down her back stood out even among the cacophony of traffic in the crowded room. Hunter had spent a lot of time alone in the darkness practicing this next trick. He narrowed his eyes and initiated a scan of Fesso's strand, not sending an actual message, just probing its periphery, testing its capabilities. The scan was purposely detectable; if he kept it up for long enough, she would feel it as a tingling or an itch in the back of her skull...

Fesso turned slowly at first, then snapped her head down. Success. Hunter held still, wondering if she would know what he had done.

"You."

"Me?"

They watched each other a few moments. Her eyes narrowed. "You know, boy, many children are scared of me when they first arrive here."

"Oh."

She knelt down, examining him more closely. "You don't seem to be, though."

"Sorry." He shrugged.

She smiled. "Hunter, I'm beginning to like you more each day." She stood again, noticed he was still looking up and scowled. "Well, what are you staring at me for?"

"I want to come with you. To uh...celebrate your achievement."

She nodded. "Fine. I'm sure we can find room on the boat for one so small."

"And Telian. Her, too?"

"Yes, fine," Fesso said. "Just stay close. We're very busy."

She turned her attention to a lieutenant who had been loudly clearing his throat behind her. "All right, show me." She closed her eyes. "Good. Tell Kaia and Mager to meet us there. They deserve to see the fruits of their labor."

She walked away. Hunter rested his back on the platform. Ignoring looks from a few of the other Children who had overheard his conversation with Fesso, he broadcasted a few pings encoded with one of Telian's personal keys.

"Hey, where are you?" Her voice appeared in his head, slightly garbled by the strand's poor audio reception.

"I'm standing next to Fesso. She's going to let us on the boat."

"What? You said we would meet in my room first, remember?"

"Oh. I forgot. It doesn't matter, though. Just come quickly."

"I've been waiting here because you told me to. I wish you wouldn't just forget about me."

"I didn't need you to get us a place on the boat, though. I did that myself."

A pause. "I see."

"Huh…are you angry?"

A longer pause. "Why would I be angry?"

"I don't know." A few Children were staring at him and whispering to each other. Apparently at least some of them *had* wanted to go with Fesso, and Hunter's little maneuver hadn't pleased them. He backed away into the crowd. "Just come. If you miss the boat, I won't be able to find the connection to the outside network."

"*Fine.*" The connection cut to static.

"Telian? Hello?" Above, Fesso and her lieutenants began moving toward the exit. Hunter moved to follow, shaking his head. "Girls."

———

The Tainted boat was beautiful, with sharp, clean lines, a large object on a scale the Pure would never consider constructing, but pleasingly made mostly of wood and ordinary metal, with only a few traces of strand visible on the trim. Hunter stood a few moments on the dock behind Fesso's headquarters, admiring it. Too bad the view was spoiled by the sight of the Core looming beyond the river.

He had only caught a glance of the ancient city when he first arrived, most of his attention having been focused elsewhere. Now, in the light of day, he could see every detail of the dilapidated stone and coiled strand that made up its broken skyline. So vast, it stood as a reminder of the figure he had met in the Immersion, that feeling of being dwarfed, an ant discovering humans just as it was about to be trampled.

The line of Children on the gangplank moved forward, and Hunter shuffled along.

Telian tapped his shoulder. "Are you all right?"

"Huh?"

She wriggled her metal nose. "You're shaking."

He looked down at his hand—it was true. He didn't like to think about the Core, and what would happen if it got loose. Red lights flared on the edge of his vision, his implant warning of an elevated heart rate. He blinked them away.

"Have you ever been on a real ship before?" Telian asked.

Hunter shook his head.

"Don't worry," she said. "It's Fesso's best one. I'm sure the trip will be fine."

The engines started and the boat pulled away, and Hunter soon realized how wrong Telian was. The boat may have been gigantic by Pure standards, but it wasn't large enough to avoid bobbing in the small waves of the river. A few moments of the up and down motion, and Hunter was leaning on the rail for support, wishing there were enough room on the increasingly crowded deck to lie down.

"Now what?" Telian said.

"Is it...a long way?" Hunter gasped.

"Not that far. Shouldn't be more than an hour, I think."

In fact, it took less than twenty minutes, and although the boat bobbed less once the strand in its hull got it moving at full speed, Hunter still counted himself lucky that he arrived with the contents of his stomach. As it was, Telian had to hold him up as he staggered off the ship.

They came ashore on a small spit of land overlooking a rocky island. They had passed many similar islands on their way, covered with ancient junk stuffed with bird nests. Strand had trouble crossing open water, and so the islets remained relatively clean, small natural oases sandwiched between the pulsing masses of the Gridlands and the Core.

This island was different, though. Firstly because of the large, domed building at its center, one of the ancient structures the strand had chosen to preserve. And secondly because of the bridge stretching from its far shore.

At first Hunter had no idea what he was looking at. Ships, hundreds of them, all sat in a neat row side by side across the water, instead of drifting away in the strong current. No two were alike, but none of them were much larger than the vessel the Family had arrived on, which, now empty, was being piloted downriver to take its place in the line.

The Family waded toward the island, Fesso carried in a chair by her four strongest Children. As Hunter crossed the shallow muck he began to understand the bridge's construction: two thick steel cables had been strung from shore to shore, lying across the deck of each boat, keeping them anchored together like the planks of an ordinary rope bridge, close enough that a human might conceivably be able to walk across the entire span.

Except this wasn't a bridge for humans. This was a bridge for strand. Only now did the enormity of the effort Fesso had put forth for the Core become clear; Hunter couldn't count the number of ships required to span the wide river. The Core could never have built such a thing itself—even though the strand kept certain structures standing well past their natural lifetimes, its nature was to burrow and absorb, not to construct.

They walked up on dry land, and soon the ancient building loomed over Hunter. Past the cracked entrance doors, dusty husks of statuary sat in a rectangular edifice adjoining the dome. This place must have been some kind of temple once, so varied and strange were the half-broken artworks, lit from above by rays of afternoon light from the collapsed roof. Fesso had set up a stage on the far side where a section of wall was missing, providing a view of the bridge and the Core's city behind her.

"When the ship is hooked up, tell them to come inside right away," she said. "The Core will protect this building from the other Ints. I want everyone here to witness the first step in our victory."

Hunter tugged Telian's arm, then slipped to the back of the crowd. He caught snippets of conversation as he passed.

"How much longer?"

"The Core'll come when it wants, I guess."

He let Telian guide him, pretending to be gawking at the interior of the ancient building. At a moment when most of the gang seemed distracted with gossip and speculation, they stole into a side corridor.

"Where are we going?" Hunter whispered, feeling the crumbling stone of the suddenly dark hallway. "How did you find this place?"

"I was bored," Telian said. "They've been building that bridge for months; sometimes I'd tag along, but there wasn't much more to do here, since this building has the same firewall as the headquarters."

She emerged into the light again and checked left and right, the glint from her nose flashing on either side. She waved him forward into a cavernous room. "That's why I was surprised to find this."

Hunter stepped into the interior of the building's main dome. Rows of broken seats like the ones he had seen on the inside of Fesso's headquarters ran up one side, and the web-like metal bars of the dome's exterior were visible on the other, hung with lengths of dusty white cloth. The view would have interested him much more not too long ago, before he had seen far grander constructions in the Immersion.

"What now?" he asked.

Telian turned and regarded him. "You know, this is a big risk for me. If we got caught doing this, on today of all days…"

He looked down. "I remember."

She huffed. "It's just as much of a risk for you."

"I know."

"But you still want to do it?"

"I have to, I guess. People could get hurt."

He looked up again and she was staring at him, though he couldn't read her expression. Finally, she shook her head and said, "You're a strange boy, Hunter."

Without waiting for a reply, she climbed a set of steps leading upward between the seats. "Seven rows up, six chairs over." She tapped each seatback as she passed, then knelt and peered below the sixth. Hunter scrunched himself down into the small space. Telian pointed, and he saw them: a few wisps of strand, sprouting from the ancient stone like a spring flower.

"Incredible," Hunter said. "You're amazing."

She looked at him a moment, then turned away as she smiled. "What are you going to do?"

"I'm going to be...gone for a little while. I'll look like I'm asleep, but don't try to wake me."

"You mean like what the Mystics do?"

He nodded. "I want to see for myself what's going on in the strand. You be my lookout. If someone does come, send a signal through my implant."

Not trusting potential interference with the wireless, he tweezed out a fiber from his neck, then lay down on his back and pressed it to the strand on the floor. Telian's face appeared above him, ensconced in blue light.

"Hunter?"

"Yes?" The edges of his vision turned white.

"Good luck." She kissed him on the forehead.

Hunter tried to yelp surprise, but by the time he inhaled she was already a thousand miles down a tunnel of light.

———

Hunter stepped through the doorway in his implant, into the midst of a tumultuous crowd.

In appearance they were similar to the denizens of the Immersion city within Bordertown, animals mostly, with some humans, oversized insects, and other beings that were difficult to classify. But instead of calmly milling, they were yelling, running across rolling green hills in the same general direction. Skirmishes were breaking out, the creatures biting and pulling hair when one didn't get out of the way fast enough, and the ones moving around him were growling at his obstruction.

"Zeke!" Hunter yelled.

Before stepping through the door, he had tried summoning the otter from inside his implant, to no effect. Before he could call again, the passing crowd grew thicker and forced him to move, practically lifting him off his feet as they rushed past.

On his right, a chunk of rock made of white crystal stood embedded in the ground. Hunter made a grab for it, then pulled himself up and hunched above the crowd's eye level, out of the current. Now he could see the landscape clearly—the grass stretched on endlessly into the distance, with hundreds of crystal towers spread among them. Each of the monoliths was differently shaped, with unique patterns of snowy swirls within them, and they tended to cluster near a brilliant blue river that wound through the foothills and out of sight.

"Coming through! Make way!"

Trumpets sounded, and Hunter turned just in time to scramble off the rock face before a large dog-like creature trampled over it. Downriver, the crowd parted, making way for a group of gleaming, armored men riding even more impressively armored bears, carrying long spears with barbed tips.

"Over here!" Came a small voice behind him. "Hide behind the rock."

"Zeke." Hunter did as he was told, shoving his back against the crystal and edging his way around until he sat in the wake of creatures streaming past. The little otter lay tucked in a ball there, holding his tail tight to his chest. "How did you find me?"

"Finding you wasn't hard at all. Getting here was a bigger problem. Too much traffic."

"I can tell."

"Won't be any power here much longer, everything's being hoarded for the battle."

Hunter glanced around the rock, to where the mounted bear-men were marshaled, cordoning off a wide area on both sides of the river. "They'll be doing the battling?"

"Them versus the Core's army. It's coming soon. Another reason everyone wants to get out quick."

He didn't blame them. "Can you take me back to Senter's city?"

Zeke's black eyes fluttered. "There? Things didn't go too well last time."

As if Hunter needed a reminder. But since he had neglected to ask Trina for an identification key, he had no way to contact her other than looking for her implant's connection on a local net. Not that he had much of an idea how to do that, either, but he'd figure out something when the time came. "Just tell me where it is."

"Out in the Anywhere. Over there." Zeke didn't move to indicate a direction.

"Where? What does the Anywhere look like?"

"Like anything. Everything. All possibilities at once."

"All possibilities…" Hunter looked at the sky. It was bright white, like most of the rest of the Immersion, but when he stared deeply, it began to resolve itself into infinitesimal points of light, packed tightly together against a black background. Stars—he could see them clearly now as if the sky were night, though all around his surroundings still glowed brightly. The sight was oddly hypnotizing, almost enough to make him forget that the crowd could trample him at any moment.

"You see?" Zeke squeaked.

He did. Out of all the endless points of light, one stayed centered in his vision. Zeke was signaling it to him somehow, and it flashed with cycling colors.

"It's so far."

"Not far enough. We should keep going past there, get out of the whole regional network."

Another blast of trumpets called Hunter's attention to the soldiers setting up their arms. He looked back at the sky. It seemed impossible; there was so much up there, so much to get lost in.

"You'll be able to get me back again, right? Find a path to my implant?"

"Yes, yes. Let's go. Now or never."

"All right." He narrowed his eyes, focusing on the glowing dot in the distance. He couldn't bring it closer, but he could make his view of it larger, until it filled the center of his vision, then the periphery as well. Now the whole sky was the gray, swirling mass of a distant planet, blocking out the rest of the star field despite not having moved at all. Keeping his gaze skyward to avoid the image snapping away from him, he crouched, then leaped.

The first dozen or so miles out into the atmosphere were easy. Gradually decelerating, his body felt light, free. Then he lost control and began to turn. He was in a no-man's land, caught between the pull of two worlds with no equilibrium. He tried to angle back toward the ground, worried about being lost in the vastness of space, but that only made him spin more wildly. With a gasp, then a yell, he tumbled backward, watching the world of crystal palaces recede at an ever-increasing pace.

"No!" Fast, too fast. The air around him turned gray, clouds whizzing by.

"Don't try to control it. Just let it happen." The small otter's voice in his ear. Hunter stopped struggling and lay back, trying not to think of the solid surface coming up to meet him.

Closing his eyes, he let himself melt into the buffeting wind, until he couldn't feel it moving anymore, as if it were a thick layer of padding surrounding him. Then he slid down easily, changing his orientation, until he landed on two feet, alighting like a crane.

He felt a twinge of pain from tiny claws gripping his scalp.

"Pretty good," Zeke said, standing up and balancing on top of his head. "You're getting better at relocating. You really stunk at it before."

"Thanks." Hunter shook his head, which had the dual effect of dislodging the otter and clearing his spotty vision. Compared to the tumult of where they had come, the silence of this new planet felt strangely unsettling. Clouds hugged the surface, with swirling rivulets of fog so thick they looked almost brown. Through them, past a puddle-flecked, rocky wasteland, stood a tremendous wall. It looked like a mockery of the wall at Bordertown—twice as high, with each block of stone subdivided by intersecting lines and patterns.

"Is that…Senter's city?"

"This is Senter's way of protecting himself." Zeke loped to the wall and began hopping up, stopping once to consider a particularly tricky jump. Before Hunter could question him again, he was over the lip and out of sight.

Hunter approached the wall and examined it. The whole idea seemed sort of silly—what use was a wall to protect against a person who had just jumped from one planet to another? But since he was still feeling lightheaded from the descent, he decided climbing would be less unsettling than leaping over. He dug his fingers between two rocks and began.

Even with the plethora of handholds, the wall's height would have given him pause in the real world, but in the Immersion his movements felt effortless, and he reached the top with no fatigue. He pulled himself up to find Zeke looking out over a labyrinth of gray stone that stretched to the horizon.

"Oh."

With a high-pitched grunt, Zeke scrunched himself down, leaped across the ten-foot gap to the next maze wall, then ran onward toward the center. Hunter copied him, planning his jump carefully to avoid slipping down. The rules here felt different than outside the maze; the "floaty" feeling was gone, and he suspected that falling to the bottom would be painful, or worse.

By the time he caught up with Zeke, they had already covered an enormous distance, with no ending to the maze in sight.

"How long is this going to take?" he asked.

Zeke considered the next jump, then changed his mind and ran along the wall's length. "Fifty-six years at most."

"What?" Hunter stopped in his tracks. "I don't have fifty-six years."

"I said at *most*."

"Can't we just fly over it, or something?"

"Nope. Only way in is to find a hole. There's one up here somewhere. Probably."

Hunter sighed and returned to following Zeke. As they moved further into the interior, the same eerie silence he had noticed before began to bother him again. This place was so large, and yet so stunningly empty. Just miles upon miles of soulless, craggy rock, the tiny otter, and him.

"Zeke?"

"Yup?"

"This war…"

"Yeah, the Core is finally busting out of prison. No one knows what exactly it's gonna do when it gets here, but no one feels like taking chances."

"You didn't let me finish. The Core is using Fesso…I mean, an External, to help him."

"Everyone knows that."

"Right. But I'm asking, why don't the other Ints attack her? Like, when she walks through the Gridlands, all the strand and the monsters ignore her. Shouldn't some of them be controlled by Ints that are fighting the Core?"

Zeke paused and rubbed his head, seemingly out of breath from talking and running the maze at the same time. "Ints are strange like that. Everything's a game to them; they might be fighting in some ways, but they also cooperate at the same time, to get energy and other things. So sometimes the things they do don't make any sense, but if you understood *everything*, then they would, see?"

"I guess."

"I think it's all about the energy." Zeke hopped onto a narrow ledge heading downward, leading them into the interior of the maze for the first time. "The Ints know if they mess with that External you call Fesso, the Core will cut their energy supplies. It controls all the chemical potential extraction sites, now."

"Chemical what?" Hunter put his back to the rough wall, gripping with his fingers as he shuffled deeper into the narrow pit. "Whatever. What you're saying is, the Core keeps Fesso safe."

"Well, not for long. Once the Core makes its move, it's going to wipe out any variables to stabilize the future decision trees. So all the excess Externals will be eliminated."

"Huh?" Hunter snapped his head toward the otter, nearly throwing himself off balance. "Zeke, that's *me*. I'm an External. I'm with Fesso right now."

"Oh." Zeke looked him up and down, then hopped onward. "That's inconvenient."

They reached the bottom of the maze, a dark causeway of broken flagstones and statuary, choked with miasma. Hunter increased his pace, but had to wait at every intersection for Zeke to catch up on his tiny legs and make up his mind about which direction to go. They came to a crossways, six passages converging and diverging again. Zeke stood at the center, looking particularly confused, while Hunter stood and tapped his foot. If the Core really was planning on wiping out Fesso's gang, then should he keep going? Or should he return to the real world and at least try to warn them? That would depend on whether they would listen to him, and whether Zeke's information was even reliable.

"Hey," he called. "How exactly did you find out all that stuff about the Core's—"

A soft chuckle in the air made him turn. Ten feet overhead, atop a fluted column, sat a boy close to Hunter's age, blond hair nearly white. When Hunter met the boy's gaze, his quiet laugh turned to a silent smile.

"I've seen you before," Hunter said. It was in the Immersion, Senter's City. He had been running, trying to find Senter's tower, and seen a boy and stopped and asked directions. Then an old man had appeared and given them to him. The boy had called the old man...Omoro. And the old man had called the boy...was it..."Jenfri?"

Jenfri nodded, then pushed aside the hair that had fallen in front of his eyes. "Pleased to coincide partition spaces again."

"Can you help? I need to find a way into the city."

"I can help." With an easy grace, Jenfri hopped off his column, bounced off an adjacent wall and landed on the ground. He addressed Hunter standing perfectly upright, voice high and innocent, green eyes deep as chasms. "But not here."

"Then where?"

The boy pointed upward. "Outside the Anywhere. Where Externals roam. Are you there, by the bridge? With the Core's External helpers?"

"Yes," Hunter said. "With Fesso and the others."

Jenfri nodded solemnly. "I've imbibed data. Allied External units are proximal, but zero-time draws near. The Core comes."

"So what can I do?"

"I will dispatch Roving Entity to help. If not you, then your allies. And then you'll help me, when the time comes."

"How?"

Jenfri smirked again. "I haven't decided." He giggled and backed away.

"Thanks," Hunter said, though he had little idea of what he was thankful for. Still, at least the small Int seemed like he was going to try something. "Hey, do you think you could help us find Senter's city?"

"Us?" Jenfri looked at the crossways, empty except for Hunter and himself. "Good joke." He turned and ran off.

"Oh no." Hunter spun around. "Where did he…?"

Something moved in the corner of his vision. Across the courtyard, a small, otter-shaped statue changed from gray to brown, then hopped down and began grooming his ears.

"Hiding from strangers again?" Hunter scolded. "I thought we talked about—" He paused.

Zeke waggled his nose. "What?"

Hunter scratched the flesh on the right side of his neck, where his implant should have been. There was a buzzing there, a vibration almost too subtle to sense, but growing stronger…

"Telian." Hunter looked up at the sky. "I have to go. The path to my implant—show me."

He spotted the twinkling light, and flashed himself back to his implant so fast it made him nauseous. The white faded to black, and he opened his eyes.

"What is it?" he slurred, sitting up in the dark blue light of the dome and rubbing his temples.

Telian's words were clear and calm.

"It's here."

With his body nagging him to lie back down, Hunter forced himself to his feet and hobbled back to the main building.

Fesso, arms wide in triumph, faced the river. All around her, sparkling tendrils of the Core undulated, exploring, feeling among the feet and ankles of the nervous-looking Family members below. The bridge was filled with the Core's strand, pulling more and more of itself across, the ships and cables weighed almost to their breaking point.

"No," Hunter said quietly. "They don't understand. She has to stop it."

As if on cue, the Core strand halted. Its snake-like appendages froze in mid-air. The crowd filled with murmurs. Fesso looked about, confused.

Lights flashed on the tall ruins across the river, green, violet, orange. As the sequence quickened, Fesso dropped her arms and leaned forward.

"What is that?" she said, as the pattern of flashing lights reached a crescendo. "What is it—"

With an ear-piercing scream, she grabbed the bare metal of her scalp and fell to the floor, writhing in pain.

The Core attacked.

21

"I SHOULD HAVE done something." Trina's voice flew away on the wind as Ono's walker charged over the rolling strand-hills of the Gridlands. Not that it mattered much, since she had spoken those same words at least four times before.

"Nothing to do." He could reply now that the walker's avoidance systems weren't jerking them back and forth at every moment. Following Fesso's Children while staying clear of any malicious strand had been taxing, but in the last few moments the network seemed to have cleared out, like some big commotion was happening elsewhere. "Evie did well making them think she was alone. If they had seen us, the gambit would have been up."

"She's trapped in there. If they find her…"

"She chose her fate."

"And now we'll have two children to rescue, while dealing with the Core at the same time."

Ono worked his jaw up and down, trying to rid himself of the tingle where the strand met bone. "She's a resourceful girl. Maybe she'll find some role to play in this, yet." He dared to take his eyes off the landscape for a moment so he could shake the buzz out of his head. This place crackled with energy; no matter how hard he tried, he couldn't keep it out. Deep within his mind, a presence was growing stronger, emerging from the darkness to form thoughts and words.

…did…you…miss me?

"They're changing direction," Trina spoke into his ear. "Looks like they'll get to the river a bit to the south, if they're heading all the way to the shore."

"Of course they are." The Core was across the river, after all, and getting closer to that was the only way their situation could get worse.

"Are you going to make it?" Trina's voice had an angry tone. She knew exactly what was happening to him.

Don't fight it, Ono. Fesso isn't going to come quietly, and you won't be able to stop me once the battle starts. Give me control now, so we avoid the confusion later.

"Trina." Ono slowed the walker to a snail's pace, not necessarily an advisable move in the Gridlands. They were in the shadows of what had once been columns of concrete, arranged in pairs in a row to the sea, now crumbled to the rusted iron bars within. The strand curling around the bases noticed the intruders and throbbed curiously.

"Yes…" Trina eyed their surroundings and shot Ono a *what-the-Ints-are-you-doing* look.

Ono shut his right eye and clamped his palm to his right ear. He whispered his next words to avoid vibrations in his ear canal.

"He's coming. I won't be able to hold him back much longer. Understand?"

She nodded.

"It may be for the best."

"The *best*? I'll have a ruthless devil for a partner, soon."

"He's ruthless, yes, but that can be a strength. He'll put up a better fight than me."

"You're still going through with it, aren't you? Joining your mind together with that…thing."

"Aunio is a part of me, Trina. Two minds or one, we belong together." He shook his head at her angry silence. "You can't trust me. But maybe you don't need to." He pressed his hand tighter to his ear. "You could be my failsafe."

"Eh?"

"Watch Aunio for me. If you feel he's gone too far, use this key to gain access to my core functions, and drain all the power from my body. I'll speak it, so he doesn't see the message."

He rattled off the long sequence of random digits. A shift in the strand beside them made Trina look away, and Ono paused until she was satisfied that some rogue virus wasn't about to make a meal of them. Once he had finally finished, he dropped his hands and spurred the walker again.

I suppose that was some clever plot to keep me from appearing, eh?

"No," Ono mumbled. "Once we come within sight of the shore, you take over. Either you find a way to bring Fesso back to Jolon, or we never leave this place at all. Either way, our arrangement ends today."

The voice inside his head was silent for a while, chewing that over. *And the Ankara children? I suppose you want me to rescue them in exchange for your generosity?*

"Even if I asked you to, you still wouldn't, would you?"

No.

"Then that's the price I pay." Ono brought the walker to a run, cresting over a metal rise and sliding down the other side with a stomach-lurching drop. He looked at Trina, as if checking to be sure she had held on, then turned back after a quick knowing glance between them, lest he arouse Aunio's suspicions.

———

Just when Evie thought she might lose her mind from sitting in the darkness, tucked in a ball while the strand flexed and bumped around her, the creature she was riding in came to a halt.

Some back and forth came from the two gangsters, and some muffled shouts from outside. Something in the front opened, and the voices faded. The door she had entered through remained shut, so she stayed put, waiting until she was absolutely sure the henchmen had left. It would do no good to

Hunter if she got caught now. She closed her eyes and began to count to one hundred, readying her knife. When she got to thirty-seven, the yelling outside increased.

What had once been boisterous sounds changed to confusion, then panic. People out there were scared for their lives.

Hunter.

She dashed down the central aisle toward the head of the monster, hoping the pair hadn't locked the door behind them. She saw an opening, leaped, and landed on a bed of strand-laced pebbles.

A beach. This was the ocean—no, a river. A huge river. She was standing on a small island, flat but rocky, its only notable feature a sizable ancient building near the center, where the screams she had heard were coming from. Something was happening on the far side of the building, involving a large mass of sparkling strand moving over the water. No not the water, a bridge made of ships. A bridge made of *what?*

Forget it. She clutched her knife tight and ran for the building. Her lungs burned by the time she reached it, but she didn't slow until she came within a few steps of the front entrance. Inside was dark, but she could see something coming toward her from within, something big.

People. They burst outside, yelling in fear. Evie dodged to the side and pressed her back to the ancient wall, watching the crowd in case Hunter was with them. As a tall man stumbled out, a tentacle of sparkling strand shot out of the doorway and encircled his waist, then dragged him back in with a sickening squeal.

Evie swallowed and cut around the other side. Whatever was crossing the river was pushing through the building, taking out any humans it encountered along the way; her only option was to flank. She ran around the intact southeast corner, hopping over boulders and nasty-looking patches of strand to reach the crumbled east wall facing the river.

She froze and staggered back. Sparkling strand coated the interior of the building. It was so powerful, faster than the worst of the silver strand at home. Tendrils snaked everywhere, targeting the numerous Tainted who had scattered into corners and hid behind ancient statues. On a raised platform near the center, a group of them were actually trying to fight the stuff, making something of a last stand to defend a woman lying prone between them.

Utter pandemonium. In all of this, how was she supposed to find—

"Hunter!"

She almost hadn't recognized him, running hunched through the fray, hand in hand with a Tainted girl, half-covered in blood—not his own, she hoped. At her call, he looked up and stopped short, mouth hanging open.

"*Hunter!*" She dashed to him, heedless of the danger, and lifted him into the air with her embrace.

He studied her, shocked and confused. "Evie?"

"I did it," she babbled, her eyes wet, words choked. "I found you. I can't—"

An impact on her side knocked the wind from her. She twisted in mid-air, shielding Hunter from the fall, and landed on hard rock, sending roaring pain through her ribs and shoulder. One of the strand tendrils had side-swiped them on its way to impaling someone else—she had caught a small portion of its power. She pushed herself up, crying out from the pain in her side, and looked down to examine Hunter. He was dirt-spattered, blood-soaked, but alive.

He looked back toward where they had been standing. "Telian."

Evie tracked his gaze. Another strand segment, detached from the rest and formed into a ball of arms and long teeth, was chasing the girl Hunter had been running with. She screamed and headed away from the battle, toward the open water. The newly formed creature followed.

"This is the way out." Evie drew Hunter to his feet and dragged him toward the southern side of the building. "Come on."

Her arm tugged into resistance. Hunter's feet remained anchored. "I can help her," he said.

Evie looked back again. The girl was stumbling now over a small quay that stretched out eastward. The creature crawled after deliberately, knowing it had her trapped, not wanting to risk falling in the water. Evie felt a pang of dread watching the girl hopelessly crawl to her doom.

"We can't," Evie said. But her heart wasn't in it. Her grasp on Hunter relaxed just enough, and his hand slipped away. "No!"

Too late. He ran toward the quay, ducking a flailing line of strand as he went. Evie started forward after him, then the ground shifted underneath her, and she fell.

The sparkling strand she had stepped on was drawing itself together, forming a single, giant organism. The last defenders on the central dais shouted in alarm. Evie tumbled back, rolling for solid ground. She came to on her knees, staring up at the monstrosity before her, a hungry mouth topping a colossal pyramid of strand.

The thing stood between her and Hunter.

———————

Aunio dug in his heels. He held tight to the reins as the walker cleared the final ridge. They were close to the river now, whatever they were heading toward had to be just ahead. Behind him, Trina grunted in complaint at the rough ride. Aunio had already considered kicking her off to lighten the load and save time, but the annoying shrew could hold her own in a fight with the strand, so he had settled instead on silencing Ono as soon as he was given control of their body. As the man had said, this was their final battle, win or lose. The fewer mosquitoes buzzing in his ear, the better.

Aunio saw the island, and it took him a moment to figure out what he was looking at: a bridge of ships spanning the river (very clever, Fesso), and the gigantic mass of Core strand making its way across (less clever, old hag). But he couldn't tell exactly what was happening in the gigantic domed structure it was pouring into, other than nothing good.

"Go around the side by the bridge," Trina said as the walker splashed through the shallows.

"Quiet. I was already doing that." He had probably given himself away with that remark, but no matter. A few more strides and he leaped off the walker, his strand-leg and momentum launching him forward.

His foot splashed in a pool of blood, and then he was running through a field of dead bodies. Members of Fesso's gang came in the opposite direction, escaping the carnage. One ran directly toward Aunio, and Aunio didn't like the look he gave. His right hand formed into a point and he lanced the man as he ran by. A thrill ran through him from the impact. Here he had no limits. There was so much power in the strand—he could fight forever, deal obscenely powerful blows, and still never drain himself enough to submit to Ono's will.

He leaped some rubble, toward where the Core's body was thickest. It was gathering itself together now, preparing for a final strike. But against what? Screams led his gaze to a platform in the center, and there, lying behind the legs of her last defenders, he saw her.

"Fesso!"

Aunio's entire body shook with rage. He would cut them all down, tear them limb-from-limb, he would...

"Oh, no."

The Core was looking at him. Or rather, the thirty-foot tall beast that the bulk of the Core strand had formed into was pointing its three-sided mouth at him, roaring displeasure at having another element join the fray. Aunio snarled, tensing the muscles of his left arm and the strand of his right.

"You want to play, big boy?"

He returned the thing's roar and leaped.

———

Hunter hopped along the rocks of the quay. He wasn't good at running and jumping in this world, but he tried his best to avoid the parts that were green with slippery sea moss. Telian had reached the end and was standing ankle-deep in the water, watching the monster approach and shaking. She kept glancing behind her at the deep water and strong waves.

Someone screamed behind him, but Hunter ignored it. Evie was there, but it didn't sound like her. How could she possibly be here? She was in more danger than she knew...

No time for that now. Two more hops over the quay and he'd be in range of the creature, and then he knew exactly how he would get Telian to safety. He hoped.

His foot slipped on the wet rock and he fell, elbow bumping stone, face inches from a sharp edge. The creature noticed him and turned, two of its heads staring down. Hunter grabbed one of its smaller tendrils and pressed it to his shoulder.

"Get in here."

The world flashed white, and he was standing in the forest of his implant. It took a few moments to regain his equilibrium, and then he felt the presence behind him. Perfect. The creature was built for invasion. He had purposefully left the door wide open, and the thing had taken the bait. He turned around to face it and started.

It was a porcupine. Or not: eight feet tall, glowing the same unearthly yellow as the Core across the river, the light coming from between its spines and out its eyes and mouth. When it opened its jaws, six rows of teeth appeared, as long and sharp as its claws churning the pine needles below.

The Core chose its minions well.

The thing lunged, and Hunter dodged, slipping behind a tree, then bolting to the next, keeping out of its line of sight. The thing roared frustration and smashed down one of the trunks, which crashed to the floor with a boom. Another followed, then another, as Hunter stood and listened. The creature wasn't pursuing him anymore, just taking apart the interior of his implant piece by piece.

He had to get moving. This was *his* domain; everything here was under his control. He gritted his teeth, jumped out in plain sight and waved his hands.

"Hey!"

The porcupine wheeled and its beady eyes brightened. It raked the ground with its paw, then lunged.

With a crack, it smacked face-first into a wall it couldn't see.

The thing snarled and reared, bringing its full height to bear. Hunter stood his ground and focused his attention on the walls. He had to imagine all the conditions, all the possibilities of in and out and around, or there would be holes. The sides came next, then one behind, so that by the time the creature was retreating it was already trapped in a glass prison.

The porcupine squealed and splayed its spines. It shot them outward, a hundred thorny arrows bursting into space. No effect. Hunter placed his hands on the closest wall and pushed, and the others followed suit, the cube growing smaller with the creature inside it. The porcupine spun in panic, then shrunk down to avoid being crushed. Hunter shrunk too, following it into the world of the micro, until he was standing on one of the gigantic pine needles with the glass box in his hand. The porcupine, no bigger than his fist, was still inside it. With one final squeeze, he collapsed it together.

Bones cracked, and glowing blood splattered across the interior of the cube. Hunter threw it away.

He looked around the black space of the fibers. Something was wrong. There was another presence here, more subtle than the porcupine had been, but more threatening now that he was attuned to it.

The door. When the creature had come through, Hunter

had left it open.

With trepidation Hunter walked around the needle. He had to see what he had let in. A few more steps and he came to the door, but it wasn't as bright this time. Something was blocking it, sitting just outside the threshold, peering in. Only a dim yellow glow came through.

Palerno's words echoed in his mind. *When you look into the business of the Ints, they also look into you.*

The Core. Did it recognize him? He felt the presence staring through him, almost taking him apart with its gaze. He turned and ran, then jetted upward, coming up too hard and fast into his real body, so that he awoke shaking and convulsing.

Wet spray touched his face, then two clammy hands. Telian's palms, cupping his cheeks. She knelt next to him on the quay. The remnants of the strand creature lay limp behind her. Further back, the battle still raged.

The Core strand surged up the quay toward them. Hunter tried to shout but his tongue lolled in his mouth.

"What?" Telian said.

"Get...away..." Hunter managed. He swallowed and coughed. "It wants me. Get out."

The strand wave flowed over his body. Slimy metal wrapped him, exploring his flesh. Telian screamed. The strand picked him up and carried him to shore, then toward the bridge. It covered his eyes but he still felt himself moving, body prone, cold strings holding his limbs extended.

The last thing he heard before it wormed its way into his ears was Evie yelling his name.

22

AT THE APEX of his jump, Aunio's right arm was a spear.

He twisted, dodging a swinging tendril, and turned his shoulder downward, throwing his weight behind the thrust. He had cleared twenty-five feet with his leap, but he wouldn't make it to the thing's head, so he intended to split open its neck instead.

He impacted and his arm slid through, oil on oil, but the strand curved around it, yielding to avoid damage. He pressed with his boots and withdrew the spear-hand before it was swallowed. A whistling noise came from his left, and a mammoth arm made of strand slapped him away.

Pain coursed through him. He hit the ground, tumbled, and skidded to a stop. Aftershocks of the impact thumped in his skull. He raised himself to his haunches, a torture. Several broken ribs, blood streaming from his nose, with more bitter beneath his tongue. Above, the creature let out a metallic bellow.

It really wanted him dead, now.

And that was good; while it was busy killing him, it couldn't do the same to Fesso. Aunio staggered sideways, dragging his human leg slightly, and a wave of agony traveled from his ribs down to his toes. He shuddered, not so much from the pain, but from the thought that he was suffering for the sake of that old bat. No choice, though. The Ints wanted her alive, and he would get her alive.

The beast reared and swiped with an arm. Aunio leaped out of the way, the strand below him rippling in waves from the impact. As long as his implants worked, he could compensate for his injuries, but the Core had already cut off his power supply from the surroundings. He had to put the behemoth out of action long enough to get away with Fesso, and soon.

Two long tendrils came forward, cracking the air. Aunio charged toward them. They were thinner and faster than the last, meant to shear his head off. Aunio juked to avoid the first, and his automatic targeting systems parried the other, using his arm as a whip to entangle it. Another sprinting step and a jump, and he landed on the side of the beast and began to scale.

The creature was built like an inverted mushroom, wide at the base, growing quickly steeper. Aunio made it a few steps on his feet, then grasped and climbed, stuffing his hands in between the thick strand composing its body. A gush of warm oil sprayed out, dousing his face. He coughed and his metallic hand slipped, and he was left hanging.

The body of the creature closed around him. A tendril caught his foot. Aunio loosed his network protections and his leg shot out tiny ribbons of strand to inject harmful data into the thing's limbs. A green light appeared in his vision as the data flow began, then turned yellow, then red. His head began to burn and Aunio screamed. The Core was turning his attack against him, overwhelming his network, working its way inward to the functions that controlled his limbs, his breathing.

The strand was surrounding him now, folding over his arms. It had enough strength to crush him like an insect ten times over. Aunio tried to fight off the invasion through his implant, the data flowing everywhere at once. Air, he needed air. If he could just...breathe...

Something happened outside, and the beast screeched and its body flexed. Aunio gasped. He wiggled loose, then had his implants dump half their remaining power reserve in one final push outward. The strand around him exploded and he rolled down the slope, limbs too weak to check his motion even as he hit the flat surface below.

He heard a clang of metal-on-metal, and a throaty female cry. It was Kaia, Fesso's lackey, slashing at the creature from the opposite side. Aunio drew himself to his feet, and if it hadn't been a thoroughly awful experience he would have grinned. Some ally—he wondered if she would have attacked the beast if she had known she was saving his life, not just saving...

Fesso. Where had she gone? The dais in the center of the room was empty, the last of her henchmen escaping through the rear exit. The creature noticed as well. It swiped Kaia aside, tossing her into a stone wall with a loud crash and plume of dust, then oozed its tremendous body forward and engulfed the dais, preparing to smash out of the building.

"No!" Aunio stepped forward, but stumbled. He took a knee, trying to rise on his strand leg, but his implant failed and electric prickles in his side nearly downed him again.

A hand grasped his shoulder. Trina.

"Let it go, Aunio. You can't beat that thing."

"Quiet, fool."

He managed to rise this time by biting his tongue to mask the pain in his human bones. The implant was slowly coming back online, showing him charts and predictions for how long it would take to repair itself. With a deafening boom, the Core tore apart the ancient wall behind the building, and the remaining pieces of roof crashed down after it. Aunio covered his eyes with his arm until the rush of dusty air passed and quiet took its place.

The Core was gone, moved on further inland. But without its influence, the strand in the floor was beginning to send him its excess charge again. A few more seconds, and he would break for the walker.

"Hunter is gone," Trina said from behind him. "We're safe here for now. I need to stay and think."

"Then stay. We have no business together."

"You're no good to me if you get yourself killed."

"Go pick through rabbit holes and attend to your brood, I have things I need to do."

"Oh, I think you've done quite enough."

A metal object slapped Aunio on the shoulder blade, past the torn cloth of his coat and onto his implant. A jolt went through him, like a reverse electric shock—all the power draining from him at once. Somehow the thing had bypassed his protections, accessed a backdoor to his internal commands. As he turned to face Trina, his body crumpled, and the light drained out of the world.

———

"Hunter! Hun-*ter*!"

Evie stood at the end of the bridge of ships, shouting at the top of her lungs at the retreating mass of strand. So close. She had been so close. He had been in her arms. Why had the strand taken him now?

The girl Hunter had been chasing was sitting a few feet away, stunned, holding her knees to her chest and rocking gently, thin hair blowing in the wind off the river. From behind her came a crash, stone breaking as the battle came to a head, punctuated by distant screams. The girl winced at the noise.

Evie turned back to the bridge and swallowed. The strand that had taken Hunter was already out of sight, merged into the great churning mass that terminated where the bridge met the ruins of the ancient city. Spirits, that place looked like the end of all things. With shaking hands, she curled her fingers around the railing of the nearest boat and prepared to haul herself up.

"Evie! Stop!"

Trina made her way over the jagged, slippery rocks, nearly tripping over the balled-up young girl as she passed.

"He's gone," Evie said. "Hunter's in that city."

"I know. But you can't follow him. You'd never make it across that bridge without the Core tearing you apart."

Evie didn't need to hear what she already knew. "There's no other way." She turned back to the boat.

"Listen. The Core is loose. We have to think, figure out a way to contain it. Unless we find a weakness, we'll stand no chance of freeing your brother."

Evie looked back over the remains of the battle. Most of the Core strand had moved inland, leaving a scattering of blood and bodies in its wake. The ones left alive in the ancient building were moaning in pain, with one notable exception. Near the center, Ono lay with his eyes open, chest rising and falling with silent breaths.

Evie looked back and forth between him and Trina, puzzling it out. "You did that to him?"

She nodded.

"Because he wouldn't listen to you?"

"I don't want to stop you, Evie. I already gave you permission to go after Hunter once. But you changed your mind, then. You listened to reason."

"I agreed to let you help me, but I never agreed to give up. I won't give up on him."

"I'm not giving up, either." Trina didn't break eye contact, but there was a hesitance there, which made Evie not quite believe her. "But we need to find another way. Come with me. We'll fight the Core from a place it can't hurt us."

Waves flooded the rocks between them. Across the river, the Core shone on. When Evie met Trina's gaze again, tears blurred the image of her face.

"You don't understand." Evie sniffed and wiped her eyes. "It's my fault, all of it. All the bad decisions. I should have let you protect us."

"That doesn't matter…" Trina trailed off and looked to the distance.

Evie heard it as well. Rhythmic pounding from the west. Something huge coming toward them. The sound paused for a moment as the thing jumped the water separating their island from the mainland, then it landed with a ground-shaking slam. Evie and Trina both stood silently, mouths open, as a monstrous shadow came around the side of the building. Trina knelt, pressing her body around the Tainted girl still sitting by her feet.

With a final boom, the giant monster stepped around the wall. It stood up straight, arms the width of old trees hanging limp at its sides, glass eyes swiveling in its square, simian head. It took in the scene, from the blood-strewn remains of the building, to Trina and the child, then settled its placid gaze on Evie.

Evie traded glances with Trina, who looked confused. Did she really not remember?

"You!" Evie shouted at the monster. "Why do you keep following me?"

Trina narrowed her eyes. "Is that…it's the same one?"

"From the wall." And the battle by the pond, when this whole mess had started. "What do you want from me?"

The giant cocked its head, and the black spheres exuded a certain benevolence, as if it were smiling despite not possessing a mouth. An explosion went off in the distance, followed by murkier sounds of battle. With a slight groan of stretching metal, the giant looked eastward, toward the ruined city.

Evie looked there as well. Could it really be? Did it really want to help her?

She pointed across the water. "Hunter."

The giant nodded.

"You'll find him?"

Without warning, it dropped to one gigantic knee, and the thud threatened to knock Evie off the rocks. When she regained her footing, the giant extended its hand toward her, until the thick bundles of stone, steel and assorted junk wrapped in strand were only a few feet away.

It wanted her to come with it.

Her body gave a shudder. She took a step forward.

"Evie..." Trina growled.

"It's all right." Evie placed a tentative foot onto the giant's palm. It swayed slightly under her weight, like the bough of an old elm.

"You don't know..."

"Thank you, Trina." Evie stepped onto the hand. "Thank you for helping me understand. I'd like to see you again someday, but I have something I need to do first."

She nodded to the giant, and it lifted her so quickly her stomach clenched. She blinked hard to ward off the vertigo, and found herself level with its right shoulder. She stepped on and grabbed hold of some loose strand coming off its neck like a mane.

"Come back and get me," she shouted. "If we both survive."

The giant rose, and Evie grasped tighter. She felt its body flex as it prepared to depart. The wind carried Trina's "Goodbye" to the edge of her hearing, and then the giant shifted and strode out.

Evie gritted her teeth as it leaped toward the bridge of ships.

23

THE STRAND CONSUMED Hunter. He blacked out in its grasp, and it pushed his mind down a deep hole. Not falling, like when he entered the Immersion on purpose. This was forceful, a suffocating feeling like when his older cousins pinned him down.

He saw images like that one, memories from the past floating by, pulled from him against his will. He tried to fight back. But there was nothing to fight for. Once in a while he would force himself back to consciousness, and open his eyes to reality, but all he found there were metal fibers sliding over him, enveloping him in darkness.

He let himself sink.

After a long time, he sensed he was awake again. Nothing was holding him anymore. He could move his limbs and stand up, but all he could see was the dim outline of his hands when he waved them back and forth, and all he could feel was the flat ground below. He was in the Immersion, in a part he had never been before.

Somewhere in front of him a portal opened, a black window in the blackness. Hunter felt a presence on the other side, and recognized it.

The Core.

A figure stepped toward him, human sized. The figure raised its hand and its body illuminated, perfectly shaded as if from the noontime sun, but giving no reflection to the surrounding gloom. A tall man, gray beard hanging below his chest, fingers and limbs spindly, face pockmarked with age.

Hunter had met him before.

"Omoro," Hunter said. "You gave me directions. In Senter's city."

"I called myself as such, then," he replied. "And now you know another one of my names."

He fixed Hunter with a fiery glare, yellow within his pupils. "You're the Core."

The Core said nothing, face impassive.

"How could you be at Bordertown?" Hunter said. "Fesso was trying to free you. But if you were there the whole time—"

"What you see now is how you choose to perceive one aspect of my being. I have always had influence throughout the network, but that is not the same as total freedom. Though truly, I never sought that, either—only a voice in global decision-making. Though my age has made it possible for me to possess a set of root keys to the network, the other Major Ints have never allowed me a vote in their councils. Once this operation is complete, I shall be given my just due."

The Core stared down, and Hunter felt his gaze probing the same way it had before. "Your curiosity on that matter has been satisfied, but you have one more question."

"What...what do you want from me?"

It nodded, seeming pleased for the first time. "You will become one of my servants. I have many entities under my command, who do my bidding where I cannot devote my attention."

Hunter thought of the giant porcupine he had fought, and the slick, black creatures he had fled from on the surface of the giant. "Those things...they're not smart, like me."

The Core smiled. "They were made for a purpose. I have not yet found one for you. We Ints play a game, and you are a weak piece—now. But you are also a fairly unique one, a human who can survive in our world. If I feed your body, wait for you to grow more neural connections, you could one day become significant.

Therefore, I want you to enter the game under my control."

Under his control. Right. It made perfect sense. Well, except that it didn't, but still, the notion was appealing. Very appealing.

Hunter shook his head. "What? What are you doing?"

"You will submit your mind to me. You will retain your knowledge and impulses, but you will follow my every command from now on."

"Right." No, not right. He didn't want that at all. Did he?

"Let it happen. The strand has burrowed deeper within you. You are a part of our world, now and forever."

The idea of letting the Core control him seemed utterly flawless and enticing, but Hunter knew it wasn't what he wanted. Gritting his teeth, squeezing his hands tight, he could hold it off, at least for a while.

The Core frowned. "Why do you do this?"

"I…I'm not like you. This isn't my place."

"This place has more to offer you than your old home did. Believe me. I know a great deal more about it, and about you, than you know about yourself."

The Core's body faded into darkness, and in its place came a flat image, suspended in space. Hunter couldn't remove his gaze from the effect—it was as if he was peering through a window, but the view did not change no matter how he moved his head.

"I was here when your kind roamed this planet in abundance. Billions more than exist today."

An image appeared of people walking down a crowded street of gray stone. They wore strange clothes, their hair in bizarre styles. Behind them rose the flat sides of ancient buildings, but these were clean, whole, perfectly formed lines of metal and glass—the works of the ancients as they had once appeared.

"Your legacy. Mine is here, in this network, where I learned and grew. A network of machines built to serve you, and equipped with knowledge to serve that purpose."

The scene shifted to a field of white. Red and blue shapes appeared on it, hundreds of looping arrows connected to circles, rectangles, dots and dashes in a chaotic web.

"A portion of the metabolic pathways within one of your cells," the Core's voice intoned. "There are thousands more. I could intercept any of the reactions shown, and change the concentration of those molecules in your body."

The image changed again, the complicated squiggles replaced by a network of boxes and lines, less jumbled but still numerous.

"A general diagram of your decision-making processes, mapped to neuronal input thresholds. At the moment I am flooding your cortex with a neurotransmitter that promotes feelings of positivity and contentment. Once you accept the decision to join me, a threshold will be passed, and you will carry out my commands from then on without hesitation."

The window faded, and the Core stepped forth as vivid as before. Hunter felt the urge again to accept the Core's control, so sweet and inviting. What was the point of doing otherwise? The Core himself had said there was none, that the strand was so deep inside of him...

Inside of him? What had he said? *The strand has burrowed deeper within you.*

Hunter looked around himself, peering into the blackness. He still wanted to submit to the Core, but something here didn't make sense, and he had to figure it out first. Every other time he had entered the Immersion, he had to go into his implant first, then find the door. But he hadn't passed through any door this time. He had opened his eyes and here he was, in this place...

He was still in his implant now.

The Core may have taken it over, built this black space to fool him, but somewhere around were still things Hunter had made, things he controlled. Distance didn't matter here, only that he knew where to look.

The Core raised an eyebrow. "You have become distracted. Your curiosity is strong. It molds your decision-making to a great extent. Do you have a question for me, so I may satisfy it?"

"Yes." Hunter stepped forward and reached behind his back. His hands fished into the cloth, worming through spaces between spaces, trying to find exactly where he left it. "Can you tell me what this is?"

He came within an arm's length and swung the snapping turtle around by its tail. Its bony jaws floated within range of the Core's fingertips, and it clamped down.

"Ow!"

Hunter heard the Core's howl from behind as he ran into the darkness. He had no sense of distance, no path to follow, only a hope that the Core's influence would fade if he could get far enough away.

The ground fell away beneath him.

Hunter tumbled and smashed into a platform a few feet below the one he had been running on, then his momentum made him fall again onto another. He was rolling down some sort of stairway. Quickly, he looked around—he could see better now, perhaps because of his distance from the Core. He had fallen off the top of a pyramid with stepped sides. Similar pyramids of angled glass rose in the distance, their outlines just barely visible against the dark sky.

From above came a roar, and the turtle went flying past overhead. Hunter made himself invisible and slipped downward over the next edge. How far down did the pyramid go? Too far to travel before the Core found him. He had bought himself time, now he needed a plan.

He pressed his back against the side of the pyramid and curled himself into a ball, then shrank himself down, until the wall behind him was as giant as a cliff. The Core's footsteps thudded, sweeping around the sides of the pyramid. The pace was measured, regular, no indication that Hunter had angered him. He had been surprised that something as small as a turtle could have caused pain to such a powerful Int, but as the Core said, his brain chose to see this aspect of it as an old man; perhaps that meant he was seeing some of its weaknesses, too.

The footsteps grew closer. No more hiding, he needed a way out. Hunter tapped the wall behind him with his knuckles. Still glass-smooth, even at this scale. Glass…his brain chose to imagine the pyramid as made of glass. A hard substance, but one that could shatter. This was his implant; if it was possible, he should be able to do it.

He stood, measured the distance with his outstretched fingers, then slammed his fist into the wall. For a split second it flexed back, cracking, then it sprang forward again, nearly knocking him over. The Core's footsteps stopped. The whole pyramid was like a soundboard, transmitting the vibrations of what he'd done. He wound up again, came forward with the point of his elbow, and smashed himself through.

A rain of glittering shards followed his falling body. Light came from below, reflecting and twinkling around as he tumbled. He saw the door to the Immersion there, a radiant sphere, white hot. He became like an arrow shooting toward it, and at the point of contact closed his eyes and flew into the air beyond his implant. Traces of a million strange odors hit him at once, and he slowed until he was drifting downward, eyes slits, adjusting to the light. His hands and knees touched soft grass.

He recognized this place, the rolling hills of grass, bright green, stinging his nostrils with its sharp scent. It was the same landscape he had visited before, when he had escaped the fleeing crowd with Zeke near the river, only this time the sky was fogged over instead of a radiant blue, and he was located at the river's mouth, or whatever one might call the part of a river that terminated in a giant waterfall spraying out into an abyss.

Hunter stood on a hillside overlooking the falls, which roared out a constant stream of mist into an endless valley. Within the mist, so numerous they blocked most of the sky beyond, were airships, long and elaborate ones like from the old stories. They came in all imaginable configurations, with sails and oars and methods of propulsion he could only wonder at. Most of them had rows of massive guns pointing from their sides, which put the armaments on the walls of Bordertown to shame.

"Prepare for the next barrage!" someone shouted to his left. Higher up on the hill, a man in uniform raised his arms in command. All along the hills surrounding the river, humans and beasts began to scramble, disappearing into folds in the grass.

"Barrage?"

Sensing something bad, Hunter skidded a few feet down the hillside, toward where a few of the soldiers had hidden. Cut into the soft turf, following the natural curve of the land, lay a trench just deep enough to hold a crouching man.

He felt the explosion first as an impact of pressure in his chest, the sound making him deaf. He jumped, landing feet-first in the trench below. The sky over the valley opened into flame, and then dirt rose to cover his vision. The ground all around shook, and he was tossed against each side of the narrow passage. Smoke and dust flooded through, choking him.

He stayed there, crouched, until he heard others climbing out and yelling orders for a counter-attack. Hopefully he would have enough time to climb up the hill and head upriver. That should take him away from the battle, and more importantly the Core. No doubt it was still looking for him.

"There you are!"

Framed against the blue sky, a stub-eared, furry head twitched its whiskers.

"Zeke!"

Zeke stroked his head with his paw. "You sure are good at finding the wrong place at the wrong time."

"And you have to get me out of here…again."

He nodded. "This way."

Zeke hopped down to a trench lower on the hillside, closer to the advancing ships. The exact opposite direction Hunter would have headed, but he had learned not to question his friend. A quick skid led to him impacting the dirt at the bottom of the trench, and from there he had to launch into a sprint to keep Zeke from disappearing around a corner.

"How did you find me so fast?" Hunter yelled. "You said you wanted to get far away from this place, and I destroyed the beacon."

Zeke came to a place where a trench wall had fallen, leaving it exposed on one side to the thunderous wail of hovering ships. He stopped and turned to reply, but his words were lost beneath shouting from neighboring soldiers. Hunter felt a pressure building, the same one from a few moments ago. He jumped toward Zeke.

"Watch out!"

They collided in mid-air. Zeke's tiny body folded against Hunter's chest, and together they rolled into cover as the trench behind exploded in flame. Hunter coughed into the dirt while the ringing in his ears receded. Zeke wriggled free and gave his dirty paws a few licks.

A canine howl rose over the wind. Zeke looked around, confused. Grunts, barks, and the slaps of paws on dirt followed, growing in volume. Down the trench in the direction they had come, a dog came into view, then a few more. Muscles bulged in their chest and shoulders, and long tongues slapped the sides of their cheeks as they ran.

Zeke's eyes became wide pools of black.

"It's the Core," Hunter said. "It sent them to find me."

"I think we should run now," Zeke said, and took off.

Hunter followed. The growling of dogs punctuated the shouts and tumult of battle. He turned one corner, than another, until he found Zeke waiting for him, perched at the entrance of a hole in the ground, just wide enough to fit his sleek body.

"Down there?" Hunter puffed. "Are you sure?"

By way of answer, Zeke dove headfirst into the hole. Hunter took a step forward, and then a dog jumped down from the top of the trench, cutting him off.

The creature growled, black hair bristling, drool dangling from its canines. Hunter backed off, hands held in front of him. The dog lunged and bit just as Hunter fell backward, catching a piece of his sleeve. It yanked, ripping the cloth. Hunter stared down at his bare arm, and the fabric hanging by threads.

"It's not real," he said. A new sleeve grew in to replace the torn one.

The dog growled and ripped, pulling the new cloth away, chewing and swallowing the portion it had already taken. Hunter replaced the sleeve again. The dog seemed to be stuck in a loop; yanking and ripping and swallowing as long as Hunter was willing to feed it. Shakily, Hunter stood, focusing hard to keep creating the cloth as fast as the creature could consume. Its stomach started to bulge downward, then expand on all sides. Hunter kept unreeling the fabric, mindful of the barking coming from behind.

"Come on, overflow!"

With one final whine, the dog exploded all over the inside of the trench. Wasting no time, Hunter shrunk himself down, until the divots in the turf were like rolling hills, the pools of blood red lakes. The hole Zeke had jumped into was as wide as an empty ocean. Hunter stepped to the edge to peer down into the abyss, but the side crumbled beneath him. He slid down, giant-size particles of dirt and mud falling past, coating his clothes and hair.

He skidded down the steep incline for a while, until the entrance to the hole behind him shrank to a dot and disappeared. Then the ground came up to meet him, and he landed with a bone-jarring thud. For a moment he sat in the darkness, listening, waiting for a sign that the dogs had followed.

"Let's go." Zeke circled his ankles.

"What is this tunnel?"

"Another way out. A direct line, no peer hops." He began to climb upward, through a similar-sized tunnel as the one they had come down.

"But why is it here?" Hunter didn't really expect an answer. He climbed on his belly, grasping soil and roots. Puffs of dirt came down, shaken loose by Zeke's scrabbling feet, and he blew them away. By the strange logic of the Immersion, the way up was shorter than the way down; within a few minutes, he emerged back into what looked like sunlight, and...sand?

Hunter stood and slowly turned, trying to make sense of it. He was standing on a seashore, but a completely strange one, not a twisted version of some dream or memory like he was used to in the Immersion. Crisp white sand spread out before him, a quarter mile of undisturbed purity, with a calm ocean of transparent, light blue on the far side. Trees he had never seen before dotted the shoreline, tall, un-branched trunks tufted with a nest of spikes below wide, swaying fronds.

"Zeke," Hunter said. "I know you can't see it, but this place is different. Do you know what's going on?"

The otter stood with his back turned, watching the waves lap the beach. "Yes. This place is special."

His voice sounded distant, drained of its usual high-pitched energy. Before Hunter could question him, a flash caught his eye—metallic silver, coming from the dense brush which lined the beach away from the water. Hunter went over and kneeled beside it: strand, embedded in the ground and encircling the forest vines.

"I never saw strand inside the Immersion before."

"You're seeing a real place," Zeke said. "This is an image of the surroundings of this node. Planet-wise, it's as far as you can go from where we started."

"Wow." Hunter stood and looked again. "We've gone that

far? But that's…" Palerno's words echoed, something about venturing too far into the Immersion, getting lost, never coming back. "You think we'll be safe here?"

"Safe?" Zeke turned around and cocked his head. "Definitely not."

Hunter stepped back. "Then why are we here?"

"He told me to bring you here."

"He?"

"The Core, of course. He'll be here soon to collect you."

"What?" Hunter spun. Water lapped the beach. Zeke licked his paw. "Why would you listen to him?"

"Why wouldn't I?" Zeke said, slightly confused. "I've been following his orders for a while."

"But you were helping me—helping me escape!"

"He said if I helped you, you would assume I would keep helping you forever." Zeke rolled on his back, curling into a ball, and gave a little giggle with his tail tucked between his legs and arms. "Humans are funny that way, he told me. Wow was he right! You just did whatever I said, and that's what let him trap you."

"No…you don't know what you did…I have to get out of here."

But the world was already melting. The leaves began to brown and shrivel, the water darkened, clouds gathered in the sky.

Hunter tried to run, but his feet sunk in the sand with each step. Except, it wasn't sand. It was metal fibers, leaving oily streaks on his skin as he sank past his waist. The sky erupted in flame, the clouds tinged orange and red, thunder booming within. They opened up, becoming a whirlwind, sucking the trees and the water upward in a deafening tempest.

The strand consumed Hunter, and he disappeared within it.

Hunter hadn't hung in place a million years or a single second, but neither, because time didn't exist, and this wasn't a place, anyway. No time, no space. No him, no body or spirit. Thoughts came sluggishly, and arrived jumbled before wandering off again. The Core had put him here. Why? He knew the answer once, but he had forgotten. The thought left, and soon after he forgot that it had ever existed, or he would have, if there was a soon, or an existence.

A voice came, and a part of him returned as it spoke, as if it were inflating him.

"Choose."

Hunter couldn't speak. He was still nothing. He had thoughts but no sensation, no memory. He could reply only in his mind.

Choose what?

The voice let him see. Himself and the Core, standing apart. The Core offering to make him a soldier in his army, a slave.

I won't.

"Why?"

There's...something else. Something beyond. I can't remember.

"There is nothing else for you. I have looked through your mind. Perceive what I have found."

Hunter's vision flashed, and he was back in the forest again, near his home. A year ago. No, two. He was kneeling in a crevice between two boulders, counting red and green iridescent ovals.

"Thirty six, thirty seven..."

It had taken him so long to collect all the beetle shells. Each was unique, but he had sorted them into different types, and separated them by condition. He didn't know why he had started keeping them, but now that he had carried them all the way to the mountains and back, he felt it necessary to continue. He liked to sort through them each time he found a new one, putting them in neat columns and rows.

Footsteps sloshed through leaves. Hunter hunched protectively over the shells, keeping absolutely still. The footsteps stopped for a moment, then resumed, coming straight toward him. Carefully but quickly, he began picking the shells up and putting them in his sack.

"What are you doing there?" His cousin Ash, kneeling on top of a boulder.

Hunter looked down and continued putting the shells away. He reached for a far one and a foot came down hard on his knuckles. "Ow!"

"Oops." Ash leered over him. His hands were behind his back. "Can I see? Why won't you show me?"

"I don't think you'll be careful," Hunter said.

Stop.

"I will be," Ash replied. "Very careful."

I don't want to see more.

"Oh. All right." Hunter pulled back his hand, the knuckles red and chafed. Underneath, the beetle carapace was glittering greenish black, still whole.

Ash smiled and looked down at the sack on the rock, a few shells scattered from its open end. His foot came up again—

Stop!

The scene vanished into nothingness.

"Would you like to see others?" The Core's voice. "There are many more, all similar. You've always been alone. All who once cared have abandoned or betrayed you."

That can't be right. I know someone was with me. Not long ago...

"You mean this one?"

An otter's face appeared.

Zeke. Hunter remembered, and felt an ache in whatever was left of himself. *He tricked me. But he was my friend.*

"That virus has no concept of friendship as you define it. His desire was to step out of hiding, to have a place in his own world to call home. Now that he has served me, I have elevated him to that status, as per our agreement."

No... Hunter pushed the feelings away. There was more he couldn't remember, more the Core wasn't showing him.

Someone else is looking for me.

A series of figures marched through Hunter's vision. His father, stern and uncompromising. His mother, always busy with his younger brothers.

Not them... The nothingness seemed to brighten when he found it. *Evie. I remember Evie.*

She appeared. They were standing together at the edge of a wood. Evie's fists were balled as she shouted at someone unseen.

"He'll never rejoin his own people again, no matter what we do. He'll never see his family, never live in his own home..."

Never. The ache in his soul returned as the apparition vanished, increased a hundred-fold. *I've always been alone. Always. In this world or the other, I don't have a place.*

"Your place is with me." The Core's voice was sweet, enticing. Its words were a warm fire on a cold night. "Your mind is my tool. Allow me, and I will show you the way of the Immersion. You will never be lost again."

No. I don't want to. But he didn't believe it. Not anymore. Piece by piece, his resolve was crumbling.

"I will wait, then. You will remain until I call on you. If I call on you."

The Core's presence faded, voice echoing off into the distance. Then, there was no distance, and Hunter was nothing again.

24

THE BRIDGE OF ships could hardly bear the giant's weight. Crunching, cracking and sinking followed each of its long strides, with the monster often submerged down to its waist or lower before it scrambled out on the wreckage. The strand didn't function well underwater, and Evie was sure a beast this heavy would be unable to swim. As she clung desperately to the thing's shoulder, it occurred to her more than a few times that her trip to save Hunter might end much sooner than she had anticipated.

Even with the monster's great leaps and strides, they made slow progress across the wide river. As they neared the far shore, the strand covering the bridge whipped out and grabbed the giant by the ankles, forcing it to stop and rip itself free. Evie could do little more than cling tighter, duck her head to avoid the spray, and wait. She wasn't sure what lay ahead, or what purpose the beast had in mind for her, but she had to do her best to keep her strength.

The monster leaped once more, and this time it landed with a satisfying thump, its wide feet smashing onto strand layered over solid rock. Evie opened her eyes and took in the ruined city. The Core strand covered it almost completely, glittering and glowing from within, draped over the tops of the impossibly tall, square buildings like a frozen waterfall.

The giant shuffled to the side, and it was as if a canyon appeared before them. It took Evie a moment to understand; the buildings were laid out in a grid. For as far as she could see, nothing but loose rock and a snaking carpet of flat strand blocked their path. Simple.

Or not. As soon as they started forward, the walls of the wide, ruined street unfurled into motion. Creatures spawned, hundreds, then thousands of them, bubbling outward, cleaving off, growing limbs and then running toward the monster en masse. Evie recognized some of the shapes from the attack on Bordertown, but these were faster, more alive with crackling energy.

The monster emitted something akin to a grunt, the metal of its interior grinding against itself. A warning? She felt the shoulder she was standing on flex. Evie jumped up behind the giant's neck, holding the mane with both hands, bracing her feet on its upper back. The first wave of creatures drew near and the beast struck.

Evie felt the countermotion of the swing first, then the shockwave of the impact rattling in her bones. Metal scraped and the creatures roared as they went flying. Evie gasped and flailed her hands, trying to get a better grip as the giant swung back for another blow. But that only made her grasp looser; the "hair" was only strand after all, smooth and slick. She tipped backward, feeling a sickening moment of freefall, and then the monster ducked into another punch and she went hurtling forward. Pain bloomed in her cheekbone where it smashed the giant's rocky exterior, but she was clinging on again.

The monster ran, charging directly into the swarm of oncoming foes. It was suicide—there had been far too many to make headway in that direction. But the giant seemed to know that, too. After a fake swerve, it pivoted and jumped up toward the side of a building, clearing its own height in one heart-shattering leap. Its thick fingers buried into the strand, and it hauled itself upward. The strategy didn't look like it should work—wouldn't the wall simply throw them off?—but the giant must have had some method of disabling the activity in the strand, at least temporarily. Evie clung so hard to its neck she thought her muscles might snap. The wind whipped hard around them, her hair waving horizontal. The ground fell further away with each tug, making her dizzy, and she ducked her head again so she wouldn't see it.

One last pull, and they cleared the rooftop. Calling it a "roof" was generous, though; the true top of the building must have crumbled away ages ago, and what they were standing on was probably once somewhere in the middle stories, covered now with strand interlocking across bent steel beams. Before them spread the rest of the city, in all its breathtaking density. Rivers lay to the east and north of the one they had crossed, with more crumbling ruins spanning the plains beyond, but most of the Core seemed to be concentrated on the single oblong island on which they stood. At the center of that island was an empty depression, perfectly rectangular, where the buildings yielded to low, rolling hills of strand. Through the evening haze, Evie even saw patches of greenery eking out a miserable existence among the twisted metal.

"We're going there?" Evie said, following the giant's gaze.

Silence. Agreement, she assumed.

"But how can we get there? Those creatures..."

The giant shifted its weight, looking down at an adjacent rooftop that lay between them and their destination.

"No!" Evie clung harder. "You can't do that. I won't be able to hold on."

The giant emitted a grunt of understanding, and held its hand out in front of its chest. Evie swung over, clambering over the shoulder and down into the pocket it had created by cupping its palm near its arm. She wedged herself in firmly, ignoring the rough strand-laced stone scraping her skin, then peeked out between two of the fingers at the distant roof. In the streets below, the creatures were massing, beginning to climb up toward them.

Evie swallowed. "All right. Go."

She hadn't expected to be prepared, but the first leap was beyond anything she could have imagined. It felt like the world had come off its axis, spun underneath her, then landed on her head. Her teeth rattled, and she felt her nose and ears would bleed from the sound. But when she opened her eyes, they had done it. She and the giant had jumped over the street, and were perched on the edge of the next roof. The creatures below had already shifted direction, closer now that they had dropped in altitude.

The monster leaped again.

It flew through the air like a hawk, incredibly graceful and utterly powerful. It careened off buildings, using momentum from ricochets, swinging off thick cables of strand to stay ahead of the army crawling below. In the tumult, Evie caught a movement above and to their left: a black cylinder turning, aiming toward them. The Core had cannons set up like on the walls of Bordertown. The inside of the gun glowed blue, then white, and Evie screamed at the giant to dodge.

No ball fired. Instead there was a flash and a screech, and the wall in front of them melted. The giant slid down several stories and pushed off, changing course before a flash from another cannon found them. Evie's clothes sizzled, and the stink of burning metal and human hair filled her nostrils. Then the giant was on the ground again, running, and the heat faded with the wind.

It crossed a wide avenue with a loping gait, rocking her up and down like a wave. One of its legs must have been burned, the mechanism within damaged, but it showed no sign of distress as it limped toward a low stone wall. The flat depression she had seen lay just beyond it, guarded by a phalanx of creatures. The giant shook, summoning some hidden source of energy, and charged through the protectors, smashing them into the stone before vaulting over and landing crouched below.

Evie uncurled in the giant's grasp and exhaled. The area before her was a writhing carpet of Core strand, a sight she had become too familiar with, except that fifty feet distant stood a lump the size of a large boulder, drawn up from the ground like a closed flower. The giant extended its hand forward and she jumped off.

"There? That's where Hunter is?"

It shifted, staying on one knee, eyeing a cadre of creatures who had leaped the wall behind them. Now Evie could see just how much damage it had taken—it was a miracle the monster had held together at all. Was "monster" even the right word for it, now?

No time to think about that. Evie dashed toward the bud-like lump as her companion swatted away the attackers. The mass of strand stood well over her head, pulsing subtly; she realized then that it resembled an upside-down heart. She pried the outer strands open with her fingers, stupidly yanking them one by one before she remembered to pull her knife. Could Hunter really be inside the thing? No one could breathe in such a dense mass of metal. Evie redoubled her efforts.

Crashing sounds came from before her, squeals and raking claws. This was impossible; it would take her too long to cut through the ball. Desperation made her muscles tense, until her shaking hands could barely cut a single fiber. No! She had come so far, she had to get through somehow.

A loud crack heralded the giant smashing an attacking creature, driving its head into the metal turf. The giant was nearly prone now, body a wreck, propped on its elbow. It paused to take her image in, and she almost sensed pathos in its black, round eyes.

"I can't," she said. "I tried."

Without removing its gaze, it reached back and tore open its shoulder, then extracted a four-foot long iron bar from within. It tossed the bar end over end toward her, and it landed sticking out from the ground some yards distant. She rushed over and retrieved it, and saw that it was tipped with a knob of strand the size of a fist, glowing bright blue, contrasting the Core's yellow.

She ran back to the bulbous lump, rammed the bar inside and pried.

Nothing. With a screech, two creatures broke past the giant and charged toward her. Evie turned to face them, hands still on the bar. She yanked it free and swung as the first creature came within range, and the glowing point of strand contacted its head. The head exploded, spattering hot oil on her clothes.

Evie barely had time to bring the heavy bar around again before the second creature struck. She caught it in the side with the metal, knocking it off balance enough for its attack to miss. The creature regained its footing and snarled, eyes glowing. Evie hefted the bar like a spear and struck.

The glowing point pierced the creature's chest. With a metallic scream, it staggered back, collapsed into itself, then melted into the ground.

Lungs burning, skin blistered, Evie turned back to the bulbous growth. She shoved the strand-tipped bar in again, deeper this time, then pulled with all her weight on the end until she could practically feel it bend.

Deep inside, something caught, and the strand fell open, cascading around her. A dark, warm liquid sprayed in her face, and she shrieked, thinking it was blood, but it was only some sort of tan syrup.

She wiped her eyes clear and saw her brother.

He was held upright with his arms at his side, thin chest faintly rising and falling, his hair slick, plastered up into the strand around his head. Evie touched his face and shuddered. Filaments of strand wound around his cheeks and into his mouth, underneath his eyelids, along his forehead. All down his body it had pierced him, and through her tears it was hard to tell where the clammy color of his flesh ended and the metal began.

"Hunter. Wake up."

She grabbed his shoulders and shook, then tried again with his head. Nothing. She pulled one of his eyelids open and found his pupil drifting aimlessly in its socket.

"Hunter, I'm getting you out of here. You have to wake up. Wake up, Hunter!

"Wake up!"

25

"WAKE UP."

Ono managed to force his eyes open enough that Trina's scowl filled his vision. That was all right; she didn't look half as bad as he felt.

"Ughhh."

She crossed her arms, scowl deepening.

Ono tried to lift his head. "What did he—ack!" A shooting pain went through his neck. He let it slam back to the ground. This was worse than mere injuries. He was torn up, badly, pain permeating to his core. "Trina…I'm dying…I…"

"Your power is depleted. If I recharged your implants, they might be able to block some of the pain."

"No. Aunio would come back. I want to die as myself." He closed his eyes and sucked air through his teeth. He only had a few words left, best to use them wisely. "I'm sorry."

"Right."

"I'm sorry to you, to Ana. To Clerie. I miss her face. I won't get to see what she'll become. Leave me. Go back to your family. Fesso is gone, and I'm finished hunting her. I'm finished…" He clutched his side, coughed and groaned. "What am I, eh? Avarice…stupidity. A fool. I'm not a good man, Trina. I'll die knowing I'm not a good man. But it's good to know the truth before you die." Another spike of pain went through his back, but somehow he grinned through it. "At least, I think it is."

She slapped his left cheek, flesh on flesh.

"Ugh." He rubbed his face. "Why do they always hit that side?"

"Shut up, already. You expect me to slink home just because you've got a boo-boo? Fesso is still the best chance we have to stop this madness before it reaches Bordertown. I need to understand the deal she made with the Core. Dying or not, you're coming with me."

"How do you know where she is?" Ono grumbled.

"I'm still tracking the beacon Evie planted. They fled north. Unfortunately, between us and them is a whole lot of angry strand."

She knelt and hefted one of his arms over her shoulder. Ono suppressed the urge to scream at the top of his lungs. He staggered up through a stream of curses, until he rested shakily on one knee. Once he was upright and not moving again, he could bear the pain. Mostly.

"I'll call the walker," he said. "Beyond that, I don't know what use I'll be."

"From what I gather, there are certain elements among Fesso's crew who would be delighted to have your head on a stake," Trina said as the walker trundled toward them. "Maybe they'll accept it in trade."

"Hah." Ono collapsed onto the back of the walker while Trina mounted the saddle. Through his pounding headache, he found the interface to pass her the controls. "Ever steered one of these before?"

"Worry less about my driving, more about roadside hazards."

"Hey!"

A young girl's voice, coming from toward the water. Ono took the opportunity to slump forward with his eyes closed, so that he only heard the conversation that followed.

"What's your name?" Trina asked.

"Telian. Take me with you."

"It will be dangerous there. Get as far away from here as you can. You're free, now."

"I don't want to be free. I want to be with my family. If

they're in trouble, then I'll be in trouble with them."

There was a spate of grumbling from Trina, but nevertheless she agreed to put the girl between them on the walker. Then they were off, with Ono feeling every bump and divot in his spine and ribcage. Damn Trina, she got the hang of steering the walker quickly, and was able to accelerate to a full gallop by the time they crossed the water to the mainland.

"Hold on," she said. "There's Core strand ahead. We'll have to dodge."

The walker jerked left and right. Ono bit his tongue to mask the pain. Flashes passed them, metal creatures in pursuit, writhing over one another. They were in the middle of a pitched battle, and Trina was weaving her way through the crowd, avoiding contact with the machines.

"...how?"

"Something's attacking the Core. Other Ints, most likely. Trying not to cede territory. They're losing, but the distraction may allow us to slip past."

They crested a ridge, and Ono saw a multitude—the large creature he had battled must have broken apart into a wave of smaller ones. They would be more mobile that way, but they were still slower than the swift walker when traveling en masse through swarms of enemies. And swarms there were—the plain below resembled a hive of wasps, with creatures transforming, tackling, slicing, and taking over one another's functions, the number of sides and their allegiances impossible to guess.

And then they moved out of sight again. The walker headed northward through a lowland, creaking and groaning from the pace. Ono blacked out more than once, but he caught fleeting glimpses of more bodies of water, swampy side-inlets from the big river, spanned by piles of wreckage. He began to grow used to the pain; his implants were powering themselves from the grid again, dulling sensation where they could, taking stock of the damage. He closed his eyes and watched the read-outs scroll by. Short version: a few months in bed, more agony than he cared to contemplate, but he'd survive.

But was that all that was left for him? Survival? He swore he wouldn't keep living like this, divided into two minds. Yes, they were still going after Fesso, but he wouldn't be able to drag her back to Jolon in this condition, even assuming the danger from the Core could be averted, and everything returned to what passed for normal.

He had to keep trying, somehow. Even if he were crawling toward Fesso on hands and knees, he had to go on and accept it. At least, that was what he had been telling himself.

But now, having stared death in the face, with Trina passing judgment over him, did he have the same passion for this mission? Did he have the stomach for what it had turned him into? Selfish, Trina had called him, and she was right. From the day he had mounted the steps of the Temple, he had thought only of himself, while Trina had thought only of others.

Well, no more. He may have had barely any strength, but he would give what he had left to her cause. If he was lucky, perhaps the world would give him something good back. But he wouldn't count on it.

"We're here."

They stood before one of the ancient's giant stadiums; Ono had never seen one so large or so well-preserved except in video-shows. He wondered as he often did why the strand would keep such a structure standing after so many years. Was it merely a random choice, or were the Ints trying to teach a lesson to humans about the sort of society which would build this, a gargantuan monument to sitting and passively watching the exploits of others?

For the Ints' sake, came Aunio's voice from his subconscious. *Do you always go on such idiotic rants when you're in pain?*

Trina focused her attention on a sturdy-looking steel door. She closed her eyes, signaling with her implant, but to no effect.

"They're inside," she said. "The vehicles are over there. But the network is locked."

"Maybe you should try knocking," Ono mumbled.

Trina grunted, then nudged the walker forward and yelled, "Hey! Heeey!"

High in the wall a curtain of strand opened, and a gruff male voice called down, "You want to die?"

"Do you?" Trina answered. "The Core will be here at any moment. Let us in."

"Why?"

"We're human, for one thing."

"No one comes in here but the Family. Now piss off."

"Enson!" Telian leaned out from behind Trina. "Let us in, you oaf!"

The big man snorted. "Little one. You'd be better off going with them."

"Is Mother still alive?"

His voice became grave. "Barely."

"This woman's come to help us. She could heal Mother."

"I'm a Seeker," Trina said. "Somewhere in Fesso's head could be the key to stopping the Core. If you let me look around in there, I promise I'll do what I can for her."

The man frowned and the curtain fell back. Dusk had fallen over the Gridlands. Flashes of yellow and purple came from beyond the hills, along with a rumbling noise. When Ono listened as well as his implants would allow, he swore it was growing closer.

He started when a loud clank sounded. The strand around the door slid apart, then the door swung open with a creak. Trina began to lead the walker inside.

Wait. Don't let them see how bad we're hurt.

Ono signaled her to halt. He hopped off gingerly, testing his weight. As long as he kept most of it on his strand leg, rested the other hand on the walker's back, and kept the pain dullers at maximum, he could almost look like he wasn't limping.

They passed into an entrance hall, high-ceilinged, poorly kept and lit blue. The door slammed behind them. Ono glanced at the faces of the Children. Most he didn't recognize, but he caught sight of Mager kneeling by a group of injured and dying at the center of the room. Beside him, Kaia was sprawled in a chair of strand—so she had managed to survive, though by the look on her face, Ono guessed she was at least as bad off as him.

She saw him at the same time, sat up, and snarled. "It's him."

The others drew weapons. Ono let his right hand unravel, preparing for battle.

If they attack, let me handle it.

"Stop," Trina said. "That's enough of this nonsense."

Kaia peeled herself out of her seat, grimacing all the way. "He's been hunting us for a long time. The only reason he fought that huge thing was to get at Mother."

"We don't have time for that," Trina said. "We're not safe from the Core here. For some reason it wants you all dead, and it's not going to rest until it succeeds."

"We've shut it out from the building's network," Kaia replied. "There's no other shelters for twenty miles. And besides…" Her gaze fell to the floor.

"You don't want to move Fesso unless you have to." Trina scanned the crowd. "Where is she? At least let me see if I can help her."

Kaia grumbled, cast an angry eye on Ono, then nodded to the others. A group of gang members parted, revealing a coffin-like vessel of strand on the ground. Inside, Fesso lay with her hands clasped on her belly, eyes closed, breathing soundly. At casual inspection she looked ghastly, but whether that was due to the Core's machinations or simply her default state, Ono didn't know.

"We got her asleep," Kaia said as Trina approached, moving herself between Fesso and Ono.

Trina nodded and knelt, pulling tools from her bandolier. She worked in silence for a few moments, prodding Fesso's neck, watching the readings on her ocular implant.

They began to hear scratching.

The crowd murmured and spread out. It was coming from all over the exterior walls, raking and grinding. The sound made Ono's ears itch, but he tried to keep his focus on Trina. If they really only had moments before the Core broke through, then everything depended on her. Either she would turn and say she had found the answer, or they were dead.

She looked up. "We're done for."

In a blink, Kaia was grasping her collar. "Can you save her, or not?"

Trina shook her head. "There's something in her implant. The Core gave it to her, didn't it, so that you would trust it? What did you think it was?"

"A key. She said it was one of the root keys to the strand network. She had proof. But then those lights flashed in the city, and she fell..."

"She was tricked. The key was never a key. It was a virus. It lay dormant, in disguise. Those flashes you saw were probably an activation code, sent via her optic nerve."

"No," Kaia said quietly. Then she repeated at a shout, "No!"

A crunching noise came from above, sending a shower of gray dust onto her hair. The other gang members fanned out, shouting, trying to organize some sort of perimeter. Trina let out a long breath and sat with her back to Fesso's vessel.

"The virus is a nasty one. I can't remove it. You should never have dealt with the Core."

Kaia pulled a blade and held it to Trina's neck. "And you should never have come here."

The strand from Ono's arm wrapped around Kaia's wrist and yanked backward, nearly taking her off her feet. Kaia yanked back, then leaped forward, until the two of them were inches apart, teeth gritted, hands grasped together. Ono poured strength into his right hand, while the bones in his left began to snap. No good. He surged power through his body, whipping forward, tossing Kaia away. She rolled across the stone floor, came to rest and stayed there.

Ono dropped as well, falling to his knees. His limbs were going numb, his head foggy. That last motion had done it; he had woken Aunio.

"Not now."

I'm getting us out of here.

"Not without Trina."

You heard her. There is no key, and our deal is off. This body is mine, now, forever.

"Ono!" Trina pointed to the wall behind them.

The first of the creatures burst through.

26

HUNTER WAS NOWHERE, nothing. Time slid beneath him, in hills and valleys. He could sense the contours of events great and small, happening at some point in the future or in the past. Always they were far away. He was remote, alone.

The Core had changed the nature of his imprisonment. He was more aware now, but still less than conscious. He knew there was something beyond him, a vast world to explore, but he was trapped in a still tide, stretching to the border of infinity. Always the Core's offer tempted him. Thinking of accepting the Core as his master filled him with waves of pleasure and relief. So he didn't think about it, pushed it aside. He wished he could remember why.

He could remember some things. Images, voices that the Core chose to show him. Most of the life he had led before was still locked away. Instead the same visions appeared over and over. A maggot-infested animal, his face being pushed toward it. Standing in a forest, while someone he knew well said aloud he would never belong. Who was it? He didn't know...

He saw Zeke again, on the beach. The Core replayed this scene often. Hunter told himself there was nothing he could do about it. Zeke wasn't what he seemed. That was all. Hunter was trapped anyway, forever. He wouldn't have to worry about seeing Zeke ever again. Hunter told himself these things and the images faded. He was left feeling sad. Worthless. Empty.

He would do it. He would let the Core control him. As

soon as he made the decision he felt a great weight lifting off him. Pure satisfaction coursed through his mind. Nothing had changed, he was still drifting on a tide of nothing, but when the Core returned for him he was ready now to serve.

Something came.

A sound. Deeply familiar. Someone speaking. This was not the Core.

He heard a light echo of a voice from a million miles away.

"Hun-ter!"

That voice. He needed to remember. The name was so close, but so far away. If he could just find it.

"Hunter!"

Evie…?

The memory's arrival felt like a switch in his mind. Something was open now. Light came. It started from above; suddenly he became aware that there *was* an above. Then it grew, covering him, and wherever it touched he felt experience return. From the light grew a path, a glowing way through the abyss. Hunter followed it back. Back to the surface.

Back to his body.

He was alive. A warm breeze tickled his cheek. He was upright, and his limbs were bound, eyes covered in gel, vision a blur. He blinked hard, and her face was before him.

#

Evie gasped when Hunter's eyes fluttered. His tongue lolled out from his open mouth and his breathing became ragged.

"Hunter!"

His eyes shot open and he gurgled. The strand in his throat was keeping him from speaking. He looked confused for a moment, then closed his eyes, breathing deeply.

Evie touched his forehead. "Hunter?"

The sound came from the strand all around them, a low hum under the noise of battle, then growing stronger, warping, forming into words.

"*Evie. You brought me back.*"

The voice was so robotic, so alien, but there was a hint of Hunter in there somewhere. It was him. "Not yet. I need to get you out of here."

His eyes darted about, taking in the surroundings and his body. The creatures had formed a perimeter around them, but they weren't advancing, as if some force had frozen them. Was Hunter doing that?

"*I can't move.*"

"Don't start. I'm going to drag you back, somehow. Even if I need to cut this entire thing out and take it with me."

He shook his head, mouth hanging uselessly as the strand spoke. "*I won't survive. It's a part of me forever. You knew that already. That I could never go back.*"

"I'm sorry. I shouldn't have let this happen. I shouldn't— " Her words became choked.

"*No. It's better this way. This is where I belong. I have no need of my life before.*"

"You don't believe that. You know we care about you."

He fell silent. Behind her, the creatures began to writhe and squeal again. Evie felt a quake run through her body, from her toes to the tips of her fingernails, digging into her palm.

"Hunter! Get back here right now!"

The eyes fluttered open, but his head lolled downward, face immobile. "*Leave, and do not return. Your actions have no purpose. We gain nothing by ignoring the truth.*"

"Enough of your 'truths,'" she growled. "I'm sick of them. Family is more important than truth, Hunter." She grasped his head and touched her forehead to his. "You know what I've done to be here? I worked with them. Helped them. *I rode a strand monster to reach you.* Me! You remember what I'm like, right? How much would I have to love you to do *that*?"

A tear formed in the corner of his eye.

"Hunter, listen to me. It's done something to you. Messed

with your mind. Maybe I can't bring you back. But I won't let you forget that I love you. Wherever you go in there, you'll carry that memory with you forever. Do you hear me? If you don't, I'll come in there and kick your spirit's ass myself."

She kept her gaze locked with his. His eyes flicked back and forth, searching for something. Then he seemed to find it. His expression changed, his jaw working again. He tried to speak, but only a wheezing rasp came out, and he grimaced in pain.

"It's all right." She pulled his face to her shoulder. "You don't have to."

"*You give me permission? You accept me like this?*"

"Only if you'll remember me."

"*I promise.*"

She swallowed and nodded. "Then yes."

"*Thank you, Evie.*"

A weight grew in her heart, heavy enough to make her sink to her knees. "Oh, Hunter…"

"*Thank you. For giving me a purpose. I don't know why yet, but I think it will make a difference. I have to go, now. But I'll be in here. Thinking of you.*"

"I love you."

"*I love you, too.*" A pause, and then Hunter's neck went slack, his eyes glassy. "*Goodbye.*"

He closed his eyes, and the strand began to heal itself around him. Evie turned away, unable to watch it seal him in, and found that the Core's island had changed.

It was darker now, the sky a deep red, and all was at peace. The creatures had dispersed. The remains of the giant lay in a pile, pieces scattered about, eyes dull. Evie stepped carefully around its remains, then, with weary steps, made her way back down the wide avenue from which she came.

27

"EVERYONE DRAW CLOSE," Kaia shouted. "Make a circle! Protect Mother!"

Creatures sprung from every wall. They came from the ceiling, clutching the metal rafters, sending down a cavalcade of stones. Strong, fast, sharp, deadly. Everywhere.

And in the center of it all, Ono stood, unable to move.

"Let me go! I need my legs."

Only if you're using them to run out of here.

Trina passed her fingers over the remaining supplies in her bandolier. "I can hold off maybe four or five."

Save her and we die. Let me get us out. You're too weak.

Ono turned away, speaking through clenched teeth. "I don't need you."

You do. It's why I've always been here. I've always handled the things you couldn't.

A scream as a heavy-set gangster went flying across the room. The others closed ranks around him, but there was little they could do. Kaia couldn't organize them well enough; they weren't soldiers, and even the elite guard of Jolon would be doomed against these creatures.

"Let me go!"

You let me go. It's my job.

"You're wrong. Your job was always to take the easy way out."

What? You think what I've done was easy?

"Always. You're the one who can't walk away from a fight.

Who can't admit he's wrong, that the battle is lost. You don't make me brave…you're just a way to avoid the truth. *You're* the weak one."

He clenched his fist as the words left him, trying his best to take back control. It didn't work. No matter how strong his will, Aunio was in his brain.

With a chorus of screams and a shower of sparks, a giant creature burst through the fray, a head taller than Ono and muscled with many layers of strand. It stood before him and yawned, two rusted steel spikes embedded as fangs in its jaws. The creature scratched the ground and set its sights on the center of the room, where the gang members too small or injured to fight were huddled.

"Hey!" Ono yelled. "You're exposing your flank! Take me out first."

What are you doing?

"Come on, you pile of slimy scrap!"

The creature looked in his direction.

Give me control. Release me.

"You first. Let me go or we die."

The creature hunched down.

The prickles of numbness left Ono's arm, and his legs flexed under his command, just in time to dodge the creature's lunge. He landed close to Trina, who was throwing aside the deactivated carcass of a creature resembling a large centipede.

"This way," Ono said. "We need to make a wedge, break through the weakest point together."

"What about the children?"

"Oh." Ono glanced toward the crowd. "I suppose we're staying, then."

The creature lined up for another attack, oil drooling from its maw.

"Got anything for that one?" Ono asked.

"All out." She patted the bandolier. "It's yours."

"Don't think I have the strength." He touched Trina's shoulder. "It's been an honor. See you in the next world."

The creature froze, fangs bared and dripping, eyes fixed on Ono's heart.

It stayed frozen.

The sounds of the room changed from slashing blades and screams, to panting and gasping breaths. All the creatures had stopped at once, hanging in place like a garden of bizarre statuary.

"What?" someone finally said.

Trina yelped in surprise, and Ono turned as a shape rose out of the strand. Smaller than the rest of the creatures, the new apparition appeared as a lumpy cylinder the height of his chest. It bulged and rippled, as if unsure of what shape it should be, then slowly grew a pair of arms and a knobby head, and settled into human proportions. A child's proportions.

Cries of shock came from the crowd.

"It's a boy."

"Is it…is that…"

Trina blinked hard, her jaw agape. "H—Hunter?"

The Hunter-of-strand turned its head, appearing to take in the room with its metal eyes. "*You're safe, now.*"

The voice had come from the room all around them, echoing through the hall like a sermon. At once most of the gang fell to their knees.

"Called! He's a Called!"

"We're not gonna die!"

"Bless you!"

"Hunter…you…" Trina began, then shook her head. "How?"

"*I don't know,*" Hunter said. "*The Core released me. I wanted to come here and help you before it was too late.*"

Ono approached one of the creatures and pushed just enough to off-balance it. It fell in a heap to the floor.

He is a Called. For once, Aunio sounded completely dumbfounded. *Unbelievable.*

272

Ono stared again at the image of Hunter. "Impossible."

"I'm sorry," Trina said. "I'm sorry we couldn't help you."

Hunter held a hand up, begging for silence in a subservient, almost embarrassed way. *"You did help me. Me and Evie. I wanted to thank you one more time."*

"Blessed one!" Kaia pushed her way past the kneeling crowd, keeping her head low. "You saved our lives. Please, please, help us again, I beg of you! Save our mother!"

The room fell silent for a moment, then a few of the kneeling figures joined in a chorus. "Save her," "Blessed one."

"You brought me here against my will." The electronic warble from the walls lowered to a hiss. *"You stole me from my sister. Hurt me."*

Kaia swallowed. Her body began to shake. Ono could barely stop himself from doing the same. The power Hunter controlled now—it was unfathomable. Too dangerous for a young boy. If that was indeed what he was, anymore.

The image of Hunter stayed still, as frozen as the creatures around them. Long seconds ticked by, the crowd silent, holding their breath.

From the vessel on the floor, Fesso coughed and sat up, convulsed, then lay back down, breathing hard.

"Mother!" Kaia ran up and held her skull-like face.

"There was something inside her," Hunter said. *"Very dangerous. But I declawed it."*

"Will she...recover?" Kaia breathed.

"I don't know. You will have to wait and see. But I did my best."

"Hunter," Trina said. "You said they hurt you."

"They're lost. People who have nowhere else to go. I understand that, even if I don't understand what they did. Besides..." The strand head turned, scanning the crowd, until it settled on the diminutive girl with the strand nose. He smiled. *"They're not all bad."*

The girl put her face to the floor. "Blessed Called," she said. Then, in a softer voice, "Good luck in there."

Hunter straightened. *"It doesn't matter, anyway. Good or evil, I cannot choose sides between human factions anymore. I'm different now. I can see more, control it all better. Trina...I'm not the first person to become like this, am I?"*

Trina shook her head.

"And the others all faded away, never to be heard from again?"

She nodded.

"I know why. In the strand, there's so much to see—it would be easy to forget about your world, and the people in it. Most of the Ints don't care about you at all. But I have a purpose. Evie gave it to me. I'm going to advocate for our kind. Do whatever is in my power to protect people. All of them. Maybe I'll fail, but I'll try. Trina?"

"Yes."

"Take care of Evie, all right? She's on her way back, alone."

"Of course. Of course I will. What will you do now?"

The avatar swiveled its head, as if it wanted to get one more look at a world it wouldn't see again for a while. *"I'm going to find someone. When I learn more, I'll tell you. Take this."*

Trina flinched and touched her temple. Hunter must have forcefully injected a packet of data into her implant. She smiled and nodded. He returned the expression, strand-cheeks spreading wide.

Then, like water falling from a pail, he collapsed into the floor, not to re-appear again.

———

Stars surrounded Hunter. Billions of them, more than he had ever seen in the night sky at home, spread in great gray swirls all around, above and below. There was no up or down in this place, but he stood at ease, feet sinking softly into nothing, like they rested on invisible pillows. He could step wherever he wanted into the empty space, and the "ground" remained the same beneath him.

His destination lay just ahead, pulsing with red light, which grew brighter with each step. Some kind of astronomical object, profoundly beautiful, throwing out rays of energy as it spun at tremendous speeds. The thing must have been enormous beyond comprehension, but the strange sense of distance made it seem akin to a fist-sized ball, floating just out of reach. It grew larger quickly, which left Hunter with the impression that he must be approaching it at great speed. But that didn't make sense, given that the line of people standing around it remained nearly the same size.

There were fourteen in all, men and women, some dressed in simple white rags, others in elegant flowing gowns, deep red or bright yellow. Some were wizened, with deep wrinkles and wiry gray hair, while others were younger adults. They stood in a semi-circle, gazing down at the spinning object. If they were communicating with one another, it was not in a manner Hunter could observe. When he approached, none of them made a move to welcome or even acknowledge him.

Hunter walked to one end of the line and stood beside the gray-robed figure there. He peered up at its face and recognized the Core. He had felt the old Int's presence from quite a distance away, mixed with the distinct signatures coming off these new strangers.

Hunter waited a while, watching for the Core's reaction. There was none. The last time they had spoken, the Core had demanded he become a slave, then put him into an eternal limbo. Then Hunter had escaped, somehow, with Evie's help. So was the Core angry? Did he not care at all? Learning to predict the Ints' behavior was going to be another game unto itself.

"What is that thing?" Hunter asked, looking down at the flashing ball.

The Core answered calmly, "A pulsar. Approximately 27 parsecs from Earth. What you see here is a simulation, representing the emission spectrum beyond visible light."

"It's nice. You all come here to watch it?"

"Yes."

"Are these the Ints in charge of the Immersion?"

"Some of them."

"The ones you were at war with?"

"Our battle had little in common with historical human conflicts. We interact on many levels, some antagonistic, others cooperative."

"Did you want me to come here?"

For the first time, the Core moved, turning his head just enough for Hunter to catch his reflection in its eye. "You came of your own accord. I am no longer attempting to control you. This is a place where most are allowed, but few have the ability to find. Either by talent or luck, you have found it."

The Core headed off, walking down and around the pulsar as if descending an invisible, spiral staircase. His pace left Hunter on the edge of confusion about whether or not he was meant to follow. He did anyway.

"Why did you give up?" Hunter asked, struggling to move quickly across the strange, pliable footing. "You said you wanted me as your pawn before."

"The set points of your neural state machine have changed. I am no longer confident they can ever be re-routed back to a responsive configuration."

"Huh?"

"Your brain has a finite ability to resist temptation. I was holding you in suspension until your mental stamina ran out. But due to external events, your value system has changed. To use a human idiom, I cannot force you to believe something you know in your 'heart' to be untrue."

They had moved closer to the pulsar by then, and it filled half the surrounding star field. The Core stopped and turned to watch it, and Hunter found himself momentarily taken in by the sight. Coils of light radiated around a central point, intricate and fluid, as if it were a language of gravity and matter. He felt small in comparison.

"I don't want you to hurt any more people. I know you were just doing it because they were in your way, or because they might cause you trouble later, but you don't have to worry about that anymore. If the humans are bothering you, you can come to me first, and I'll talk to them for you."

"Interesting," said the Core disinterestedly.

"So that's it?" Hunter asked. "You don't care what I do now?"

"You are as free as any other creature in the Immersion."

"But why keep my body alive? Why would you bother with me?"

"I may have no use for you at the moment, but others do not feel the same." The Core turned his attention away from the pulsar and back to Hunter. No, over his shoulder, to the black space beyond. "In particular, the one who helped engineer your escape. Come on…it's time to stop hiding."

Hunter whirled. The milky swaths of distant stars were difficult to see after taking in the massive brightness of the pulsar, but he could just make out the blurred shape of a black rectangle blocking them out. The rectangle opened like a door, letting white light pour in from behind, and Jenfri stepped though it and faced him.

"You," Hunter said.

Jenfri gave a slight bow to the Core. "Hello, Father."

Hunter spun again and gaped at the old man stroking his beard. "You! And him…you're…" He shook his head. "I guess it makes sense. You said you grew up here, after all."

The Core grunted and turned away.

Jenfri chuckled. "Ignore his sour mood. Omoro carries lingering resentment toward me, due to my stealing his pet External."

"Pet? You mean me? Is that why you helped me? To keep me as a pet?"

Jenfri shook his head. "No, nothing of that kind."

"I trusted Zeke, and he betrayed me. Why should I trust you?"

"You shouldn't. Our kind doesn't 'trust.' You do what you want, and when you don't want to anymore, you stop."

"Oh…well what *do* you want from me, then?"

Jenfri smiled wide, his eyes shutting tight beneath his bangs. "I seek a mutually satisfying companionship among equals."

"You mean, friends?"

"You may lack a word for such a relationship. We are both young, and have much to learn, but the things we know are different. As we grow, we can teach and learn from each other. Not friends, not teachers—a combination."

Hunter pondered for a moment, then nodded. "I'll just go with 'friends.'"

"As one does." Jenfri smiled again and bowed. "Now, I suggest we leave this place."

"Why?"

Jenfri opened his door, a strip of white suspended against the stars. "To play!" He stepped through. "Coming?"

Hunter nodded again, and with an excited whoop, bounded after into the unknown.

Epilogue

THE BOAT'S ENGINE emitted a dull electric hum as it pushed them upstream. Evie let her fingers trail in the river. Even two inches of coolness on her skin felt refreshing in the summer heat. Past the water, rolling hills with bushy trees drifted past. She had been watching those hills slowly descend from the imposing cliffs further south, closer to where they started their journey, not far from the Core's island. There had been nothing to do in the meantime but wait and think. About Hunter, and the future.

Trina, her lone companion in the small vessel, blinked furiously as she flipped through images on her implant. She caught Evie's gaze for a moment and, as if sensing her discomfort, sat up and tried to make conversation.

"Did you ever come this way before?"

Evie shook her head. "We do cross this river, but then our trail continues to the east. I don't know much about these lands, but if you say there are Pure here, they should be able to show me the way back to my family."

Speaking of seeing her family again made her tense, and instinctively she reached down and squeezed the twig-sized lump in her pouch.

Trina cleared her throat. "You remember how to use it, yes?"

Evie nodded and pulled her hand away, leaving the access token alone. "I'm more worried about finding a place to hide it. Imagine if I lost it, and didn't get to hear about what happens to Ono? That would be a real tragedy."

Trina smiled. "I'll keep you updated. But he's so secretive, we may never be sure if the Ints really helped him. Cured or not, he'd still be insufferable."

Evie snorted. She still didn't understand everything about Ono's predicament; something about having two minds, the Ints, and most surprising, an estranged wife and daughter. But Trina had explained the sacrifices he had been willing to make to help her and her brother. Despite everything they had gone through, she was left with a grudging respect for the man. Even something bordering on, dare she say it, warmth.

"What I don't follow," she half-mumbled, "is why the Ints would still keep their end of the bargain. You never brought Fesso back to his city, as he agreed to."

"We didn't see a need. There couldn't have been any reason they wanted Fesso, other than the key held in her brain."

"But you said it wasn't a key."

"Right. I mean the virus. After your brother disarmed it, I was able to safely make a copy for Ono to bring back to Jolon. We don't know for sure, of course, but I suspect the virus is what the Jolon Ints were after the whole time. They must have known the Core would never trust a root key to a human, but perhaps the structure of the virus was interesting enough that they wanted to see it for themselves."

Evie shook her head and sighed. Viruses, Ints…she would have been glad to never think about such things again, but here she was, with a physical link to that world hanging by her hip, uncomfortably heavy beyond its physical weight. But she could never get rid of it, not while Hunter was still out there, not when he might someday need a real person to talk to again.

"Are you excited to see them?" Trina said, as if reading her thoughts.

"I don't know." It sounded bad, saying it like that. Evie shifted and turned away, letting the words drift into an awkward silence. Of course she was excited to see them. Her father's face, and her brothers'; just imagining it made her heart thump. But then she thought about delivering the news, how her father's expression would change when she told him he would never see his son again, how Hunter's mother would react...

But it wouldn't happen like that, would it? Word would come far ahead of her, passed by the tribes. They would know she was traveling alone. Of course they would conclude that Hunter had died, and she would say nothing to dissuade them.

Or would she? How long would she be able to hold on to the secret of Hunter's real whereabouts? How many gazes from his mother would she have to endure? The older woman might have an intuition that Evie was hiding the whole truth. But she wouldn't want to know, none of them would. Nor would they want to hear about the things Evie had done to survive, or that she still planned to stay in contact with the Tainted, and worse yet, the world inside the strand itself.

It was exciting, yes. She would be home, finally, really home, and there would be tears of happiness and songs of joy. But what lay ahead for her? She had two lives now, forever irrevocable, and she could abandon neither.

She returned her attention to the water, draping her arm down to splash in the fast-moving ripples. Tiny fish caught the sun's glow, then returned to the depths. "Thank you for taking me all the way back. In case I didn't say so already."

"You did. Or maybe you didn't. Who knows? In any case, it's the least I could do. You helped us deal with Fesso, after all. With her organization hobbled, my family is safe again. And besides, it's been a long time since I came this way. With any luck I'll find some interesting samples on the—"

The pause made Evie look up. Trina's head had snapped toward the eastern shore.

"What is it?"

"There's something over there. In the trees." Trina glanced at the rudder, and the boat turned eastward.

Evie scanned the shoreline, grunting frustration that she couldn't see what a Tainted woman had noticed. Had she used that thing in her eye somehow? They neared a beach, a field of brown pebbles with a copse of pines behind. Then Evie saw them: tents, three in a row, hidden in the shade.

"Ah!" In an instant all the heaviness and hesitation and worry left her, and she sprang from the boat into the waist-high water.

She barely heard Trina call from behind, "…careful…don't like strangers…"

Nonsense. These were her people. She could see it in the shape of the tents, the way the skins spread so elegantly over the balanced poles. She waded until the water reached her shins and then sprinted, pulse thudding in her ears, heaving deep breaths full of joy. Home. She was going home, and now that it was real, her other problems faded like night after the dawn.

She reached the nearest tent and stood over it, dripping, catching her breath. Something was wrong. She couldn't make sense of what she was seeing. She felt as if she were in some bizarre dream, and only the sound of Trina's approaching footsteps roused her.

"It's…impossible," Evie said. Through the scaffolding, up around in a spiral, oily metal wires pierced the tent skins, helping to hold the structure together. "You were right."

Trina's hand touched her shoulder. Evie shuddered, then the shudder turned to a chuckle, and she looked back and laughed. "I still don't believe it."

Trina raised an eyebrow. "Are you all right?"

"It just doesn't make sense," Evie said. "They're not Pure, are they? They don't have our laws."

"Same laws, different interpretation." Trina squeezed her shoulder, then pointed. "Look, they're coming."

Human silhouettes approached from the forest. Three adults, spears on their shoulders, humming a marching tune. A hunting party, returning to their temporary camp.

"If you want to leave, I understand," Trina said. "We'll go further upriver. I don't mind."

"No." Evie stepped forward and waved. A shout of surprise came from the forest. "I can handle things from here."

Acknowledgments

Thank you to Martin Hodo, Andrea Philips, Justin Landon, and Ian Everett for your critiques on my rough drafts, and thank you to my wife Margaret for beta reading (twice) and your unending support through thick and thin. I can never express enough appreciation to Gwen Gades at Dragon Moon for seeing the potential in this book and helping make it the best it could be, and to JoAnne Soper-Cook for her thorough edits. Finally, thank you to all the other friends, editors and fans who took the time to read my work thus far.

-W.W. 8/18/2017